Cardboard City

JOE CANNON

YELLOW BRICK PUBLISHERS

First Published 1993 by:

YELLOW BRICK PUBLISHERS
2, LONSDALE ROAD
QUEENS PARK
LONDON
NW6 6 RD.

British Library Cataloguing in Publication Data:
A catalogue record for this book is available from the British Library.

ISBN: 0-9520560-3-8

Typeset by Lonsdale Press Ltd.
Printed and bound in Great Britain by Cox & Wyman Ltd, Reading, Berkshire

This book is dedicated to all the homeless, may they soon find warmth, happiness and peace...

FOREWORD

Based on a true story.

Adapting an Orwellian attitude to research rather than the cosier BBC style: 'I spent two months living with the people there, its a bloody disgrace that in the 1990s this is actually happening, looking around there is so much poverty, it just doesn't make sense.'

THE AUTHOR. LONDON 1993.

CHAPTER 1.

The tiny hamlet of Anscombe nestles on the northern edge of the Sussex downs, some four miles from the urban and industrial sprawl of the new town of Crawley.

It is not easy to find. A dirt road which appears to be the entrance to a farm is unmarked. There had been a signpost at one time, but that had been taken down during the war and had never been replaced. Travel a mile down the unmade road and there is the centre of the village, a grassy square on the four corners of which stand the local pub, the village store and post office, a hairdressing establishment catering for both sexes and a public toilet with separate entrances for Ladies and Gentlemen.

Anscombe had the air of having been forgotten by time. Its two hundred and fifty inhabitants maintained a stubborn indifference to the march of progress, though they were not averse to benefitting from such aids to easy living as electricity, gas and piped water. Visitors were few and far between, for there were no tourist attractions, not even lunch in the Anscombe Arms. The good citizens of the village believed in the virtues of home cooking and Josh Hamilton, the landlord of the pub, was content to go along with that. Besides, it made life easier for him and his buxom wife. He had more time to spend on keeping his ale in first-class condition and the wife was able to pass many happy hours in gossip with the widow Fawcett who presided over the hairdressing salon.

There really wasn't much to gossip about for the villagers by and large led fairly uneventful lives. None the less, Dora Hamilton and the widow were experts at wringing the last drip of juice from the tiniest scandal. As Josh Hamilton was prone to remark, as long as his missus and the widow Fawcett were spared, the village would never need a local paper.

The Parish Council met once a week in the front room over the bar of the Anscombe Arms. Its chairman was the headmaster of the village school, an austere academic by the name of John Masefield Lewis, a bachelor and a rigid disciplinarian who terrorised his small staff of two assistants and still had sufficient spleen left over to hold the forty or so pupils in subjection. The other three members were respectively Commander Philip Reece (RN, retd), Miss Agatha Thynne-Williams and a pale young man who was employed in the Borough Surveyor's office in Crawley and who answered to the name of Seymour. He was so addressed by his fellow members of the Council.

The Commander was anything but the bluff old seadog which his naval rank implied. Indeed, most of his service had been spent on land in various dockyards up and down the country. He passed through the war unscathed, which was not surprising since his war effort was directed from the safety and comparative comfort of an office in the Admiralty building. Short, slight and very dapper, he was given to nail-biting at times of crisis. He reminded one of a rather frightened ferret.

Miss Thynne-Williams would have been outstanding in any company. She was six feet tall and as straight as a ramrod. At sixty-five, she looked not a day younger than eighty.

Enormously wealthy, she devoted herself to Good Works and Charity on which she spent a considerable amount of other peoples' money. She covered her shapeless body in equally shapeless garments which looked as though they had been purchased from one of her own jumble sales, as indeed some of them were. Her wrinkled face was set in a gentle, kindly smile, and she possessed a mind like an adding machine.

Young Seymour was a newcomer to the Council, having been roped in by Miss Thynne-Williams who regarded him as an unpaid lackey. If there was fetching and carrying to be done in connection with the lady's charitable efforts, then Seymour was on hand. For the rest, he was little more than a head which nodded in agreement with the views expressed by whichever member of the Council happened to be speaking.

The matter occupying the Council's attention this Monday evening was important in so far as it affected Miss Thynne-William's pocket. Grange Hall, in which the lady lived surrounded by a retinue of servants, was a listed building within the meaning of the Act and, as such, rated certain financial contributions for the up-keep of the house and grounds, such contributions being met in part from the local rates. Here a conflict of interest arose. The chairman wanted money for his school, and the Commander looked with disfavour on even the smallest rise in the rates he paid on his farm and outbuildings.

The debate had reached a point at which the Commander was chewing his finger nails down to the quick, Lewis was about to explode and the lady member's kindly smile had changed to a ferocious scowl, while Seymour looked as though he was on the verge of tears.

'What exactly needs to be done at the Hall?' enquired the chairman, in a tone of voice which implied that, whatever it was, he was against it.

'I have discovered dry rot in the kitchens,' said Miss Thynne-Williams. 'Extensive remedial measures are required to cure the present rot and prevent any further incidence. My estate manager has prepared an estimate...'

'How much?' said Lewis abruptly.

The lady's tone was icy. 'If you'll kindly have the manners to let me finish, I have a copy of the estimate here.' She rummaged in her handbag, which had the dimensions of a small suitcase, and produced a manila folder which she passed to Seymour who in turn handed it on to the chairman. Lewis wasted no time in reading through the schedule but glanced at the total. His face turned a deep shade of purple. The estate manager, a cunning Scot by the name of Galbraith, had been lining his pocket at public expense for years, but this time he had gone too far.

'Twenty seven thousand two hundred and fifty three pounds and sixty pence! Good Lord! Are you looking to rebuild the Hall?'

'Sarcasm doesn't become you, Mr. Lewis. By today's standards that is a very moderate sum.'

Lewis took a deep breath but refrained from further comment. He was well aware that at least five thousand pounds would find its way into Galbraith's retirement fund, adding to the considerable sum stashed away over years of taking backhanders from venal builders who regarded the Hall as a bottomless well of revenue. This most recent assault on the parish purse had to be scotched. But how? He stared at the preposterous total for a while, then came up with the clincher.

'I'm afraid the Council cannot endorse this application, Miss Thynne-Williams,' he said.

'And why is that, pray?'

Lewis delivered the coup de grace.

'Because, dear lady, any request for a sum greater than five hundred pounds must be accompanied by two independent estimates. Isn't that so, Seymour?'

4

The miserable Seymour could only nod his head in agreement. Miss Thynne-Williams looked towards the Commander, but that worthy was busy inspecting a fragment of thumbnail which had escaped the attention of his marauding teeth. In any case, he was at one with the chairman in disliking the odious Galbraith.

'This is quite monstrous,' said Miss Thynne-Williams. 'Why have I not encountered this difficulty on previous occasions?'

'New regulations. Designed to prevent unscrupulous persons from cheating.' Lewis was cock-a-hoop. It was not often that he was able to defeat the redoubtable Miss Thynne-Williams. 'Any further business?' he enquired of the meeting at large. There was an ominous silence as the lady member gathered up her papers and stuffed them in her reticule before making for the door, which she slammed behind her with a bang that indicated her disapproval of the proceedings.

'I declare the meeting closed,' said the chairman. 'Next Monday as usual. Goodnight, gentlemen.' Seymour and the Commander exchanged glances.

'There'll be some bloody ructions over this,' said Reece. Seymour, to whom the gesture had become part of his behaviour pattern, nodded his head.

The following day news of the rift between the headmaster and the self-appointed Lady Bountiful of the village was a main topic of conversation. The Commander had spent an hour after the meeting downing a few gins in the bar of the Anscombe Arms and chatting to the incumbent. During the course of the conversation he had incautiously let drop a few remarks anent the business of the application for a repair grant by Miss Thynne-Williams. Josh Hamilton had casually mentioned the matter to his good lady as they were preparing to go to bed. Early the following morning Dora

5

Hamilton had lost no time in imparting the news, with embellishments, to the widow Fawcett. The rumour passed from mouth to ear and by the afternoon almost everyone in the village was apprised of the fact that John Masefield Lewis had engaged in a stand-up fight with Agatha Thynne-Williams and had emerged a clear winner.

Grange Hall's lady was not a popular person among the denizens of Anscombe, nor was the agent Galbraith held in any esteem. The general feeling was that Miss Thynne-Williams had finally got what had been coming to her for a long time and nobody was going to shed any tears over her. The gossips waited on the sidelines for the next development in the saga while the protagonists prepared to do battle at the next meeting of the Parish Council. Lewis was happy to leave decisions to the bureaucrats on the County Council. The Lady of the Manor, on the other hand, was a great believer in the power of the purse. She made an immediate beeline to her solicitors.

Tommy Hutton leaned his bicycle against the doorpost of the Anscombe Arms and made his way inside. After the ride from the factory, it was his habit to sink a half-pint of bitter before going home for his evening meal, which was on the table at seven o'clock every weekday. Tommy was a personable young man of twenty-six who lived with his wife Jean and daughter Elizabeth in a small house some hundred yards or so from the local.

'Alright then, Tommy lad?' said Josh Hamilton as he pulled a glass of bitter and placed it on the bar. Tommy nodded, paid for the drink and took an appreciative gulp.

'Heard the latest?' said the landlord.

'Is it out yet?' said Tommy with a grin.

6

Hamilton smiled. 'Seems old Daddy Lewis and her ladyship had a bit of a row at the meeting last night.'

'Yeah. What's the old bat up to now?'

'She reckons the Hall is falling to pieces. Wants a repair grant. About fifty thousand, so I heard.'

'So Daddy Lewis said you're welcome?'

'Not according to the Commander. Lewis said she couldn't have it, so she stormed out of the meeting without even a goodnight.'

'Well, it'll be interesting to see what happens,' said Tommy. He finished his beer and put the glass on the bar.

'I'll be off, then,' he said. 'See you tomorrow.'

Cycling down the narrow lane that led to the Home Farm, where Commander Reece pretended to farm some thirty acres of fine arable land on which he returned a substantial loss every year, Tommy passed the bungalow of his nearest neighbour, a retired civil servant who had settled in the village some ten years previously. It was a neat and tidy residence, the front garden devoted to flowers while the plot in the rear was given over to the production of vegetables in orderly and well-spaced rows like a line-up of desks in a Government department.

A shiny Joseph Grimstone and his equally shiny wife were in the act of climbing into their car, but they paused to give Tommy a cheery wave. Just off to the cinema in Crawley, thought Tommy, all dressed up and somewhere to go. He drew up at his own front gate and surveyed his little house with pride.

He was the third generation of Huttons to occupy the property. Grandfather Hutton had been a carpenter, an industrious worker who, in his spare time, thought of himself as a modern day Chippendale or Sheraton and busied himself with furnishings for the home. Had he set his sights lower he might have created more durable though less pretty chairs and tables and whatnots. As it was, the house became full of ostentatious carvings in expensive woods adorned with bosses and curlicues that harboured dust and were a constant threat to the ankles of the incautious.

When Tommy's father inherited the property he sent off the furniture to auction where a lunatic with more money than sense bought up the lot and paid handsomely for the privilege. The auctioneer's stooges, sensing the presence of a genuine muggins, skilfully forced up the bidding. Tommy's father came out of it with sufficient cash to re-furnish the house with a tidy bit left over.

As a child, Tommy conceived a great affection for the house and in particular his own room which had windows to both front and rear, each commanding a splendid view. Arthur and Dorothy Hutton idolised their only son. Within the limits of their modest means they gave him anything he desired. He made no great demands on them. A serious and thoughtful child, he did well at school, displaying a natural talent for painting and drawing and, strangely enough, a love of mathematics in which subject he excelled.

Arthur Hutton died after a short illness when Tommy was sixteen, and the boy was obliged to go to work to supplement the family's income. There was a vacancy in the drawing office of a nearby engineering firm. Equipped with a glowing reference from 'Daddy' Lewis, Tommy applied for the job, sailed through the interview and was duly appointed a junior trainee draughtsman.

The work suited his talents. A large blank sheet of paper on the drawing board he looked upon as a challenge to his artistic abilities and, as he was entrusted with more intricate tasks as he progressed through the ranks, so he took greater pride in turning out impeccable work. The time arrived when the men on the shop floor were able to identify his drawings with their distinctive lettering and neat instructions without having to glance at the initials T.H. in the bottom right-hand corner of the blueprint.

In the five years during which he was ostensibly 'learning the job', he attended night school and sat the City and Guilds examinations. At the age of twenty-one, he was not only a fully-skilled engineering draughtsman but was also engaged to a pretty brunette by the name of Jean Mortimer, secretary to one of the directors of the company. She was an eminently sensible young woman, a year younger than Tommy and had all the makings of an ideal partner. His mother approved of her whole-heartedly, but the approval was not to last for, just one month after he had celebrated his coming of age, Dorothy Hutton died from a brain haemorrhage.

During and after the funeral Jean was a tower of strength. Three months later she and Tommy were married and Jean moved into the little house in Anscombe. She settled down, gained the good wishes of the community as an ideal partner for one of their favourite sons and, nine months later presented Tommy with a daughter whom they named Elizabeth.

This, then, was the young man who opened the gate on to his own property and wheeled his bicycle to his own front door, a young man who had suffered his share of unhappiness but had, over the past five years, found great joy in marriage and fatherhood. Leaning the machine on the porch he opened the door and passed through a passage between the ground floor rooms which led on to the kitchen. Jean was standing over the electric stove putting the finishing touches to a concoction which smelled good enough to eat.

He went up to her and put his arms round her slender waist, bending slightly to kiss her on the cheek.

'Hi, there,' he said. 'How's my favourite house-wife?'

'Busy being a favourite housewife,' she replied.

'Elizabeth in bed?' he enquired.

'Just ten minutes ago.'

'I'll pop up and say goodnight.'

'Alright, darling. Supper'll be ready when you come down.'

He went out of the kitchen and mounted the stairs. As he entered the room which had once been his personal domain the child sat up in her bed and put out her arms towards him. He perched himself on the bed and embraced her.

'How's my little sweetheart tonight?' he said.

She did not reply but merely snuggled closer, her head beneath his chin, her tiny body wriggling as though she wanted to get right through to his heart. He felt a deep glow of satisfaction. This was their child, his and Jean's, a living proof of their devotion to each other. There was a lump in his throat as he gently disengaged himself from her arms and fluffed up her pillow.

'Sleepy-time, little one,' he murmured. She snuggled down in the bed as he gently drew the blanket over her shoulders. She looked up at him, lids already beginning to close over sleepy blue eyes.

'Goodnight, daddy.'

'Goodnight, my darling. God bless you.'

For a few moments he stood gazing at her, then turned abruptly and left the room, closing the door gently behind him.

The supper was excellent, veal in a white sauce with sautee potatoes and baby carrots. Jean smiled as he chewed on one of them.

'Courtesy of Mr. Grimstone,' she said. 'First of the season. I could see he hated to part with them.'

'Next time you see him tell him the carrots were marvellous. That way he'll feel better - then you can ask him how the spring cabbage is coming along.'

'Guts,' said Jean.

'I know. Isn't it lovely,' said Tommy.

In the view of the town-dweller, the rustic life is simple and uncomplicated. Flowers bloom in their season, spring sees the burgeoning of life as the trees burst into leaf, there is the sowing of the seed, the reaping and mowing, the gathering of the harvest, the roistering in the village alehouse and the pastoral calm of Sunday morning with the solemn procession of the faithful wending its way to render thanks to the Almighty for his many blessings.

Alas for the unfortunate townie who escapes to the expected peace and tranquillity of the countryside, these illusions are quickly shattered. Beneath the calm of the village existence lurk many fearsome undercurrents. Old feuds, the causes long-forgotten, force a wedge between rival factions. Gossip, starting as a mild infection, becomes a raging epidemic.

Josh Hamilton, mine host of the Anscombe Arms, hit the nail on the head when he said that anybody was free to hold an opinion so long as it agreed with the majority. He himself was a master of the art of rural diplomacy. Whether agreeing, dissenting or merely sitting on the fence, his inevitable reply to any and every expression of opinion was a nonchalant 'Oh, aye'. He was regarded as a man of great wisdom and considerable common-sense. As he disagreed with nobody, everybody agreed with him. It was, in any case, extremely difficult to come up with an effective counter to a laconic 'Oh, aye'.

In the art of pouring oil on troubled waters, Hamilton was almost equalled by the owner of the village store. Gareth Evans, Newsagent and Post Office, was a comparative newcomer to Anscombe, still referred to by some of the elders as a 'furriner'. He retained in his speech some of the characteristics of his native Wales, he was always effusively polite to his customers and he systematically cheated them right, left and centre. A tall, spare man in his middle forties, half-moon spectacles perched precariously almost on the tip of his beaky nose, he had never been known to express disagreement with any of his customers. His wife, also from the green valleys, was a tiny, plump woman whose pride and joy was their son, an eighteen-year-old rapscallion with an acne-scarred face who occasionally helped out in the shop when he was not careering around the Sussex countryside on an ancient motorbike.

On this particular morning Evans was attending to the wants of the wife of one of the jobbing gardeners at Grange Hall. As he listened to the string of complaints, Evans managed to slip a couple of tired tomatoes in amongst the sound ones. He hated waste, which was why he always passed on the old stock to his customers. The butt of the lady's complaint appeared to be the estate manager at the Hall, who had instituted new working practices.

'He'm a slave-driver, that Galbraith. My man don't have no time for a proper lunch,' she whined.

Evans gave her the full benefit of an unctuous smile, at the same time turning over in his mind the possibility of off-loading a few packets of Quick-Snack which had passed their 'sell by' date. He decided against the idea and placed the bag of tomatoes on the counter.

'Dear, oh dear, Mrs. Groves,' he said. 'Poor Tom. Still, you do keep him well-fed at home I'm sure. Now, that'll be three pounds and six pee exactly.'

Mrs. Groves counted out the money from her shabby purse. She had been overcharged twenty-six pence but, as Evans would freely admit, everybody can make a mistake. The fact that these errors in simple addition invariably turned out to his advantage was, Evans reasoned, just one of those things and part of the proper conduct of a successful business.

Mrs. Groves was the last customer of the day. Evans put up the CLOSED sign on the door and retired to the upper part of the premises to enjoy a good meal at wholesale prices and an evening in front of the outsize colour television set.

Coincident with the closing of the corner store, the evening session at the Anscombe Arms was shifting into top gear. The cribbage school was already in progress, the four participants crouched over the table, glasses of their favourite beverages at their elbows. Their game would continue until closing time, punctuated at intervals by noisy altercation when one or other of the players was guilty of breaking the rules. Josh Hamilton leaned on the bar deep in conversation with two of his cronies while the evening help, a young woman from the village earning a tax-free emolument, pulled the pints and washed the glasses. The bar was wreathed in smoke from pipes and cigarettes.

'I'm telling you, Josh,' said Frank Gilliam, head gamekeeper at the Hall, 'that bloody Galbraith is getting too big for 'is boots. Guess what 'is latest game is.'

'No idea,' said Josh.

'Putting in what 'e calls time and motion for the staff. We've got to fill in daily returns - account for every hour of the day. Daft idea. You can't run an estate like a bloody factory.'

'Oh, aye,' said Josh.

Ted Oakes, Gilliam's assistant, put in his two pen-north.

'Galbraith's 'ad it all 'is own way for too long,' he said. 'Gone to 'is 'ead. Going to come unstuck in a big way I reckon.'

'Should 'a seen the gardeners' returns,' said Gilliam. 'All muck an' manure. There's only one of 'em can write an' he can't spell.'

So it went on, rumour feeding on gossip which in turn was bolstered by half-truth and innuendo. By the time the pub closed, many reputations were in shreds, with Miss Thynne-Williams and her agent streets ahead in the unpopularity stakes. Unaware of the seething discontent in the village, the lady spent hours with her solicitors trying to find some loophole in the law with which to slaughter the chairman of the Parish Council while Galbraith pressed on with his crackpot schemes to harness Dame Nature to a time schedule.

Tommy Hutton was not a great socialiser, and his wife seemed to be quite content to stay at home and care for their daughter while ensuring that her domestic duties were not neglected. In the result, they were known in the village as a nice young pair who kept themselves to themselves, didn't poke their noses into other folks' business, and were a model couple.

Tommy was quite happy with the daily routine which, ever since his marriage, had scarcely varied from one weeks end to another. At work he was an ideal employee, diligent and conscientious, finding great satisfaction in executing drawings which in themselves were works of art. It was generally accepted that, when the chief draughtsman reached the age of retirement, Tommy would step into his shoes.

This is not to say that Tommy was a dull fellow. He got on well with his fellow-workers, shared their jokes and laughter and was regarded as a young man who possessed all the requisites for a successful career in his chosen profession. At the age of twenty-six he had come a long way. There was every indication that he would go much further.

Saturdays and Sundays were special days in the Hutton household. This was when father, mother and child shared a mutual happiness, when Tommy pottered in the garden or played games with Elizabeth while Jean prepared delicious meals in the kitchen which was her pride and joy. She was forever experimenting with new and appetising dishes using herbs grown in her own section of the garden. She was never at a loss for fresh vegetables, since they flowed in a constant stream from the Grimstones next door. The retired civil servant took great pride in the growing and an even greater pride in his neighbour's fulsome compliments on the quality and freshness of his produce.

On this particular Saturday in early April, Tommy strolled up to the Anscombe Arms where it was his habit to spend an hour before the evening meal downing a couple of pints of bitter and indulging in inconsequential chat with the landlord and those of his customers who happened to be among those present. Josh Hamilton, who was careful not to play favourites, nevertheless showed some small preference in favour of young Tommy Hutton who, in his estimation, was a credit to the village and destined to play an important part in its development. Tommy was one of the few who merited meaningful discussion in place of Hamilton's usual 'Oh, aye'.

When Tommy entered the bar the only customer present was the head gamekeeper at the Hall. Frank

15

Gilliam was, as usual, holding forth on the iniquities of the estate manager, and Hamilton welcomed the entrance of one of his more favoured clients as a happy diversion.

'How are you then, Tommy?' he said as he pulled a pint and set the glass on the bar.

'Fine, thanks, Josh,' replied Tommy. 'What are you having?'

'Not just now. Got a long evening ahead.'

Tommy turned to Gilliam.

'What about you?' he asked.

'The usual,' said the gamekeeper. Josh was already pulling another pint. According to well-established protocol, Gilliam would pay for Tommy's second pint and honours would be even.

'Alright for the game next Saturday?' Josh was addressing Tommy, the game in question being the first match of the cricket season to be played against an eleven from Crickham some seven miles away. Josh took a keen interest in local sport. He had, in his younger days, played Rugby for the county and, as captain of Anscombe's cricket team was keen to field the best possible side in what was an important annual event. Tommy had proved himself to be a useful middle-order bat but, more importantly, was a medium-pace bowler who knew how to make full use of the bumpy wicket carved from Commander Reece's meadow.

'I'm available,' said Tommy. 'I hear Crickham have got Matthias playing for them.'

Charlie Matthias was an ex-county player who, in his day, had sported an England cap.

'That'll be a ruddy good wicket for you to take,' said Gilliam.

Tommy laughed, and curled his fingers round an imaginary ball. 'We'll see,' he said.

'Is that right Galbraith's joined the club?' said Gilliam.

'I've got his name down,' said Hamilton. 'Twelfth man. He can bring the drinks out.'

'Bit of a come-down for the mighty Galbraith,' said Tommy. 'He won't like that.'

'Then he can lump it. He won't put a pair of pads on as long as I'm captain.'

The spectacle of the mighty Galbraith trotting from the pavilion bearing a tray of drinks for the thirsty players was altogether too much. The three men were still roaring with laughter when the door opened and Gilliam's assistant entered.

'What's the joke?' he asked.

'Josh 'ere 'as just given Galbraith a place in the eleven for next Saturday, Ted,' said Gilliam.

'Give me a pint, Josh,' said Ted Oakes, 'then you can cross my name off the list. Bad enough to 'ave to work with the sod. Damned if I'll play in the same team...'

''old yer 'osses, Ted,' interrupted Gilliam. 'The feller goes in tenth wicket down.'

'Bloody 'ell. Twelfth man. 'e won't swallow that.'

'All the same to me,' said Josh Hamilton.

The subject of the conversation in the Anscombe Arms was closeted with his employer in the latter's study. Ian Galbraith, a short, stocky man in his middle forties, had a mop of flaming red hair and a temper to match. There were no signs of temper here, however. Galbraith knew which side of his bread was buttered and his attitude to Miss Thynne-Williams was quietly subservient.

'It appears that you made some errors in your estimate of the extent of the dry rot,' the lady was saying. 'I've had an independent estimate prepared and it would seem that your figures are on the high side by something in the order of five thousand pounds.'

Galbraith thought furiously for some seconds; Damn the old bat, she must have sneaked a surveyor into the Hall during one of his absences from the estate. Just the same, he had to have an answer to Miss Thynne-Williams charge.

'Well, ma'am,' he said, 'nobody can be quite sure when dealing with dry rot. I admit my estimate did take account of contingencies, but as I see it, it's best to be on the safe side. After all, it is my job to protect your interests.'

Miss Thynne-Williams was mollified, but not convinced. There still remained the hurdle of the Parish Council endorsement of her application for a grant, and she put the matter squarely to her estate manager. As usual, he was not lost for an answer.

'If I may suggest, ma'am, you could get another estimate from other sources and present both of them in support of your application. That would comply with the rules. If there should be a shortfall I'm sure I could make it up in - er - other ways.'

The lady glanced at the documents spread out on her desk. Galbraith's suggestion possessed some merit and would provide her with a weapon which could be used to defeat the chairman of the Parish Council. On the other hand, and taking the long view, she might have to dip into her private resources, and that was unthinkable. She came to a decision.

'Very well, Galbraith. I will do as you suggest. However, I must make it quite plain that I look to you to ensure that I do not become liable for any of the costs in this matter.'

'I can guarantee that, ma'am.'

'Excellent. Now there's just one more small problem. About the seven-acre meadow grazing rights...'

18

As his employer droned on, Galbraith permitted himself an inward satisfied smile. His mind was already working on a scheme necessitating an approach to a cowboy firm in Crawley who would pay handsomely for the privilege of winning a contract to repair the Hall's ancient fabric. A few sweeteners in the right direction would make it certain that the contract would be awarded to his nominees. As to the bunch of wankers on the Parish Council, he was confident that Miss Thynne-Williams would triumph over them. He looked forward to the coming summer with keen anticipation.

Tommy had thoroughly enjoyed the weekend. The meal on Saturday evening had been delicious. Sunday had been spent on the Downs with a picnic lunch prepared by Jean. Little Elizabeth had scampered over the turf, squealing and giggling as she chased the tennis ball which Tommy gently lobbed in her direction. The child had fallen asleep in his arms as the bus wended its way back to Anscombe. He had never been so happy in his life.

Now it was Monday morning and back to work. As he pedalled his bicycle along the main road to Crawley, Tommy gave some thought to an idea which had been on his mind for some time. With a comfortable balance at the bank he could well afford to buy a small car which would add another dimension to family life, weekend trips to the coast, perhaps a motoring holiday on the Continent and, of course, an easy journey to and from the factory every day. The more he thought about it the more entrancing the prospect became. He decided that he would take an hour off that afternoon and visit the local Ford dealer.

During the morning he was kept busy on a rush job, preparing a drawing which had to be blue-printed and on the shop floor by lunch time. The task had fallen naturally to Tommy. He was far and away the fastest and most accurate draughtsman in the office, and it was a foregone conclusion that he would step into the shoes of the chief of the drawing department when the time came for retirement. It was with the sense of having done a first-class job that Tommy went off to the works canteen for lunch.

The talk over lunch was centred on one topic. News had come over the radio of a serious train smash on the outskirts of Brighton. A passenger train had ploughed into the rear of a stationery goods train. It was said that the death roll was twenty with fifty seriously injured. Tommy gave a passing thought to the tragedy, the effect on those who had been spared and the sorrow of the mourning relatives. He nevertheless ate a hearty lunch, returning to the department precisely at two o'clock. Five minutes later he was summoned to his chief's office. As he entered the room he had a sudden feeling that there was something untoward . Standing beside the head of department was a stolid police constable.

There is no easy way of imparting tragic news.

'Mister Hutton?' enquired the officer.

'That's right,' answered Tommy.

The constable might have been giving evidence in a motoring case.

'I'm sorry, sir. There was a train collision at eleven o'clock this morning. Your wife and daughter were among those fatally injured.'

CHAPTER 2.

It was a grey dawn and a light mist hovered over the downs. In the hollow where Anscombe lay the mist had thickened to a dense fog. It was unseasonably cold.

On the sofa in the living room, where he had spent the night, Tommy Hutton awoke to another day. He opened his eyes and stared dully at the uncurtained window. A sudden fit of coughing racked his body and he retched uncontrollably for a full minute. His body trembling, he swung his feet to the floor and attempted to lever himself upright. He succeeded at the third try and stumbled into the passage that led to the kitchen, almost falling as he tripped over a couple of empty bottles lying on the carpet. Clutching at the edge of the sink in the kitchen he focussed his eyes on the draining board. Among the welter of bottles he spotted one which contained a few inches of whisky. It was unstoppered. He raised the neck of the bottle to his lips and gulped greedily then, gasping and spluttering, collapsed on to the nearest chair.

He had been drunk for five days, ever since he had formally identified the bodies of his wife and child at the mortuary. They were not really bodies, just two pallid faces emerging from coverings that hid what little remained of their mangled torsos. He had taken one look, mumbled a few words to the coroner's officer and rushed out of the building into the street.

For the next hour he tramped the streets, seeing nothing but the two masks which had been the faces of his wife and his daughter, hearing nothing but the pounding in his head. Then he came to the public house, a welcome doorway to oblivion, where he sat for hours drinking large whiskys until the pain in his temples was replaced by nausea and his stomach rebelled against the treatment being meted out to it. He had vomited on the carpet before being thrown out of the pub by an outraged barman. From then on it was nightmare all the way. Hugging two bottles of whisky to his chest he made for the station, changed his mind about waiting for a train and hired a taxi to drive him home. There he collapsed into a chair in the living room of the empty house and drank until he fell into an uneasy slumber.

He woke several times during that night, and each time he reached for the bottle beside him. At dawn he rampaged through the house, calling for Jean and Elizabeth, overturning furniture and smashing up anything breakable. He slept once more and awoke with a raging thirst. The whisky had run out, so he drank enormous quantities of water. Yet it was whisky he craved, whisky and blessed forgetfulness. He left the house and staggered rather than walked as far as the Anscombe Arms.

Josh Hamilton had been shocked by the spectacle which confronted him when he opened the door in response to Tommy's repeated knocking. This pathetic figure, unshaven and dirty, his rumpled clothing stained with vomit, was not the Tommy Hutton he had known and valued as a good and regular customer. Tommy, for his part, was in no mood for niceties. He wanted whisky and was determined to get it. There was some argument but Tommy finally had his way and departed with three bottles of Haig in a carrier bag with a final admonition from the landlord. 'Don't come back until you've cleaned yourself up,' Josh had said.

There was naturally great sympathy in the village for the unfortunate Tommy, and there were many callers at the Hutton home. They were met by drawn curtains and a locked door behind which the owner of the house, crazed with grief and bemused with whisky, muttered obscenities at these disturbances of his peace. He did not attend the funeral of his wife and daughter, which had been arranged by Jean's parents nor did he open the letters which piled up behind the front door, for Tommy Hutton had crossed the dividing line between sanity and madness.

Opinions as to what constitutes a broken heart are many and often divided. Psychiatrists, whose mental processes are subject to occasional vagaries, are apt to put it all down to self-pity, a rough diagnosis invariably followed by rough treatment, which does little for the broken heart but tends to knock hell out of the brainbox.

Perhaps the cure for a broken heart lies in large and regular doses of stimulants, dulling the senses and wrecking the nervous system, bringing to the sufferer the delusion that whatever it was had not really happened. Tommy held long conversations with Jean and Elizabeth, spectres far more real to him than the pitiable mounds beneath the shrouds in the mortuary. In his lucid moments, which were few and far between, he recognised that these phantoms were part of a life that had gone forever. A frenzied gulp at the bottle thrust him back into the dream world where the house was warm and cosy, where the chatter and laughter of his wife and daughter echoed in every room and where everything was for the best in the best of all possible worlds.

What Tommy did now, with the slow deliberation of the sodden drunk, was designed to wipe out all memories of his past life. It was early morning, the final dregs of the last bottle of whisky had been despatched and it was a time for action. Slowly he moved around the house, collecting books, papers, odds and ends of clothing and anything else that was combustible. From the

23

cupboard under the kitchen sink he took a can containing the best part of a gallon of paraffin with which he anointed the piles of rubbish in the sitting room, the dining room and the kitchen. His last act was to empty his pockets of everything save his cheque book and bank cash card before he moved methodically from room to room with a lighted taper. The fire was beginning to take hold as he wheeled his bicycle out of the front door and took the road to Crawley. Arriving at the station and leaving the bike on the forecourt, he staggered into the booking hall and bought a single ticket to London.

Victoria station is a large, main-line terminus, for many the end of a journey, for many the beginning. For Tommy it was the start of a new life which he had chosen deliberately, for here in the midst of teeming crowds he found anonymity. He was one of many thousands of human derelicts who did not rate even a passing glance from the busy inhabitants of the metropolis. There was no one to point a finger at him, to say poor Tommy Hutton, to remind him of the loss of his wife and child, to tell him to pull himself together. Now he was completely alone, his past wiped out in flames.

The train journey had been almost unbearable. He sat huddled in a corner of the carriage, his arms crossed over an aching void, which was tied up in knots of agony, craving the anodyne of drink. As fast as his legs could carry him, he hastened out of the station in search of an off-licence which would be open at this hour of the morning. He found what he was looking for in the Vauxhall Bridge Road, where a cheerful Pakistani obligingly packed two bottles of Haig in a plastic carrier bag, took his money and told him to 'have a nice day'. With salvation in his possession, there was now no need for haste. Tommy ambled round the next corner into a deserted side street, where he seated himself on the edge of the kerb, opened one of the bottles and drank deeply.

It took only a few minutes for the fire in his belly to subside and be replaced by the warm glow with which he was all too familiar. Though there was a slight nip in the air the whisky provided an effective antidote, so Tommy remained where he was for the time being. There were few passers-by and the sight of a shabby drunk clutching a carrier bag was not unusual in the area.

Though he had not visited the capital often, Tommy was aware of the general lay-out of central London. Somewhere to the east of his present position lay Buckingham Palace and the grassy sweep of Green Park, and he decided to head in that direction. Fortified by another swig from the bottle he rose to his feet and retraced his steps to the station. Negotiating the hurly-burly of traffic at the top of Victoria Street he came to Buckingham Palace Road at the end of which he could see the massive ornamental gates beyond which the statue of Queen Victoria bent a stern gaze on the court-yard of the Palace.

Early tourists were taking up positions from which they would watch the changing of the guard later in the morning. Threading his way through the excited mob, Tommy came to the broad tree-lined avenue of the Mall and thence to the park itself. Choosing a quiet spot he stretched himself out on the grass, took another gulp from the bottle and closed his eyes. He fell into a light sleep, and the phantoms that the fire had not destroyed came to his inward eye, Jean and Elizabeth running over the turf of the downs, the child lying in her cot, Jean turning from the stove in the kitchen, her dark eyes asking a question to which he had no reply.

He was brought back to his surroundings by a voice which sounded almost in his ear. He opened his eyes. The first thing he saw was what seemed to be a mass of tangled hair with a long, bony nose projecting from the centre. There must have been a mouth somewhere beneath the nose, but its whereabouts was a matter of conjecture. The words that issued from this mouth were accompanied by a waft of breath reminiscent of a compost heap.

'Anything left in that bottle?' said the voice.

Tommy sat bolt upright and surveyed the apparition that was lowering itself to the grass beside him. Apart from the hair, which stood out like a halo, there was a very large overcoat held together with safety pins and a length of string. Protruding from the hem of the coat were a pair of large and very decrepit boots. That was the complete picture. Tommy, at a loss for words, could only stare.

'Come on, mate,' said the apparition. 'I'm dying for a drink. What about it?'

Tommy was in two minds. He knew what it was like to be deprived of drink. On the other hand, the thought of watching that malodorous mouth close round the neck of his bottle turned his stomach over. He came to a quick decision. Tilting the bottle to his lips he swallowed half the remaining contents and, struggling to his feet as quickly as he could, he thrust the bottle into the outstretched hand which had appeared from the folds of the overcoat.

'You can keep it,' he said. 'Gotta be off. Good luck.'

He was away across the park as fast as his legs would carry him, which wasn't very quickly as he soon realised. He began to gasp for breath. During the past few days his physical condition had deteriorated to a point where even the most moderate exertion distressed him.

Looking back over his shoulder he saw that he had put a considerable distance between himself and the smelly tramp. He slowed his pace and began to walk towards Admiralty Arch.

Though Tommy did not know it, one of the gathering points for London's homeless down-and-outs was the flight of steps that fronted the ancient church of Saint Martin's in the Fields. The vagrants came in all shapes and sizes, some of them merely bundles of rags from which heads, feet and hands stuck out in the appropriate places, while others had obviously made some attempt to keep up appearances and were more conventionally clothed. They all had one thing in common. They had set their feet on the road to nowhere and had reached the point of no return. This was the sight that met Tommy's eyes as he laboriously climbed the steps that led from Trafalgar Square to the pavement opposite the National Portrait Gallery. He leaned on the convenient parapet, heart thumping and calf muscles aching, almost on the point of collapse. His whisky-addled brain told him that he needed to rest and get some food down his throat. In Charing Cross Road he came across a small and rather dirty cafe, where he ate two cheese rolls and drank a cup of coffee which he laced surreptitiously with a dollop of whiskey from his one remaining bottle. That need attended to, he once more launched himself on the streets without any fixed purpose other than to waste time until the evening, when he would organise a bed for the night. Beyond that he did not bother to think. Husbanding his physical resources by the simple expedient of putting one foot before the other and making frequent stops for rest, he meandered up Charing Cross Road toward Cambridge Circus. His vision was blurred but, paradoxically, his perceptions were sharpened as though the alcohol permeating his bloodstream had somehow made him more aware of the sounds and smells of the metropolis. The traffic whizzed by in both directions, vans and lorries, taxis, motor cars of every sort from the humble Ford to the majestic Rolls. Before the Palace theatre a shining stretched limousine decanted a pop group whom he recognised from their television appearances, a collection of scruffy louts who possessed little talent beyond their ability to strum three chords on their guitars and bellow an incomprehensible torrent of gibberish into a microphone. Tommy sneered, remembering the times he had switched off the television before they had got into their stride. He pressed on and, on a sudden impulse, turned left into a narrow street which would lead him into the heart of Soho, an area of exotic foreign sights, sounds and smells where on one of his rare visits to the capital he had eaten a memorable meal. What was the name of the restaurant? Try as he would, he could not remember. Then his eye lighted on a sign outside a public house. Over the representation of a bundle of golden corn, gilded lettering spelled out the name. The Wheatsheaf. This was the place where that heroic boozer, the poet Dylan Thomas, had caroused with his literary cronies. Tommy pushed open the door and went in. Whatever literary associations the place had possessed during Thomas's short but hectic patronage, they had long gone. An old man sat at one of the tables gazing morosely into a pint of Guiness. On two stools at the bar perched a brace of gaudily-dressed birds whose profession was all too obvious. Apart from these three there were no other customers in the place. Tommy marched up to the bar and ordered a double Scotch, which was served without enthusiasm by a bored young woman with a pronounced Australian accent.

Nobody paid any attention to him as he sat in a corner

cradling his glass, which was fine so far as Tommy was concerned. He had no desire to be noticed. All he wanted to do was to sail along on a sea of alcohol with only his dreams for company. He remembered that last morning with Jean before he left the house, how she had mentioned that she might pop down to Brighton to get a few things for Elizabeth. Oh, God, he thought, why did they have to be on that train, that one particular train. Tears welled up in his eyes. He hurriedly drank his whisky and left the bar.

Outside in the street he leaned against a lamp post for support, his body shaken with sobs as the tears ran down his unshaven cheeks. Then the bile rose in his throat and he was violently sick. The spasm passed, and with shaking hands he made ineffectual attempts to wipe the vomit from the front of his jacket. The spectacle he presented would have caused considerable comment in Anscombe. Here in the big city people passed him by without a second glance.

He walked into Charlotte Street, neither knowing nor caring where he was going. He crossed the street to where an off-licence had its doors open for custom and bought a bottle of Scotch. Now, with two bottles safely in his carrier he had no fear of running short in the immediate future. Outside the shop he counted his money, sixty pounds in notes and a handful of small change. This would do to be going on with, he thought, and continued on his way towards Euston Road. Automatically he put his hand into the inside pocket of his coat to assure himself that his chequebook and cash card were safe.

Anscombe was buzzing with speculation that day. By the time the Grimstones had noticed the fire it had gained a firm hold and the ancient timbers were well ablaze. When the fire engines got to the scene the fire was out of control and the roof had collapsed. Within the hour the house was gutted, despite the hundreds of gallons of water that had been pumped into the conflagration. A serious situation such as this was outside the province of the village constable, who had called up reinforcements from Crawley. Now a small group consisting of Mr. Grimstone, the fire chief, a sergeant and a constable from the county town and the village constable himself stood by the police car surveying the wreckage of what had once been the home of the Hutton family. The sergeant was addressing Mr. Grimstone.

'Was there anybody in there?' he asked.

'I don't really know,' answered Grimstone. 'Tommy had locked himself in. There was only him. His...'

'Yes, I know about that. Did you see anything of him early on?'

'No, nothing.'

'We'll be able to make a search soon,' said the leading fireman. 'When things cool down a bit I'll send the lads in.'

'They know what to look for?' said the sergeant, and there was a world of significance in his tone of voice.

'They know alright,' replied the fireman.

'Right. Now Mr. Grimstone, I'll take a statement from you later on.' To the village bobby, 'just keep an eye on the place when we've finished.' To the small knot of villagers who had gathered at a respectful distance, 'you can all go home now. There's nothing more to see.'

This was enough to start the stories going round. In no time at all the word flashed round the village that Tommy Hutton had set fire to his house and had burned to death. The gossips embroidered the simple facts, adding bits and pieces of their own invention. Josh Hamilton recalled Tommy's visit to the pub in search of

30

drink.

'Poor sod,' he said. 'Losing his wife and kid like that. I reckon he went round the bend.'

Speculation was brought to an end when the report of the incident appeared in the local paper. It stated boldly and succinctly that a fire had burned down a house in Anscombe, that there had been no fatalities and that the owner of the premises had been away from home at the time. The report went on to say that the fire had probably started in the kitchen of the house due to the failure of electrical equipment and foul play was not suspected.

Tommy Hutton was not aware of any of this activity in his home town. In fact he was not aware of anything much, being stretched out on a bench in Regent's Park, dead drunk and unconscious of his whereabouts. Twice that afternoon he had been sick, his stomach ridding itself of its contents mostly down the front of his jacket. He looked terrible and reeked like a public urinal.

As the evening closed in he stirred and opened one-bleary eye, making an effort to take in his surroundings. He saw green grass and trees. From a distance came the noises of children at play, laughter and cries which pierced his throbbing head like tiny arrows. He moved slightly and his aching bones screamed a protest as a foul taste rose in the back of his mouth presaging another bout of vomiting. He fell back on the bench with a groan of agony, then felt about him in panic. The bottle, where was the bottle? His fingers encountered a smooth round shape lying against his thigh. Concentrating his mind and every nerve in his body he swung his feet to the ground and levered himself into a sitting position.

The next problem lay in opening the screw-cap on the new bottle, on which the seal was intact. There was no

31

strength in his hands and he wrestled desperately for what seemed to be hours, though in reality it was but a few minutes. Then the seal broke. He unscrewed the cap, lifted the neck of the bottle to his lips and drank long and deep. The medicine worked and within minutes his mind was able to cope with the problem which had been nagging him the whole day. Where was he going to spend the night?

On one of his visits he had found himself in an area where every large house appeared to be an hotel. He remembered that it was not far from Marble Arch, but the name of the area eluded him. Bay something or other, he thought. Then it came to him - Bayswater, that was it. Now all he had to do was to get there. In his present state walking was out of the question.

The simple business of getting to his feet caused him to break out in a sweat, and he had to support himself on the arm of the bench until the trembling in his legs sunsided. Carefully placing one foot in front of the other and concentrating on preserving his balance he took a few steps which gradually became a shambling walk. He came to an exit from the park and emerged into Upper Baker Street, where he leaned against a wall to recover his breath. From the wall he progressed to a lamp post, to which he clung as a drowning man would hang on to anything which kept his head above water. Taxis were crawling alongside the kerb, hunting for fares, but none of the drivers paid attention to Tommy's frantic signals. All they saw from behind the wheel was a bedraggled figure, an unshaven face and the possible development of trouble. The London cabbie, an expert in avoiding the complications that beset those in his line of business, knows when to turn a blind eye. Had it not been for a compassionate driver who sensed that Tommy was in extremis, he might have remained there forever. When the burly cabbie appeared at his elbow, Tommy was literally on his last legs and on the point of total collapse. The cabbie put a massive hand under the elbow of his intended fare. 'Pissed, mate?' he enquired, not unkindly. Tommy's furred and swollen tongue refused to obey orders, and his reply was an incoherent mumble. 'Where d'yer want to go?' said the cabbie. Tommy rallied his scattered wits and managed to utter two words.

'Bayswater. Hotel,' he said.

The cabbie was not without experience of drunks and their behaviour. The two words told him that here was an alcoholic who had been out on the toot, gone over the top and now wanted nothing more in life than to get back to some miserable room in one of the flophouses which abounded in the Bayswater area. That would be Beaufort Square, on that he would bet his bottom dollar. If the punter was skint then he would lose about three quid, which was neither here nor there.

'Got any cash?' said the cabbie. Tommy nodded.

'OK then. Here we go.'

Lifting his semi-conscious fare with one muscular arm the cabbie stowed him in a corner of the cab, closed the door securely and was in the driving seat and into the stream of traffic before Tommy had fallen asleep.

Beaufort Square in the Bayswater section of the City of Westminster, is not a square in the accepted sense but a long, wide street. On either side rise massive Victorian houses once the home of massive Victorian families but now split up into a series of rabbit warrens masquerading as bed and breakfast accommodation. The shifting population consists mainly of homeless persons and families placed there under the aegis of the local authority who pay the rents, other needs being met by the local Social Security office. For the rest, there

33

was the usual smattering of eccentrics, lowly and badly-paid workers in the restaurants which abounded in the district, members of ethnic minorities who had abandoned starvation in their own countries in favour of semi-starvation in London and a hard core of derelicts who passed their days indulging in drinking when they could afford that luxury and begging for the wherewithal when they ran out of cash.

It was in the front of one of these former mansions that the cab containing a sleeping Tommy Hutton drew up. The shabby exterior with its peeling paintwork was similar to the other houses in the square, neglected, run-down and earning a fortune for the owner who, quite naturally, lived as far away as possible from the source of his wealth.

'Right, mate. Here we are,' said the cabbie, gently shaking his passenger by the shoulder.

Tommy alighted from the taxi unaided, and stood swaying slightly. He hauled a crumpled collection of notes from his pocket and selecting one at random he thrust it into the cabbie's hand with a muttered word of thanks. His only desire was to get off the street and into some quiet haven. To say that he made a dive for the sanctuary of the hotel would be a masterpiece of understatement.

The smiling Asian at the reception desk had seen it all before. There was no need for Tommy to make his wants known.

'Fifteen pounds a night, seventy-two pounds a week,' said Islam's gift to the United Kingdom.

Tommy still held a fistful of notes, which he dropped on the counter.

'More tomorrow,' he said.

The money vanished in the twinkling of an eye, to be replaced by a key attached to a sizeable block of wood.

'Room seven, first floor,' said the amiable voice.

Siezing the key, Tommy staggered across the lobby and hoisted himself up the stairs. After a short struggle with the key he managed to gain entry to the room, where the first and most welcome sight was a single bed. He fell on the soiled counterpane and closed his eyes.

Sleep did not come. Instead a grey, swirling mist wreathed itself into monstrous images against a background of intense black. Slowly he curled himself into a foetal position, his brain sharp and clear sending out messages to his arms and legs which rendered a sluggish response. His heart hammered out a regular rhythm in time with a childish voice in endless repetition, daddy, daddy, daddy, daddy... The thudding of his heart and the cries of the child merged into the click-clack of pounding wheels on a railway track, then came terrifying noises as metal ground into metal, screams and yells of mortal anguish as bodies were torn apart and then silence as the two white faces which would be part of his eternal nightmare stood out starkly against the blackness as Jean's voice whispered brokenly, sorry, Tommy, sorry...

He opened his eyes and raised himself on one elbow. His hand closed round the neck of the bottle in his coat pocket. As he poured the essence of forgetfulness down his throat his body relaxed and the incessant battering in his temples abated. Now came the maudlin tears in an unstoppable torrent accompanied by racking sobs that shook his exhausted frame. Finally the empty bottle fell from his nerveless fingers, the clouds cleared from his brain and he slept.

When he came to cautious wakefulness, early light was seeping through the one grimy window of the room. He lifted his head and groaned in agony as pain lanced through his entire being. He was still drunk, but it was not the hallucinatory intoxication of the night but another kind of alcoholic infection that permitted his mind to operate divorced from a body over which it had almost no control. He did not know it, but he was on the verge of acute alcoholism, a condition which has a profound effect on the nervous system and which, in its final stages, creates a shambling wreck out of a normal human being.

Loth to repeat the painful experience of moving his head, he stared for a while at the ceiling of the room. It was not a pleasant sight, an expanse of crumbling plaster with a pendant strand of wire supporting an unshaded light bulb and a battered section of cornice disappearing into the flimsy wall that separated his room from that of his neighbour. Within his limited range of vision was a corner where a tattered curtain partially concealed a yellowing hand basin with a dripping tap. What he could see of the floor covering was frayed carpet which had not seen a sweeper for a very long time. It was a God-forsaken dump but it was also a refuge, a hole into which he could creep at any time.

He realised that he could not lie on his bed all day, that certain matters had to be attended to, the most important being topping up his cash situation. Somehow he began to exercise control over his limbs, first flexing his knees then bending his arms until in the end he achieved a degree of mobility. In a final effort which left him sweating his feet found the floor and he sat up on the edge of the bed. The next step was to clean himself up in preparation for a foray into the outer world. After several abortive attempts, he at last managed to stand upright. He took a few tentative steps in the direction of the hand basin and promptly fell on his face.

History has chronicled the durability of heroes who fought against hunger, thirst and fatigue to reach the goals they had set themselves, proving that somewhere deep in the human psyche there are untapped resources which can be called upon in times of crisis. Tommy Hutton was no hero but there was in him something of the stuff of which heroes are made. He crawled across the smelly carpet to the curtained corner, struggled to his feet and splashed his face liberally in cold water. A threadbare towel served to wipe away the aftermath of the sketchy wash and also to remove some of the stains from the front of his jacket. Judging that he was now sufficiently presentable to face the outside world, he left the room.

He negotiated the stairs and reached the front door of the hotel without mishap. Once on the pavement he stood for a few moments breathing deeply. There was still a weakness in his knees which made walking difficult, but walk he did, putting one foot in front of the other with grim determination. After a while he came to a broad and busy thoroughfare and a bank which boasted a cash dispenser. Inserting his cash card into the slot, he tapped out the appropriate numbers and the machine spewed out two hundred pounds.

Comfortable in the knowledge that his financial position was secure for the moment, he paid a call on one of the many off-licences in the street, which he identified as being Queensway. Carrying a plastic bag containing three bottles of whisky, he dropped in on one the many pubs in the vicinity, where he rapidly put away four large Scotches which quelled the queasiness in his stomach and put a new spring in his step. On the way back to the hotel he purchased a shirt, together with a razor and shaving cream. Equipped with these basic necessities, and having paid the smiling Asian a further

37

fifty pounds, giving him a week's security of tenure of his sleazy room, Tommy Hutton embarked on his new life.

It has been said that London is a collection of villages, each borough divided into smaller districts which have an identity all their own. The City of London proper, that square mile that has been described as the financial centre of the world, is an entity in itself. No village this, no sowing or mowing or harvesting. Money is planted, nurtured and brought to harvest in the shape of more money and Mammon is the only God. In the City of Westminster, Bayswater is in the nature of a village, though there is little evidence of the rural life in its teeming streets and squares. The denizens are of all shapes, sizes, colours and origins, of various religions ranging from Muslim to Seventh Day Adventists. The principal thoroughfare is Queensway, a one-way street which stretches from Bayswater Road to Westbourne Grove, lined with restaurants, boutiques, supermarkets, the ubiqitous banks and bureaux de change and a plush casino. The area is well endowed with public houses which in turn are well patronised by the indigent population.

Tommy Hutton slotted into this scene at the lower end of the spending scale. A shabby figure, most of the time with a stubble surrounding his chin and upper lip, he attracted little attention in the various pubs in which he passed many hours. He would sit alone, nursing a glass of whisky and rebuffing any attempt at opening a conversation by the more gregarious customers. Towards the end of an evening session, hardly able to stand, he would shuffle off to his lonely room and fall on to the bed without troubling to undress. During the nights he awoke frequently and it was then that he had recourse to the bottle.

So the days passed for the pitiable wreck that had once been Tommy Hutton, a round of the pubs, junk food meals at unusual hours in squalid cafes and irregular visits to the cash dispenser to top up his funds. There came a day when he inserted his cash card into the slot of the dispenser, tapped out his requirements and watched dully and without any real comprehension as the machine swallowed his plastic friend. He did not return to his room. With his remaining cash he bought a half-bottle of whisky, made his way to the park and settled down for the night.

CHAPTER 3.

Statistics as to the number of homeless people in inner London are hard to come by. For a start there are the hard-core vagrants who pay lip service to their idea of freedom and roam the streets of the capital, one hand outstretched to receive the gifts of the compassionate. Then there is a leavening of lunatics, men and women of feeble mind released from mental institutions in order that they may be rehabilitated by 'community care', whatever that may mean. Add to that some hundreds of young people of both sexes who leave their homes to find fame and fortune in the big city, and who fall victim to a Government edict that they may only stay in one area for a period of two weeks. Many of them fall victim to another kind of predator and end up as rent boys or juvenile whores.

Whatever their numbers might be, that total was increased by one unit on an early summer morning. Tommy Hutton, moderately sober for the first time in many weeks, sat under a tree in Hyde Park and paid some thought to his immediate future. The few coins in his pocket added up to a little over three pounds. Other than that, he possessed nothing save for the shabby suit and grimy shirt which had been passably respectable when he left Anscombe but were now fit for the incinerator. With a three-day growth of stubble on his face and lank, dirty hair falling over his collar, he looked exactly what he was - a man who had opted out from life and joined the army of the lost.

With no fixed idea in his mind he wandered across the park and found himself on the bank of the Serpentine. The nagging ache in his stomach cried out for the balm of alcohol and the bile rose in his throat. After a furtive glance over the immediate vicinity he hurriedly vomited on the grass at the same moment as a pair of riders on shining mounts trotted past him. She was a beautiful young woman, long blonde hair escaping from beneath a peaked riding cap, impeccable in hacking jacket and jodhpurs. He was a handsome elderly man who sat his horse as though glued to the saddle. Her voice came to Tommy loud and clear, a high, imperious shriek that needed no amplifier.

'You dirty, disgusting old man,' she yelled.

DIRTY... DISGUSTING... OLD. Each word was like a slap in the face as he staggered from the scene of this latest humiliation. He was now desperate for a drink. But where could he get it? He emerged from the park at the ornate gate under the shadow of the Hilton Hotel and plunged into Curzon Street. The Playboy Club, luxurious mansions, towering blocks of flats, but no off-licences. He broke into a shambling trot, hearing himself muttering the one word please over and over again. He paused at the entrance to an alleyway leading to a maze of narrow streets. This looked promising, he thought, and indeed it turned out to be just what he was looking for. Shepherds Market, an oasis of pubs, cafes and shops catering for the common people, was indeed uncommon in the plush opulence of Mayfair.

The man behind the counter of the off-licence handed over a half-bottle of whisky in exchange for almost all of Tommy's remaining capital. The trembling figure with the shaking hands was no strange spectacle in the Market, for Tommy was one of many who came from somewhere or other on the way to God alone knows where. The man behind the counter had no qualms of conscience about the transaction. It was all good for business, and the money of this piece of social wreckage was as good as anyone else's.

Outside the shop, Tommy sat down on the pavement and opened the bottle. He took a great gulp and in a few minutes the liquor had done its work, quelling the fire in his guts and stopping the trembling in his limbs. Alcohol, the great poisoner, was for him the great reviver. The discomfort he had experienced the previous night passed into memory and was soon forgotten. Only the present existed and the future could take care of itself.

His musings were interrupted by a presence which forced itself on his attention. A large, shapeless figure plumped itself down beside him on the pavement, a miasmic odour of foul breath enveloped him and he turned to face the apparition he had last encountered in Green Park on his first day in London. The familiar whining voice emerged from the forest of hair that covered the creature's face.

'Anything left in that bottle?' said the voice.

Tommy felt a moment of panic. On that morning which seemed so long ago he had not been concerned about the loss of the best part of a bottle of Scotch, but now the situation was entirely different. Despite the menace of the monstrous bundle of rags leaning against him, Tommy had no intention of parting with even a drop of his precious liquor. With the courage of desperation he snarled an answer to the question.

'Sod off,' he said.

'Don't be like that, mate,' said the voice. 'We're both in the same boat.' The tone had lost its belligerence, there was a friendly warmth to be detected. Nevertheless Tommy moved away slightly, for he was in no mood for any overtures which might result in the loss of the smallest quantity of his precious whisky. It was his lifeline, and he hung on to it like grim death.

'Come on, mate,' said the coaxing voice. 'Just a drop.'

Tommy began to relent. He knew the feeling of the aching void which could only be filled by a good, long pull at the bottle. Acting on impulse, he passed the bottle from his pocket to the grimy hand which had materialised from the bundle of rags beside him. To his surprise the offer was not taken up.

'Testing, mate,' said the voice. 'You passed.'

A non-plussed Tommy returned the bottle to his packet.

'What's the idea?' he asked.

The apparition by his side made no answer. Instead, a series of convulsions took place beneath the cover of the huge overcoat, as a result of which there emerged a large bottle almost filled with a cloudy liquid.

'Share and share alike. That's my motto.'

Tommy took the bottle hesitantly and sniffed the contents. The smell was not displeasing, a strong alcoholic odour tinged with an aroma he could not place exactly. He raised the neck of the bottle to his lips and took an exploratory sip. The effect was instantaneous. A pool of fire filled his mouth and raked his throat, he coughed and spluttered and finally croaked a question.

'What the hell is it?' he said.

'Heart starter. Litre white wine. Dollop o' meths. Rubber tubing an' gas. Bubble, bubble, bubble. Bingo!' The bulky overcoat heaved as its occupant shook with laughter. Despite himself, Tommy joined in. They made a strange sight, two derelicts sitting on the pavement in the heart of Mayfair howling like hyenas.

'What's yer name?' said the apparition.

'Tommy. What's yours?' was the reply.

'They call me Matt.'

'Short for Matthew?'

'Right. Yer an educated man. What yer doing on the road?'

Tommy made no reply, but reached for the bottle and another swig at the strange brew. This time he was more cautious, allowing the liquor to roll round his tongue before swallowing. Almost immediately he was enveloped in a rich warmth that flooded his mind and his body as he felt himself floating away on a cloud as soft as thistledown. Very slowly he collapsed in the gutter. Somebody was shaking him, pulling at his arm, a voice was pleading, yes, he was late for school and his mother was trying to get him up, but it wasn't his mother's voice, it was rougher, deeper, and he heard himself saying leave me alone, mum, let me go to sleep, don't want to go to school today, and still there was that insistent tugging and then he was strangely upright and moving through a fog where strange shapes gathered round him and leering faces with distorted mouths gibbered soundlessly and the delirium took on greater momentum as he struggled weakly against the force that propelled him on and on as he heard himself saying over and over again let me sleep, let me sleep, sleep, sleep, sleep...

He came to his senses, aware that he was lying on his back, that there was grass beneath him and warm sun caressing his face. A busy pigeon swaggered into his line of vision, snapping up the crumbs left behind by some long-gone lover of eating in the open. From a distance he could hear the hum of traffic and voices drifted faintly to his ears. He vaguely wondered where he was and how he had got there, then decided it wasn't worth bothering about and moved himself into a more comfortable position. About to lapse once more into sleep, he felt a hand on his shoulder and looked round in alarm. 'All right now, mate?' asked Matt. The effort of speech was too much for Tommy. Memory returned with a rush as there flashed on a mental screen a picture of himself and the hairy monster perched on a pavement in Shepherds Market, roaring with laughter at some joke or other, then the ensuing blackness followed by the phantom passing through an alcoholic mist full of strange sounds and even stranger figures. He managed a nod of the head as he struggled to raise himself on one elbow. 'Take it easy,' said his companion. 'Passed out, didn't yer. Lugged yer down here.' Tommy licked his lips with a tongue that was at least three sizes too large for his mouth. 'Where am I,' he croaked.

'Green Park. See the Ritz. Over there.'

Tommy took his time digesting this piece of information. He was not quite sure what the Ritz Hotel had to do with his present situation but did not feel inclined to argue. He squinted into the sky where the sun was directly overhead and guessed the time at about midday, which meant that he must have been unconscious for an hour or so. He thought, with a wry grin, that Matt's heart starter was powerful medicine. How had it been described? White wine, meths and a saturation of domestic gas which, though he was no chemist, had all the makings of something lethal. His thoughts were interrupted by another short speech from Matt, delivered as usual in abrupt sentences.

'Wanna watch that stuff. Blow yer head off. Used to it, me. Drink it all the time.'

Tommy managed a weak grin. 'You're a better man than I am, Gunga Din.'

There was a stirring among the whiskers which could be interpreted as a smile in acknowledgement of the compliment.

'Knew you was educated,' said Matt. 'Shakespeare,

innit?'

'Rudyard Kipling,' said Tommy.

'Never heard of him,' was the terse reply. The huge overcoat jerked convulsively and a grimy hand emerged from its folds, the fingers wrapped round the neck of the familiar bottle.

'Time for a drink,' said Matt. The bottle neck disappeared into an aperture in the forest of whiskers and there was a gulping sound as something like a quarter of a pint of the cloudy fluid vanished down a responsive gullet.

Tommy shuddered as he reached into his pocket for the remains of his whisky.

'I'll stick with this,' he said as he swallowed a mouthful, tentatively at first, but as his stomach failed to rebel, emptying the bottle. As the liquor began to take effect his head cleared and he felt a renewed vitality flowing through his body. He knew a desire to be up and doing though he had no clear idea of what he wanted to do nor where he wanted to do it. Anyhow, for the time being he was content to lie on the grass and let the world go on around him, to bathe in the warm sunshine and to tell himself that nothing mattered except existing for the moment and enjoying it to the full. Not that there was much to be enjoyed in his present state, he thought, for he was almost penniless, the last few drops of whisky had gone down his throat and the future looked very bleak.

Lying next to him on the grass, his companion had fallen asleep and was snoring loud enough to wake the dead. Tommy wondered idly what sort of a man was this, where had he come from and what circumstances had led to his present situation. To outward appearance he was merely a tramp, a knight of the road, a disgusting bundle of rags concealed beneath a huge overcoat belted round the waist with a length of cord. From the bottom of the garment a pair of frayed trousers protruded just far enough to make contact with the ancient boots which were worn without benefit of socks. Yet inside that repellent heap of old clothes was a human being who had once, perhaps, been a neat and tidy worker, a husband and father. What the hell, Tommy thought, Matt had been right when he said they were both in the same boat, for there was little to choose between the sleeping derelict and the ex-draughtsman from Anscombe.

His musings were interrupted by a stirring under the overcoat and movement of the hairy head. Matt was awake and obviously thirsty, for the first thing he did was to produce the bottle and take a hefty swig. He held out the concoction to Tommy.

'Have some,' he said. 'Better get used to it.'

Tommy took the proffered bottle, wiped the neck and sipped cautiously. It really wasn't bad, he thought, as he sipped again before returning the bottle to its owner, who was now in a sitting position.

'Give us that empty,' said Matt.

Tommy obligingly handed the empty whisky flask to his companion, who proceeded to fill it from his bottle.

'Keep yer going for a bit. Never can tell. Doesn't do to run short,' said Matt.

Tommy agreed with that sentiment whole-heartedly, for the panic of the morning was still present in his memory. He could imagine no greater tragedy than being without drink, the panacea that erased the pain he still felt even weeks after the event which had taken away his reason for living. That he was still alive was not due to any conscious effort on his part, for it was all the same to him whether he lived or died. Lacking the will to do away with himself, he surrendered to fortune and let events take their course.

Matt was now standing over him, swaying slightly but still in possession of such faculties as were left to him.

'C'mon then,' he was saying. 'Things to do. Better get going.'

'Where to?' asked Tommy.

'Get some bread. Foller me. Keep yer eyes open.'

What turns a man or a woman into a vagrant? To some it could be the lure of the open road, the feeling of freedom that comes from shedding the responsibilities of rents, taxes, a job of work, caring and providing for a wife and kids and all the stresses heaped on the individual who merely wants to have a peaceful existence.

In the case of Matthew Dixon, the catalyst that turned him from a well-paid worker on a North Sea oil rig into a hobo was very simple. On a night out in Aberdeen and under the influence of countless pints of the local brew, he fell foul of a couple of youths whose intention was to relieve the drunken rigger of such worldly goods as he carried on his person. Matthew, a hard man, disillusioned them, as a result of which the yobbos were carted off to hospital, where one of them subsequently died. An unsympathetic judge awarded Matthew ten years imprisonment. During the time he spent in Barlinnie jail his character underwent a profound change, and he emerged into the outside world an embittered rebel, a loner with a grudge against society.

This was the man who strode purposefully across Green Park and into Piccadilly, with Tommy close on his heels. Once on the thoroughfare Matt went to work with an ease born of long experience, sidling up to selected passers-by and muttering a few words which Tommy could not hear but which seemed to bear fruit.

Reaching Piccadilly Circus Matt crossed to the steps surrounding the statue of Eros and stood waiting for Tommy to join him.

'Have a seat, mate. Let's see what we got,' he said.

Tommy squatted beside his mentor, who produced from his pocket a handful of coins intermingled with a few Treasury notes and proceeded to count the proceeds.

'Not bad, mate,' he said. 'Seventeen pounds an' forty pence. What d'yer think o' that?'

'Bloody marvellous. How do you do it?'

'Judgement, mate, just judgement. Pick the right mark. Get in close. Stick yer hand out. Whisper. Don't make too much noise. I'm starving, mister. Give us a few bob. It never fails.'

Tommy burst into laughter. In a ten minute walk along the pavements of Piccadilly Matt had picked up the equivalent of a day's wages in some lowly employment.

'It's their conscience, mate. I look terrible. I smell awful. They want to get away,' Matt went on. 'Only one way to get rid o' me. It costs. You'll learn. One thing. Never touch 'em. Stand close, but don't touch. Got it?'

Tommy nodded. He was becoming accustomed to the rapid fire speech of his new friend but things were happening too quickly for his mind to comprehend. His introduction to Matt's heart-starter had been sudden, and his mental processes had not quite caught up with the effects of the potent brew. Of one thing, however, he was very sure. All he had to do was to follow wherever Matt led, which saved him the trouble of thinking for himself.

For the past several minutes Matt had been muttering inaudibly, but now he spoke out.

'You skint, mate?' he asked. He was holding a five

49

pound note delicately between thumb and forefinger and waving it like a fan.

'You could say that,' replied Tommy.

Matt thrust the note into Tommy's hand. 'Cop for this. Come in handy,' he said. 'Let's get moving.'

'Where to?'

'See a feller. Down the South Bank.'

The two strangely-assorted figures moved away from the steps, rating a few incurious glances from the mob of drug addicts, winos and other flotsam congregated around the statue of the winged youth armed with bow and arrow, an eternal symbol of Love boarded up against the attacks of vandals. Ambling through the pedestrian precinct of Leicester Square and on into Covent Garden, the pair finally emerged via a series of side streets into the Strand, where they were confronted by the ornate entrance to the Savoy hotel. The noon traffic was at its height, a constant stream of buses, taxis, private cars and the occasional massive juggernaut, all moving at the mandatory speed of five miles to the hour. The still air was heavy with the fumes emitted by the exhausts of the slow-moving vehicles. Talk about hell on earth, thought Tommy, memories of Anscombe and fresh country air still in his nostrils, this is bloody it.

Beside him Matt was mumbling under his breath, savage expletives directed against the occupants of the taxis and shining limousines rolling into the forecourt of the hotel. He literally shook with anger as a chauffeur-driven Daimler, packed to capacity with white-robed Arabs, passed within a couple of feet. 'Bloody bastard wogs,' he screamed.

Tommy, alarmed at this outburst of hate and aware that Matt was attracting unfavourable attention from some of the passers-by, tugged at his companion's sleeve.

'Let's get going. Haven't you got to see somebody?' said Tommy.

Matt made no reply, but set off towards Waterloo Bridge. He was still seething with anger and walked so swiftly that Tommy had all his work cut out to keep pace with him. After a while the anger evaporated and what had been almost a jog-trot slowed to a moderate walk. They came to a halt half-way across the bridge and stood looking up-river.

Matt broke the silence, bitterness and hatred in his voice. 'Bloody Ay-rabs. In the Middle East I was. On the oil rigs. They caught me. Bleedin' bottle of gin. They flogged me. In the public square. All round me. Singin', dancin' an' yellin'. Bloody wogs. I hate 'em.'

Tommy said nothing, chiefly because there was nothing he could say. In his mind's eye he saw a semi-naked Matt tied to a post while a bulky Arab laid into him with a whip to the cheers and roars of a frenzied crowd. The pain and the humiliation suffered by the victim of this barbarity must have been enormous. He understood now the deep vein of resentment that had been tapped at the sight of a bunch of Levantines being transported to the lush confines of one of the finest hotels in the world and to some extent was able to sympathise with Matt's outburst. Yet that was the way of the world, and he put the thoughts out of his mind as he leaned over the parapet of the bridge and stared at the ripples of the Thames as the wake set up by a passing craft licked against the barrier of the Embankment.

His musings were brought to an abrupt end as Matt gripped his arm.

'Let's get going. Not far now. Just over the bridge,' he said.

Close by Waterloo station, overlooking the river, lies the vast complex of the South Bank, where the Festival

Hall and its outbuildings dominate the riverside scene. The mammoth enterprise was conceived and built by the London County Council in 1951, and has during its lifetime been host to millions of native Britons and foreign tourists from all over the world.

In this decade of private affluence and public squalor, the many nooks and crannies of this remarkable area have given shelter to a growing army of the homeless. Crammed into odd corners where stone bastions give some degree of shelter are to be found a horde of human derelicts whose living quarters are large cardboard boxes garnered from the detritus thrown out by large stores and supermarkets. The popular press has given this flimsy shanty-town a name - it is called Cardboard City. A saintly nun, a visitor to Great Britain, referred to it as the shame of a nation.

It was into this half-light world that Matt led the way. He moved quickly and without hesitation, finally arriving at a secluded corner almost beneath the great arch of the bridge. At first glance it appeared to Tommy to be a tidy and homely collection of large cardboard boxes fronted by two human figures, a man and a woman. The man was a strange sight. He wore a long and extremely ancient opera cloak which covered his body completely. On his head he sported a bowler hat which had seen better days. The woman, an old crone bent double with a combination of age and arthritis, was rummaging through the contents of a large plastic bag as she mumbled through toothless gums, a small pink tongue roaming like a serpent in the cavern of her mouth.

The man straightened and turned as Matt spoke to him.

Seen from the front the combination of bowler hat and opera cloak gave him the look of a circus clown, and a round, weather-beaten face with huge bags under the eyes added to the illusion. Stranger still, as the cloak fell to one side giving a glimpse of a lining that had once been a brilliant scarlet, it could be seen that one of his legs was some six inches shorter than the other. To compensate for the deficiency some genius had contrived a U-shaped metal object which was firmly attached to the heavy sole of a surgical boot. The man clumped his way towards Matt, a smile on his face.

'Matt, my dear fellow. How nice to see you.' The voice was high-pitched, the tone refined. He might have been an Oxford don addressing one of his favourite students.

'My mate, Tommy,' said Matt, by way of introduction, and Tommy smiled and nodded. Over his shoulder Matt completed the introduction. 'Ironfoot Jack,' he said. 'He's the guv'nor round here.'

The old woman decided to take a part in the conversation. She shuffled forward, screwing her head round to peer into Tommy's face.

'Wos yer name?' she said. She cupped her hand to her ear and waited for an answer.

'You heard what Matt said, Lizzie. His name's Tommy,' said Ironfoot Jack.

'Tommy, eh. Tommy wot?'

The subject of their exchange of words thought it was time to clear the air.

'Hutton,' he said. 'Tommy Hutton.'

The old woman cackled, lips writhing back from her toothless gums. 'Wot a name! Tommy Rotten. Fits yer. Look rotten to me.' She turned away from the three men and went on with her exploration of the contents of the plastic bag.

'Pay no attention,' said Jack. 'Poor old Lizzie is not fully compos mentis, not in possession of all her marbles as our American cousins would say. But what's in a

53

name? Tommy Rotten will do as well as any other. Nicknames are fashionable in our little world.'

'Tommy's skint. Nowhere to sleep,' said Matt. 'Got a place fer 'im?'

Ironfoot Jack pointed to a corner of the enclave.

'He may take up residence there. Quite a nice little spot, free from draughts.' Addressing Tommy directly, he went on to inform him that a spare box was available for which there was no charge and he (Tommy) was free to move in at once.

'That's very kind of you,' said Tommy.

'Don't mention it, my dear boy. We unfortunates must do what we can to help each other. Just make yourself at home.'

So Tommy Hutton entered a new phase in his life as Tommy Rotten, dosser, vagrant, a person of no fixed abode and no visible means of support. Now all the ties that connected him with his former life were severed. His past was but a memory, his future an uncertainty. Yet he felt at peace with the world when he curled up that night in his cardboard home and, fortified with a hefty dose of Matt's heart-starter, slept like a log.

Tommy's existence now took on an unchanging pattern. By day he wandered in the streets of the city, stopping frequently to rest at any convenient spot where he could sit and recharge his batteries. On those occasions he often had money pressed into his hand so he was never without the wherewithal to buy the liquor to satisfy his craving. When night fell he returned to what he regarded as his home, the cardboard box under the arches of Waterloo bridge. For some time his only human contacts were his near neighbours. In addition to Ironfoot Jack and Lizzie, the ancient bag woman, were a small, emaciated man who seemed to live on a diet of potato crisps and a youth from the north of England whose broad accent rendered his speech well-nigh unintelligible. The crisp consumer was known as Packet, the youth referred to simply as Boy. Ironfoot, a natural leader, had established a morning routine which he insisted all should follow. As a result, the site was spick and span with all litter cleared away and, as Ironfoot was at pains to point out, no evidence of the creation of a nuisance which might give the local authority grounds for eviction. When Tommy congratulated him on his forethought, Ironfoot had a ready answer. 'The fact that I do not recognise rules and regulations doesn't make me an enemy of society, dear boy. Let them get on with their machinations, and the best of British to them. I can't be touched because I have nothing, no house, no goods and chattels, no traceable income, in fact sweet sod-all.'

'Excuse my asking,' said Tommy, 'but how do you live?'

'By a series of miracles, dear boy, a series of miracles. I have a trusting belief in my immortality which I shall hold dear till the day I shuffle off this mortal coil. And now, since we are exchanging confidences, what are your views on life? What has brought you to this salubrious quarter?'

Tommy gave some thought to the question and for a few moments debated whether he should unburden himself to this unusual man or no. He decided against it. He saw no point in pouring out his troubles, and in any case he possessed a cure for them in his pocket, the ever-ready flask which now contained a mixture of whisky and heart-starter. He pulled the flask from his pocket and took a long, satisfying drink. In his usual pompous fashion, Ironfoot weighed in with a homily against the evils of alcohol.

'That stuff won't do you any good,' he said. 'You can

find forgetfulness in the bottle, but it doesn't last long. I know. I've been down that road. It leads nowhere.'

'That's where I'm going,' replied Tommy. 'The road to nowhere.' He took another drink and began to laugh.

'And what, may I ask, is so funny?' enquired Ironfoot.

'Life, that's what's so funny,' said Tommy. 'It's a bundle of laughs. Look at me. Look at you. Look at Packet over there and the boy. Look at the way we live. Isn't it a bloody joke?'

'There was a Greek philosopher who lived in a barrel,' said Ironfoot. 'So far as we know, most of the time he had only his thoughts for company. By all accounts he was a happy man.'

'I suppose he died laughing, did he?

'Diogenes of Sinope died in 322 BC at the age of ninety. He preached the gospel of individual freedom. Perhaps he died laughing. I wouldn't know.'

Tommy, his mind fuddled with drink, had lost the thread of the conversation, but Ironfoot was firmly mounted on his hobby horse. He now had an audience of three, Packet and the boy having moved closer so as not to miss a word of the developing argument.

'Let me explain something to you, my young friend,' went on Ironfoot. 'A lot of people think they are free, but they live in cloud-cuckoo land. They are imprisoned in a web of their own making. Rents, rates, taxes, wives, children, jobs, the paraphernalia of what we call civilisation. The free man possesses nothing.' Here Ironfoot struck an attitude. 'I am truly free,' he said. 'I live in my own world, I am answerable to nobody and I make my own rules.'

'Good for you,' said Tommy, who by this time had had enough of the pompous posturing of the incongruous clown in the grubby cloak. 'I'm going for a walk.'

'Hang on a minute,' said Packet. 'I'll come with.'

Side by side the two man left the site. As they crossed Waterloo bridge on their way to whatever the West End had in store for them that day, Packet broke the silence.

'He was on telly, y'know,' he said.

'Who?' asked Tommy.

'Ironfoot. They was doing a programme about homeless people...'

'Where did you see telly?' asked Tommy. 'Got one under the arches?'

Packet considered the question and decided it was funny.

He leaned against the parapet of the bridge and began to laugh, a shrill cackle that was of a piece with his ragged clothing and emaciated appearance. When a fit of coughing brought the laughter to a stop he sat on the pavement to recover. Tommy sat beside him.

'So, what about Ironfoot on telly?' he asked.

'Well, like, they interviewed him. They'd found out all about him, like he was a professor or something with letters after his name. We had the reporters down for a few days, getting stories like. One of 'em interviewed me.'

'Must have been a thrill,' said Tommy.

'It was alright. I blagged one of 'em for twenty quid. Told 'im a real sob story, like. Brought tears to 'is eyes.'

Tommy could imagine the scene, this ragbag of a man spilling out a tissue of lies and the reporter taking it in as though it were gospel truth. We live and learn, he thought.

'How about a mooch round Covent Garden,' said Tommy.

'Suits me. There's a gaff up there always a good touch for a bit of grub,' replied Packet.

Covent Garden was a great place to spend a sunny afternoon. The old fruit and flower market had long vanished, to be replaced by stalls and restaurants grouped around a central piazza. The atmosphere was decidedly continental. A trio comprising two guitars and a violin did its best to emulate the music of the old Stephan Grapelli-Django Reinhardt ensemble to the obvious delight of the crowd sitting and standing round the players. From the tables came the appetising odours of garlic-flavoured dishes and the chatter of the diners. Though alcohol had dulled his desire for food, Tommy felt a slight pang of hunger.

'What was that you said about getting a bit of grub?' he said to Packet.

'Round the back of that restaurant over there,' said Packet. 'Got a mate works in the kitchen. Let's go and see what's going.'

Followed by Tommy, Packet led the way to the rear entrance of one of the buildings. The double doors were wide open giving a view of part of the kitchens where a brigade of perspiring cooks laboured to produce the wherewithal to satisfy the appetites of a horde of hungry patrons. Outside the doors was ranged a line of waste bins which, even at this early hour in the day's trading, were already at the point of overflow, crammed with kitchen refuse including partly-consumed food which was still perfectly edible. An old vagrant was hovering over one of the bins, carefully selecting the choice morsels which would serve as his lunch. Packet, however, showed no interest in the leftovers, but poked his head round the doorpost and waved a hand to some-one outside Tommy's line of vision.

'Just hang about. Grub's coming up,' he said, and sure enough, within five minutes, out of the doorway came a short, stocky figure carrying a large parcel wrapped in brown paper which he thrust into Packet's receptive hands, accompanying the action with a broad grin.

'Thanks, Charlie,' said Packet.

'Don't mention it,' replied the man. His disappearance was as sudden as his arrival.

'Very reliable is our Charlie,' said Packet. 'Come on. Let's find a quiet spot and get outside this little lot.'

The little lot proved to be an agreeable concoction of fresh bread, a selection of cold meats and some fruit. In the small park not far from the Opera House Tommy and Packet sat on a bench in the sunshine, washing down their meal with occasional recourse to Tommy's flask. 'Not bad, eh?' remarked Packet. Tommy, his mouth full of roast chicken, laughed. 'Not bad. Not bad at all .

CHAPTER 4.

It was one of those mornings in late summer when the uncertain weather which is a feature of the British climate had brought low cloud and drizzle to Central London. It had been a cold night and, despite the layers of newspaper tucked inside his jacket, Tommy had spent several uncomfortable hours in his cardboard box. A hacking cough had kept him awake and, to add to his miseries, the nightmares had returned. No sooner had he drifted into an uneasy slumber than the bad dreams came, the faces of his wife and daughter in a grey haze, the rattle of iron wheels on an iron track, the scream of rending metal and the piercing yells of the injured and the dying.

As he crawled out of his ramshackle home every bone in his body ached. After several abortive attempts he managed to stand upright. He rubbed his eyes and the surroundings settled into focus. Not far away was the all-too-familiar sight of Ironfoot, perched on a wooden box and buried in the pages of the previous day's issue of the Times, while almost at his elbow crouched the bent figure of Lizzie, rummaging through the contents of one of her many plastic bags and mouthing obscenities as she searched for some long-lost object which, in all probability, had never existed.

Ironfoot was the first to break the silence.

'Morning, Tommy. Had a good sleep?'

The answer was a baleful glare which summed up Tommy's opinion of his companions, his views on the weather and his outlook on life in general. It was Lizzie who put the cat among the pigeons.

'Yer ain't so good, eh? Tommy Rotten feeling rotten,' she jeered. Lips curled back from toothless gums, she presented a horrifying picture. Tommy lost his temper.

'Shut your trap you old hag,' he shouted.

Lizzie was shocked into momentary silence. During the time Tommy had spent in the bash he had accorded the old woman a measure of grudging respect, which she accepted as her due. Anyone who picked a row with Lizzie did so at his or her peril. Ironfoot saw the danger signals and rushed into the breach.

'Take it easy, Tommy,' he said. 'She was only joking.'

He might just as well have saved his breath. Lizzie's capacity for invective was well-known, as was her tendency to violence when she ran out of words. Now she poured out a torrent of abuse directed against Tommy, all his relations, his past, his present and his future. Then, breathless, she launched herself at her luckless antagonist, arms flailing. Retreating before the onslaught, Tommy fell backwards against Ironfoot and the two men collapsed in a heap.

It was a moment of sheer comedy, but none of the participants in the scene appreciated the humour. Ironfoot was the first to regain his feet, after which he spent the next five minutes restraining the maddened Lizzie from continuing the assault. Finally, when the outraged bag lady had returned to routing among her possessions, Tommy joined Ironfoot who, now that the tumult had died, had resumed his seat.

'Sorry about that,' said Tommy. 'Dunno what came over me.'

'Don't apologise to me,' replied Ironfoot. 'Just don't give any repeat performances.'

'I won't. Had a bad night, that's the trouble.'

'Happens to all of us at some time or another,' said the older man. 'Don't let it get you down.'

'What I need is a drink,' said Tommy.

'There I can't help you. Never touch the stuff. But, if my eyes don't deceive me, here comes somebody who can provide what you want.'

Looking out across the rain-soddened terrace Tommy saw a familiar figure. Wet overcoat flapping around his ankles, hair and beard dripping moisture, Mattie strode across the concourse in front of the Festival Hall. As he came up to them he let out a great roar of welcome.

'So it's raining. Who cares. Cheer up,' he bellowed. 'How yer keepin' Ironfoot?'

'Reasonably well thank you, Mattie. And your good self?'

'Fine. Couldn't be better. What about you, Tommy?'

Tommy came straight to the point. 'I could use a drink,' he said. 'How's the bottle?'

Mattie seated himself and reached inside his overcoat. Pulling out the litre container which was almost full he handed it to Tommy.

'Drink up, son. Plenty there. Yer welcome.'

His fingers trembling, Tommy unscrewed the stopper and took a long pull. It was a stronger brew than usual and he gasped and spluttered as he handed the bottle back to its owner. who roared with laughter.

'Good gear, that. Drop o' meth. Puts hair on yer chest.'

As soon as his vocal chords had returned to normal working, Tommy stammered his thanks and, as the alcohol began to do its work, his spirits revived and the dreams of the night faded. He listened idly to the conversation between Ironfoot and Mattie.

'Been up Lincolns Inn,' Mattie was saying. 'Seen some funny sights. Blokes dossin' on the grass. Fellers in wigs and gowns walking about. Pretending the dossers wasn't there. A right giggle it was.'

'You amaze me, Mattie,' said Ironfoot. 'The sacred turf of the Fields given over to the homeless. Tents and blankets desecrating the heartland of the legal system. Whatever next, I ask you?'

'Cardboard boxes in Downing Street I shouldn't wonder,' replied Mattie.

'I doubt that. The lady incumbent at number ten has already taken precautions, which I suppose you have noticed in the course of your travels.'

'Yeah. Seen 'em. Bloody great iron gates. What's she expecting? A revolution?'

'Your guess is as good as mine, my dear Mattie. Still, who can tell? There are ten thousand homeless people in this fair city, and one day they may take it into their heads to do something about their condition.'

As Mattie pondered, Ironfoot turned to Tommy.

'What are your thoughts on the matter, Thomas? Do you feel the stirrings of revolutionary fervour? Are you prepared to take up the cudgels on behalf of suffering humanity?'

'Lets have another drink, Mattie,' said Tommy. 'I'll need it.'

Mattie obligingly passed over the bottle, from which Tommy took a healthy swig. He ran the back of his hand across his lips.

'I'll tell you what I think,' he said. 'I think we all deserve what we get in this life...'

'Or we get what we want, perhaps,' interrupted Ironfoot.

'Depends how you look at it,' went on Tommy. 'Now, for example, you've got what you want, or at any rate you say so. You prattle on about freedom, but what freedom have you got? Anytime the Council blokes can come down here and turn the hoses on you and wash you out. Where's your precious freedom then?'

Ironfoot smiled and put a finger to his temple.

'This is where my freedom is, my dear boy. The mechanism is waterproof. Brain washing is not done by workmen with hoses. It's carried out by very clever men with newspapers and the magic of television under their control. The dumb public is fed with lies, and the greater the lie the more it is believed.'

Mattie clapped his hands delightedly. He had probably understood one word in four of Ironfoot's diatribe, but it had the smack of revolution and so met with Mattie's instant approval. Tommy was more guarded in his opinion.

'There's something in what you say, but what can poor sods like us do about it,' he said.

'It's not for me to give advice,' retorted Ironfoot. 'The answer lies in yourself. Develop your individuality. Know who you are and where you're going.'

'That's the stuff,' cried Mattie. 'Don't let the bastards get you down. Up the rebels.'

Tommy looked out across the vast expanse of concrete that lay between him and the Festival Hall. The drizzle had abated and glimpses of blue sky were appearing through the clouds. He felt the urge to get away from these drab and inhospitable surroundings, to wander alone through the streets and lose himself in the crowds of people who had somewhere to go and something to do. He jumped to his feet.

' Where yer going? ' asked Mattie .

'Out,' replied Tommy. He began to walk purposefully in the direction of Westminster Bridge. Pausing at an off-licence in York Road, he counted his worldly wealth. The previous day had been good for the begging business. An American tourist had contributed a ten pound note, there was a handful of coins, in total he possessed nineteen pounds, which was a fair start for the day. He marched into the shop and purchased a bottle of Scotch, then went on his way, over Westminster Bridge, into the curiously named Birdcage Walk and finally arrived at his goal, the green and verdant pastures of Saint James'Park.

The morning sun had broken through the clouds, giving promise of a fine day ahead . Selecting an unoccupied bench within sight and sound of the barracks, Tommy relaxed on the hard wooden seat and opened the bottle. By the time he had disposed of a quarter of its contents he was back once more in a world where cares and worries no longer existed. The aches and pains which had disturbed his sleep vanished as if by magic as he fell into a light doze. He was dully aware of the sounds around him, the conversation of passers-by, the shouts, muted by distance, of the drill sergeants in the barracks, the cooing of the pigeons and the twittering of sparrows as they combed the grass for crumbs left by the picnic parties of the previous day.

He was awakened by the sound of martial music. The guard was being changed at Buckingham Palace as a military band played on the forecourt. Whether the occupants of that stately pile enjoyed the concert was a matter of complete indifference to the social outcast on the park bench. The sound merely told him that it was eleven o'clock, and time for moving on.

London is, by common consent, the finest capital in the world. A wealth of ancient buildings, a fine tradition dating back to the times when the Roman hordes vainly attempted to subject the indigent population to their idea of civilisation, a history of progress in art and culture unparalleled in the Western hemisphere, all have contributed to the hyperbole of tourist brochures which attract travellers from the continent, the United States and the far and middle East.

There is another side to this great city. London, in the opinion of a professor of Sussex University, is, in terms of its homeless population, on a par with a third world shanty town. Visitors to London are confronted with the problems of the homeless as they walk along the Strand. A visit to that heartland of culture, the Royal Festival Hall, involves at times stepping over the bodies of men, women and occasionally children who are 'sleeping rough'. The learned professor, in a report published in 1989, reveals that some 75,000 people in the capital are homeless, and of those at least two thousand are sleeping in the streets, the parks and, in fact, wherever there is sufficient space to pitch a rudimentary tent or lodge a cardboard box.

Tommy Hutton, blissfully unaware that he was merely a statistic in a learned professor's computations, trudged through Hyde Park on his way to Edgeware Road. In one of the side streets leading off this thoroughfare was a small and somewhat shabby cafe where down-and-outs were welcome, always provided that they had money to meet the modest charges for the simple fare on offer. During the three months or so that Tommy had been a member of the legion of the lost, he had frequented the place often and was known to the owner, who greeted him by name as he took a seat at one of the rickety tables.

'Now then, Tommy lad,' said the head chef, waiter and part-time washer-up. 'What would you like?'

Tommy grinned. 'Smoked salmon and quail's eggs,' he said. 'If you've run out of them, I'll have sausage, egg and chips, two slices and a cupper.'

A speciality of the establishment was speedy service. In no time at all a ravenous Tommy was wolfing a gen-

66

erous helping of two sausages, two eggs and a mound of chipped potatoes in between bites of bread and margarine and gulps of hot, strong tea from a large mug. The basis for a steady bout of drinking during the evening having been well and truly laid, he paid the bill and left. On the spur of the moment he decided to visit the Bayswater area, where he had made several acquaintances among the drinkers who were usually to be found congregated outside a shuttered cinema at the junction of Queensway and Westbourne Grove.

He was in no hurry as he made his way along Praed Street. Shuffling along, shoulders bent and eyes on the ground, he presented a pitiable picture. He made no attempt at begging, but was nevertheless halted several times by more fortunate citizens who pressed money into his hand. One of the donors wished him good luck with such sincerity that Tommy was moved to mutter a few words of thanks.

The Bayswater branch of the Society of Persistent Alcoholics was already in full session. They were three in number, all in an advanced stage of inebriation, sitting on the steps of the cinema surrounded by empty beer cans and bottles. Larry, the bane of the local hospitals, nursed a pair of crutches. He was a large man with a massive pot-belly who always found something to laugh at. As Tommy came up to the gathering he waved a crutch in greeting. Seated next to him was his constant companion who rejoiced in the name of Gimpy, a small man with an affliction of the left leg which caused him to roll rather than walk. In action he was reminiscent of an oversize crab. The third member of the trio was a character known as Raven, a black-haired and cadaverous individual whose favourite pursuits were getting drunk and assaulting the constabulary in that order. He had only that morning been released from

Wormwood Scrubs and was busy celebrating the occasion.

'Where've you bin all this time,' said Larry.

Gimpy provided the answer. 'He's got a bash down the Bullring, didn't you know?'

'That right, Tommy.'

'That's right. Haven't got my card on me at the moment, but you can get in touch care of the Festival Hall.'

'Get him,' said Gimpy. 'Why not Buckingham Palace while you're at it?'

Tommy produced the bottle from his pocket and passed it to Larry.

'Have one on me,' he said.

Larry gave himself a liberal helping and handed the bottle to Gimpy, who did likewise. Raven wiped the sullen scowl from his face long enough to imbibe, then returned the bottle to Tommy, who finished off the last drops. After a pause for appreciation of the gift and the generosity of the giver, Tommy gestured towards the crutches.

'You been in an accident, Larry,' he enquired.

Larry laughed and waved one of the crutches in the air.

'Not what you'd call an accident,' he replied. 'Felt like a bit of fun last week so I paid a visit to Saint Mary's. Hadn't seen them for a long time. I crawl into casualty on my hands and knees, moaning and groaning. Nice little nurse comes along and it's into a cubicle and a nice cupper while I'm waiting for the doctor. Course, when he comes in he susses me right away. "You again, Smithers. What is it this time" he says. Well, I give him a load of chat about my knee, can't stand on it and so on, he pokes it about a bit then he has a right go at me, calls me a malingering bastard, wasting his valuable time, then he tells me to piss off.'

'What about the crutches?'

'Well, I'm on my way when I see these crutches leaning up against a wall, doing nothing, so I nicked 'em.'

'That wasn't very nice of you,' said Gimpy.

Larry considered the morality of his action. It didn't take long.

'Look at it this way,' he said. 'I go into the hospital expecting sympathy and help. What do I get? Instead of a bed for the night and breakfast in the morning I get a load of abuse. I reckon I'm justified. What do you think, Tommy?'

Tommy, the fumes of his last intake of Scotch still clouding his thinking processes, nodded his head in what he imagined to be a sage and judicial manner.

'Quite right, Larry, quite right. What I would call compensation for loss of dignity.'

Raven, up to that moment a silent observer of the debate, weighed in with his contribution.

'What a load of cobblers. He nicked the crutches because he knows a lame beggar gets more than if he was able-bodied. Also he can flog the crutches in Portobello when he gets tired of 'em. Right?'

There came an interruption in the shape of two police officers, who obviously regarded this collection of shabby derelicts as a threat to the security of the good burghers of Westminster. They scanned the litter of empty beer cans and sundry other items with evident distaste. The younger of the two, fresh-faced and eager, opened the ball.

'What's all this rubbish, then?' he said.

'Dunno, guv'nor,' said Larry. 'It was here when we came.'

The officer fancied himself as a humorist. 'Well, it's

69

going to go with you,' he said with a grin. He pointed a finger at Raven.

'You,' he said. 'Put that rubbish in the bin over there. You three, get out of it. Come on. Move.'

Larry assembled his crutches and made ready for a quick departure. Gimpy and Tommy were right behind him. Raven, to whom uniformed authority existed only to be disobeyed, made no attempt to comply with the officer's order. Instead he twisted his lips in a sneer and spat on the ground.

'Did you hear what I said. Move that bloody rubbish now.'

The policeman's voice had risen to a shout. Raven's reply was cool and deliberate.

'Move it your bloody self, you pig,' he snarled.

A small crowd of interested onlookers had gathered. They began to laugh as Raven ostentatiously leaned back on the cinema steps and folded his arms across his chest.

Larry, Gimpy and Tommy observed developments from a safe distance. They had no intention of being involved in any further escalation of the dispute which now seemed certain to become a minor riot. Some elements in the crowd expressed their opinions loudly, and there were cries of 'leave him alone' and 'he ain't done nothing'. The elder constable cast a nervous glance at the swelling crowd, seeming uncertain as to what action he should take. His younger colleague, on the other hand, seemed to have no doubts about the measures needed to handle the situation. The authority of the Metropolitan Police was being challenged by a shabby layabout. He walked up to Raven, leaned over him and grabbed him by the shoulder.

Raven the rebel, the enemy of uniformed repression, responded to the assault on his person with remarkable

70

speed. With a single movement he swept the officer's legs from under him and, as he fell, pounced on him with flailing fists and, to the accompaniment of a stream of obscenities, proceeded to commit grievous bodily harm. The elder constable joined in the affray, there was a flurry of arms and legs, two helmets rolled into the gutter, the onlookers gave vent to a mixture of cheers and boos and, in the result, a handcuffed Raven was pinned to the ground.

'Let's get the hell out of it,' said Larry. 'The heavy mob'll be here. We don't want to get nicked.'

As the three men hurried along Queenway, Larry displaying remarkable agility on his crutches, the siren of a police vehicle could be heard in the distance. Tommy, breathing heavily, finally ran out of steam and collapsed on the edge of the pavement as his erstwhile companions legged it in the direction of Kensington Gardens.

For the next ten minutes he rested, eyes closed and completely oblivious to the the scurrying pedestrians and the sounds of passing traffic. Finally, when his breathing returned to normality and his heartbeat slowed, his first thought was that he needed a drink. The nearest pub was but a few yards away and he reached it by the simple expedient of putting one foot in front of the other, every step an agony.

At the bar he sank three large whiskies in rapid succession. Over the fourth drink he lingered, sipping slowly and making vague plans for what remained of the day. He could, of course, return to the bash, but the prospect of listening to the homilies of Ironfoot or enduring the meaningless chatter of the old bag woman was not attractive in his present state of mind. From where he sat he had a good view of himself in one of the many mirrors with which the bar was equipped, and he was forced to admit to himself that he presented a sorry sight. His eyes were deep hollows and his sunken cheeks were surrounded by a heavy growth of stubble. His hair, long and matted, hung down on either side of his face. Tommy Hutton, he said to himself, you are a bloody wreck. He finished the rest of his drink and stumbled out into the street.

There are times in everyone's life when the unexpected happens, when fate plays a trick that comes as a surprise, either welcome or otherwise. Though man's ultimate destiny is death, whatever happens between birth and the final experience is anybody's guess. On this particular day, fate had something in store for one Tommy Hutton, lately a respectable member of a small village community, now hopeless drunk and society reject.

Had Tommy turned to the right on leaving the pub, what subsequently came about would never have transpired. That he turned to the left involved no conscious effort on his part, for he neither knew nor cared where he was going. Plodding on, he came to Westbourne Grove, where he paused long enough to buy a bottle of whisky. Pursuing his aimless wandering, he finally came to Portobello Road, that most famous of London's street markets which can provide anything from an antique Georgian dressing table to a pound of apples.

Adjacent to the covered section known as the Pagoda is a small pedestrian precinct where the weary shopper can take the load off his feet on one of the rough benches, and it was here that Tommy came to rest. Through half-closed eyes he watched the bustling crowds as he took occasional sips from his bottle. He was about to drift into dreamland when he became aware that someone had sat down beside him. A voice, almost in his ear, said 'Do you mind if I speak to you?'

Tommy turned and looked at the questioner. He saw a young man, well-dressed, smiling, bright blue eyes in a fresh face.

'Talking to me?' said Tommy.

'That's right. I'd just like a word.'

Alright. Go on. There's no law against it.'

It was an uncompromising start, but the young man was persistent.

'My name's Bruce Adams,' he said. 'I'm a journalist.'

'Very interesting,' replied Tommy. 'What's that got to do with me?'

'I might be able to do you a good turn.' 'Is that so. Why me?'

'Well, I'll tell you. I'm on a story. London's homeless people...'

'Go down the Bullring,' interrupted Tommy. 'You'll find all the stories you want.'

'I've been there. I've also been down the Strand, having a word with some of the kids there.'

'So?'

'I can't get what I want from them. Just a lot of bullshit, all saying the same thing. What I need is the real human interest stuff, the tragedy and the heartache that is happening to real people, not a bunch of kids spinning me yarns about broken homes and sexual abuse or old blokes yakking about past glories. I talked to one kid, a girl about fifteen. She pitched me a helluva yarn then invited me round the corner for a quick blow job. Only a tenner, she said.'

'Did you enjoy it?'

Adams laughed. 'I'm a journalist not a pervert,' he said. 'If I want a bit of nooky I'll have it with something about my own age, not some juvenile amateur brass.'

Despite his semi-drunken state, Tommy began to feel

a glimmer of interest in what Adams was saying, so he allowed the conversation to continue.

'Look, what I'm after is the genuine stuff. For example, I've talked with you for a few minutes and you strike me as an intelligent chap, somebody who would be prepared to tell the truth about how he became... well... a down-and-out. Don't ask me how I know, but I've got a feeling that you have a good story to tell and the sense to tell it properly.'

Tommy did not reply immediately. He took the bottle from his pocket, slowly unscrewed the stopper and poured a good measure down his throat. Adams waited expectantly for a response to what he had said.

'Supposing I play along with you,' said Tommy. 'What's in it for me?'

'What's in it for any of us,' replied Adams. 'Money, that's what. If this story is a runner there's a packet in it for both of us. Come on, what do you say?'

What the hell, thought Tommy, why not. I've nothing to lose and I might pick up a good few quid.

'I'm game. Where do we go from here.' he said.

'Great. What I want first is a couple of hours with you and a tape recorder. Now I'm going to give you fifty quid on account and my card. Go and get a haircut and a shave and tidy yourself up and come round to my place this evening, say about six. That suit you?'

Tommy took the proffered money and the card, which he slipped into his pocket without looking at it. There would be time for that later, if there was to be a later. In the meantime he was fifty pounds to the good.

'That's fine. See you at your place about six,' said Tommy.

The journalist got up and put out his hand.

'Right. I'll be off now,' he said. 'Look forward to seeing you later on.'

Tommy shook hands and the journalist turned and walked away into Portobello Road.

It was a rather nervous Tommy who pressed the button beside the name of Bruce Adams at the entrance to an imposing block of flats in Marylebone High Street. His hair neatly trimmed and the stubble gone from his face he looked a different man. He had invested some of Adams' money in a new shirt, but had done nothing about replacing his shabby suit. A disembodied voice issued from the speaker above the row of buttons.

'Mister Adams,' said Tommy.

'Yes?'

'The bloke you met this afternoon.'

'Oh, good. Push the door and take the lift to the third floor.'

A buzzer sounded, Tommy pushed the door open and passed through into a spacious hall. Directly opposite was a pair of lifts, one of which whisked him rapidly to the third floor, where Adams was awaiting him. The entrance to the journalist's flat was directly opposite the lift. The two went in and Adams closed the door behind them. He ushered his guest into a large, well-furnished sitting room, one wall of which was taken up with rows of bookshelves.

Adams indicated one of a pair of comfortable armchairs.

'Make yourself at home,' he said. 'What would you like? Tea? Coffee? Or something stronger?

'Coffee'll do me fine,' said Tommy.

'Good-ho,' said his host. 'We'll have a drop of the hard stuff after we've done a spot of work, eh? By the way, I don't have a name for you.

'Just call me Tommy.'

'Right, Tommy. Shall we get down to it?

'Ready when you are.'

Adams disappeared through a door which presumably led to the kitchen. After a short while he returned to the sitting room bearing a tray on which reposed two large mugs of steaming coffee which he set down on a low table. Taking a seat opposite Tommy, he picked up a clipboard and pressed a switch on the tape recorder which lay ready to hand.

For the next two hours Adams gently coaxed the details of his subject's past life from him by way of a series of carefully constructed questions. As the interview progressed, Tommy relaxed and for the first time since the death of his wife and daughter he talked freely about the tragedy and its aftermath. A happening of which he made no mention was the deliberate burning of his home. That, he felt, might lead to some legal complications. For the rest, he told the plain unvarnished truth, pausing from time to time when a lump formed in his throat and tears came to his eyes.

The session came to an end and Adams switched off the recorder and put down the clipboard.

'That's enough for today,' he said. 'I reckon you're ready for a drink now. Scotch?'

Tommy nodded, and the journalist made his way to the drinks cabinet and poured liberal measures from a decanter into two glasses.

'I think you'll like this,' he said. 'It's a single malt. Very good gear.'

'Cheers,' replied Tommy and drained his glass, which Adams promptly refilled. They sat for a while in silence, each occupied with his thoughts. The silence was broken by the journalist.

'Fancy a bite to eat?'

'Wouldn't mind. I feel a bit peckish,' replied Tommy.

'There's a little Italian restaurant round the corner in Dorset Street. Very good grub. I think we ought to tidy you up a bit first, though. Hang about.'

Adams left the room. Tommy sank back in his chair and closed his eyes. The past two hours, during which he had re-lived the harrowing experiences of months, had not been very pleasant, yet nonetheless he felt a great sense of relief. Dully he realised that this was what he had been in need of for a long time, the chance to unburden himself to a sympathetic listener and thus exorcise the ghosts that haunted him. His thoughts were interrupted as Adams entered the room. Over one arm he carried a tweed jacket, a pair of trousers and a set of underwear.

'You're about my size, so these should fit,' he said. He looked down at Tommy's feet, which were encased in what had once been a pair of shoes but now resembled nothing so much as a couple of unpleasant and hairless rats.

'What size shoes do you take?' he asked.

'Eight,' was the reply.

'I take nines. I've left a pair in the bedroom. And socks. They should be alright. You can change in there.'

Tommy, stammering his thanks, retreated to the bedroom, from whence he shortly emerged looking totally unlike the shabby creature who had entered the flat two hours previously. The journalist expressed his appreciation of the change.

'You look a million,' he exclaimed. 'Let's go and put on the nosebags.'

The little Italian restaurant round the corner proved to be a small, family-run enterprise where the proprietor was very much in evidence, controlling what was to him the important business of eating and drinking as a conductor would control a symphony orchestra. Adams, obviously a regular patron, was greeted effusively by name and, along with his guest, seated at a secluded corner table. As they perused the menu, Adams gave Tommy a run-down on the establishment.

'They're all in the family, papa, mama and the kids. The pasta is first-class. They make it on the premises, fresh every day. The veal cutlets are the best bet. Anyway, choose what you like.'

Tommy's knowledge of Italian cooking was on a par with his familiarity with the language. He knew nothing of either.

'I'll have the same as you,' he said.

In the result they dined on spaghetti bolognese, followed by the veal cutlets with spinach and sautee potatoes and washed down with a dry Soave. The zabaglione, whisked up by the proprietor himself at the table, was a fitting conclusion to an excellent meal. Adams ordered double measures of grappa with the coffee and Tommy, to whom the fiery liqueur was a new taste, was very much in favour.

'Beats Scotch any day,' he said. 'Think I'll go on to it.'

'Watch it,' advised Adams. 'That stuff rots your boots.'

'Well, it's a good job I'm wearing yours, isn't it,' retorted Tommy, and burst into laughter.

'You know something,' said the journalist

'What?'

'This is the first time I've heard you laugh since we met.'

'Well, I haven't had much to laugh about up to now, so I've got some time to make up, don't you think?'

'You can say that again.' said Adams. 'But when I get this story off the ground you'll be able to laugh all the way to the bank.'

'Roll on the day,' replied Tommy.

'Well, now, let's make arrangements for tomorrow,

shall we? I'll transcribe the recording tomorrow morning. Can you come round about midday and we'll have another session.' He took out his wallet and extracted a fifty pound note which he laid on the table. 'Book into a hotel for the night and have a good rest.'

They said their goodnights outside the restaurant and Adams departed. Tommy strolled into Baker Street and hailed a cab.

'Take me to the Royal Lancaster,' he said.

He had almost forgotten what it was like to sleep in a real bed with clean-smelling sheets, and he revelled in the experience, yet what he appreciated most was the absolute quiet. No sound disturbed his rest, no raucous drunken howls such as were common in the Bullring. He slept like a log.

He had elected to have breakfast served in the room, and it was the waiter's knock on the door which awakened him. The trolley which was wheeled in bore a traditional English breakfast of eggs, bacon, sausage and tomatoes, there was a rack of hot toast and a large pot of coffee. As soon as the waiter, suitably tipped, had departed, Tommy sprang out of bed, slipped into shirt and trousers and tucked into the food.

Afterwards he spent the best part of an hour in the bathroom, from which he emerged free of the dirt and grime which his body had accumulated over the months he had spent living rough. He donned his new clothes and looked at the result in the full-length mirror inside the wardrobe. Tommy, mate, you look alright, he said to himself. The shoes were a mite too large but not uncomfortable, and he made a mental note to acquire a new pair later in the day. Lacking a watch, he guessed the time to be around eleven, which gave him ample opportunity for a couple of drinks before he presented himself at Adams' flat at noon.

It was a fine morning and reasonably warm for the time of year. Leaving the hotel he decided to walk the short distance to Marylebone High Street, breaking his journey at a little pub in Edgeware Road, which he entered shortly after the legal hour of opening. With two large Scotches under his belt, he left the pub and at midday precisely was pressing the button which would give him access to the journalist's flat.

Adams greeted him cheerfully. 'Had a good night?~ he enquired.

'First class,' was Tommy's reply.

'Where did you stay?'

'The Royal Lancaster. Thought I'd have a bit of comfort for a change.'

'And why not. Must have set you back a bit, though.'

'Quite a bit. It was worth it.'

'Fine. Now, a cup of coffee and then we'll get down to work.'

A couple of hours later Adams called a halt.

'I've got all I need,' he said. 'Now what I'll do is write the story up. The deadline is tomorrow, Saturday. It'll appear on Sunday in the Pictorial.' He handed Tommy an envelope. 'There's a couple of hundred in advance. Give me a ring Monday morning and we'll pay a visit to the bank.'

'How much can I expect?' said Tommy.

'Will you be happy with a couple of grand?'

Tommy's eyes widened. Two thousand pounds for four hours chat. He could hardly believe his ears.

'More than happy. Over the moon,' he replied.

On that note they parted. Out on the street Tommy was almost dancing with joy as he contemplated the immediate future. First would come the purchase of a pair of shoes, for his present oversize footwear was a constant irritation. Then he would book into one of the small hotels in Bayswater for the weekend and rest in preparation for Monday, the magical day when he would begin a new life away from the Bullring and the hardships of the past months. He did not know what he was going to do, but he could hardly wait to do it.

The mind and its workings are largely uncharted territory, a fact freely admitted by many workers in the field of mental illness and its treatment. It could have been that Tommy's sessions with Adams had a cathartic effect, that talking out his cares and troubles had exorcised the demons which tormented him. Whatever the reasons, Tommy had never felt fitter in mind and body than on this Friday evening as he prepared to go out on the town and enjoy himself. His room boasted a private bathroom, and he had bathed and shaved leisurely. He extracted from its wrappings the shirt he had bought that afternoon and put it on, carefully knotted the tie which was a reasonable match with the tweed jacket with which the journalist had provided him and descended to the lobby of the hotel with the intention of having a couple of drinks at the bar before going out to eat.

The barman was a taciturn Scot whose idea of service was to put a drink on the counter, take the money and retire to a stool with an economy of movement which would be praised by an expert in time and motion study. In response to Tommy's order he poured a large Scotch, placed the glass on the bar, put a jug of water beside it and retired from the scene. There's not much joy here, thought Tommy as he looked around him. He added water to his whisky, drank up, paid the bill and left.

As he walked down Queensway Tommy's nostrils were assailed by a variety of ethnic cooking odours varying from Greek to Indian to Chinese. In his sober state the smells increased his appetite whereas formerly they would have brought on an attack of nausea. Resisting the temptation to enter one or other of these establishments, but with a mental reservation that he might return later, he walked on, revelling in the pleasure of having money in his pocket, clothes on his back and no fear of looking the world in the face. Besides, he had time to spare for window shopping, deciding what he would buy when his boat came in on Monday.

Turning into Westbourne Grove he came across what he had been sub-consciously looking for, an Italian restaurant whose bill of fare, prominently displayed outside, included those dishes he had enjoyed at the "little restaurant round the corner". He pushed open the door and went in.

He had made a good choice. A buxom Italian waitress ushered him to a table and took the trouble to guide him through the menu. In the result he settled for ministrone followed by an escalop of veal with mushrooms and spaghetti. The waitress was lyrical about the Italian-bottled Valpolicella, so he ordered a bottle. He ploughed manfully through the enormous portions, discovered that he had quite a liking for the wine and all-in-all enjoyed himself hugely. He had intended to treat himself to zabaglione but his overloaded stomach rebelled. He settled for black coffee and grappa.

Although he had lingered over the meal, the night was still young. He settled the bill, added a handsome tip in recognition of the excellent service and sauntered out into Westbourne Grove. He remembered a pub he had often visited during his previous sojourn in the area, a bright and noisy place which would exactly fit his mood. He paused at an off-licence long enough to buy a bottle of Scotch then headed for the pub. There he sat quietly until closing time, sipping whisky, listening to the music and enjoying himself hugely.

When the pub closed he hailed a taxi and within a few minutes was deposited at the hotel. Going straight up to his room, he took off his jacket, opened the bottle of whisky and turned the switch on the television set. Shortly after midnight, having disposed of half the bottle, he went to bed. It had been a good day.

The following day he took things easily. A stroll through Kensington Gardens was followed by lunch at a pub just off the High Street, where he ate a large plate of sausage and mash and drank a couple of pints of bitter. Curiously enough he did not feel the need to pour alcohol down his throat in an unending stream, which he put down to his new peace of mind. Leaving the pub, he sat for some time on a bench in Holland Park where, through half-closed eyes, he watched the children at play and the antics of the dogs as they chased each other over the grassy slopes.

As the late summer sun declined in the west he rose from his seat and made his way to the northern gate of the park. From there it was a short walk to Holland Park Avenue, where he picked up a cab which took him to Notting Hill Gate. His destination was a pub rejoicing in the name of the Sun in Splendour, where he hoped he might meet up with some old drinking companions, and he was not disappointed. Standing at the bar were two men with whom he had passed many pleasant hours during his sojourn in Bayswater.

Jim and George were pleasant and inoffensive fellows bound together by a liking for strong drink taken in congenial company. They were only too willing to soak up as much whisky as Tommy could buy, and the three spent a couple of hours discussing all manner of topics ranging from the state of the economy to the terrible price of whisky. When Tommy finally broke away from them on the pretext of a pressing engagement, he was pleasantly intoxicated.

At an off-licence close by the pub, Tommy purchased a bottle of Scotch then hailed a cab which deposited him at his hotel. He went up to his room, switched on the television set, opened the bottle and settled himself in an armchair. For the rest of the evening he divided his attentions between the television set and lowering the level in the bottle. In the end, stupified by the twin effects of the liquor and the flickering screen, he went to bed.

He slept late the following morning and ate breakfast in his room. Shortly before noon he left the hotel and made his way into Queensway, where he bought a copy of the Pictorial at the news stand at the entrance to the Underground station. Seated in the nearest pub, a large whisky on the table before him, he opened the paper, curious to see what Adams had done with his story. He was not in doubt for long. Spread across pages 3 and 4 was a banner headline in bold type asking one simple question. DO THEY DESERVE OUR SYMPATHY? Running alongside a series of photographs of derelicts crouched in doorways and sleeping on pavements was the story of a man called Tommy, a scathing account which described him as a snivelling wretch, deserving neither pity nor assistance, a creature who lacked the moral fibre to stand up to the trials of life, choosing rather to opt out and become a homeless vagrant.

Tommy read every word with growing disbelief. He felt betrayed. Then anger took over, and he rushed to the telephone in a corner of the bar. He dialled Adams' number with shaky fingers and, as a voice answered, rapped out a single sentence.

'What's the bloody game, Adams?'

'Just a minute. Who's that?' said the voice, and Tommy realised that he was speaking to a stranger.

'Is Adams there?' he asked.

'No, I'm afraid he isn't,' said the voice. 'Can I help you?'

'Where can I get hold of him?'

'Hang on. Who's speaking?'

'My name's Tommy. He...'

'Oh, yes. He's gone to New York. Be away for about three months. He left a message for you. If a chap called Tommy rings, tell him cheerio and good luck, he said.'

Slowly Tommy replaced the receiver. This was the ultimate betrayal. He had bared his soul to someone whom he believed to be an understanding listener, and the man had turned out to be a Judas. As anger, frustration and bitterness built up, he stood in front of the telephone shaking in every limb, then hurried out of the pub and into the busy street.

What to do now? The question burned in his brain, and there was only one answer. Drink, drink, pour it down, dull the pain, erase the memories. The liquor store across the road beckoned.

The polite assistant showed no surprise at the request for a bottle of grappa from a customer who appeared to be in an extreme state of agitation. He wrapped the bottle, took the money and Tommy staggered out of the shop and into Queensway. In Kensington Gardens, which was but a few minutes walk, he chose a secluded spot beneath the spreading branches of a tree and opened the bottle, from which he drank deeply.

Grappa is a strong liqueur with a high alcohol content. Taken in large quantities straight from the bottle the effects can be catastrophic, and so they proved to be. Gasping for breath he leaned against the trunk of the tree and closed his eyes as a spasm wrenched the muscles of his stomach. His next attack on the bottle was more cautious but still determined. Sipping slowly, he went on drinking until he collapsed unconscious.

The two youths walking through Kensington Gardens were on the look-out for loot. Spotting the body lying supine on the grass they approached it cautiously.

'Is he dead?' said one to the other.

'Nark it. He's still breathing.'

'Wonder if he's got anything on him?'

'Let's have a look, eh?'

They handled Tommy none too gently as they rolled him over and went through his pockets, but there was no resistance. It was the taller of the two who struck gold. From the inside pocket of Tommy's jacket he extracted a wad of notes.

'Come on,' he said to his companion. 'Have it away.'

Dawn was breaking as a scarecrow figure shambled across Waterloo Bridge. Shirt, jacket and trousers stained with vomit, still only semi-conscious, instinct was bringing Tommy back to the only home he knew.

CHAPTER 5.

There must exist depths of degradation below which no human being can sink. The man known as Tommy Rotten had reached the lowest point in his miserable journey through life, a point where life seemed no longer worth living. Lying in his cardboard home in a pool of vomit, his body wracked by periodic spasms, he would have greeted death as a welcome relief from his sufferings. His eyes were open, but he was not awake, nor could he fully comprehend where he was and what was going on around him. A doctor could have told him that he was suffering from acute alcoholic poisoning, but medical advice is rare in the Bullring and vagrants are outside the scope of the National Health Service.

Happily, in the close-knit community of society's rejects there are those who feel some responsibility for their fellows. Ironfoot Jack had heard the groans coming from Tommy's box and now deemed it time for him to take a hand in the game. He poked his head into Tommy's flimsy home.

'You alright, Tommy' he said.

At first there was no reply, merely a succession of grunts and groans as the occupant of the box attempted to formulate something that resembled human speech. Finally Tommy managed to force out a couple of words.

'I'm... dying,' he whispered.

The philosopher, when necessary, was a man of action.

'Packet,' he yelled. 'Give me a hand.'

Packet, who had been standing nearby, responded quickly. Between them the two men dragged the limp body from its cardboard casing.

'Blimey, he's in a right two and eight,' said Packet. 'Stinks like a bleedin' polecat.'

Indeed, Tommy was in a state. At some time during his unconscious condition he had urinated and defecated in his trousers and the odour was appalling. The front of his jacket was thick with stale vomit. His pale face and shallow breathing alarmed Ironfoot, who realised that this was an emergency that called for instant action. He turned to Packet.

'Get over to the telephone box and call an ambulance,' he said.

Packet scurried away and Ironfoot went down on one knee, leaning over the semi-conscious body of his friend.

'Can you hear me, Tommy?' he said.

The reply was a moaning sound interrupted by a burst of coughing. A thin dribble of bile trickled from the corner of Tommy's mouth and his chest heaved as he fought for breath. Ironfoot realised there was nothing more he could do. He settled back against the adjacent wall and waited for the arrival of the experts.

To the ambulance men it was all in a day's work. They came on the scene, took in the situation almost at a glance, loaded the patient on a stretcher and in a matter of minutes, siren wailing, they were on their way to the nearest hospital. Packet and Ironfoot stood side by side watching the departing vehicle.

'Reckon he'll be alright?' asked Packet.

'I hope so,' was the reply.

'What was wrong with him then?'

'Self-inflicted wounds, my dear Packet, self-inflicted wounds. In crisis the weak turn to drink or drugs. In Tommy's case it was drink. Something happened to him during the few days he's been away, what it was God only knows. So what does he do? He pours alcohol down his throat to get rid of what's going on in his head and all he succeeds in doing is making himself a hospital case.'

'So what'll they do to him?'

'A good question. Now, if he were a member of the moneyed class, the answer is simple. Off to a funny farm, diet, exercise, psychological treatment, group therapy and bingo, out into the great wide world to start it all over again. As for Tommy, well he doesn't qualify. He'll go through hell for a few days, then as soon as he's fit enough to walk he'll be pitched out to fend for himself.'

At the best of times a hospital is not the sort of place in which one would choose to spend a holiday. There is little in the way of happiness in the compound of human misery to be found in the typical ward in which Tommy found himself. The doctors and nurses treated him with brusque efficiency, their attitude betraying little sympathy for a patient who had been the principal architect of his misfortunes. Their job was to save lives and, in the case of Tommy Rotten, they performed that task commendably.

Three days after admission the patient was adjudged ready for discharge. His clothing, roughly cleaned, was brought to him and a busy almoner gave him a five pound note which, she said in hasty admonition, wasn't to be spent on drink. So, at nine o'clock on a bright and sunny morning, Tommy stood on the steps of the hospital with no clear idea as to what he wanted to do or where he wished to go. His mind was soon made up for him. Across the road an off-licence had already opened its doors to cater for such morning trade as happened to be about. The purchase of a half-bottle of whisky left little change from the five pound note with which the almoner had provided him, but he had no thought for the future. It was the immediate present which was his prime concern.

He delayed taking his first drink for some time. He was in a part of London which was unfamiliar to him, though he sensed that he was not far from the heart of the capital. Wandering along a bustling street lined with shops, head bent and eyes fixed firmly on the ground, he concentrated on putting one foot in front of the other until finally his legs began to tremble and he looked round for a place to rest. A shopping arcade equipped with a range of seats for the benefit of weary shoppers solved his problem.

He did not realise how weak he was until he sat down on one of the plastic chair-shaped contrivances roughly adapted to the contours of the human frame. For a while he remained quiet, breathing evenly, one hand tightly clasping the other, until the trembling in his legs abated. Now, he thought, I'll have a drink, make me feel better. He took the half-bottle of whisky from his pocket, unscrewed the stopper and took an experimental sip.

Whatever medication had been given to him at the hospital had certainly included an element of aversion therapy to alcohol. Throat burning, he gasped and spluttered, finally bursting into a paroxysm of coughing which shook his entire body. A sharp pain shot through his temples. At that moment he felt a non-too-gentle tap on his shoulder. Looking up through tear-dimmed eyes he saw the burly form of a uniformed security guard whose face bore an expression of utter disgust.

'What the bloody hell do you think you're doing?' asked the man.

Tommy swallowed hard and, with an effort, cleared his throat sufficiently to allow him to speak.

'Just - resting,' he croaked.

'Just resting,' mimicked the guard.

'Well, go and rest some other place. Come on. Out.'

Tommy attempted to rise, only to fall back as his legs refused to support the weight of his body. The guard, with whom patience was not a strong point, took the shortest way out of the difficulty, grabbing Tommy by the shoulder and literally lifting him to his feet. From where he had been sitting to the main entrance to the arcade was a matter of a few yards which the guard covered at top speed. Before he was fully aware of what was happening to him, Tommy found himself reeling across the pavement. Had he not clutched a friendly parking meter he would have been under the wheels of a passing bus.

Added to the experiences of the past few days, this was a final humiliation. He had only one thought, to get away from his present surroundings as quickly as possible, to seek the safety and anonymity of his bash in the Bullring. There he would find friendliness and understanding from those who were in the same situation as himself, outcasts from society, unloved, unwanted and unnecessary.

Four hours later he came to Waterloo Bridge. He had walked some six miles, pausing frequently to resort to the bottle. He was at the end of his tether and his exhaustion was apparent as he staggered across the concourse of the Festival Hall to the recess under the arches of the bridge. All was as he had left it some four days ago, though he had only the haziest memory of the event. Now he was comforted by the sight of Ironfoot, perched in his usual position on a concrete slab, his nose buried in a book. He looked up as Tommy shambled into the bash.

'My God, Tommy, you look awful,' were his first words.

'I bloody feel it,' replied Tommy, and managed a feeble grin. 'How've you been?'.

'Just the same. Nothing much changes round here.'

'Where's Lizzie and Packet?'

'Out on the scrounge I'd say. Haven't seen either of them since early morning. How did you get on in hospital?'

'Bloody awful. Glad to be out of it.'

'Your bits and pieces are all here, just as you left them. Lizzie wanted to poke around. I put a stop to that.'

'Thanks,' said Tommy. The thought of the old crone turning over his few possessions was not particularly welcome. Now all he wanted to do was crawl into his box, close his eyes and escape from the world for a few hours.

'Going to have a kip. See you later,' he said.

Ironfoot nodded and returned to his reading as Tommy bent down and prepared to worm his way into his cardboard refuge. He was half-way in when the commotion broke out, a storm of voices yelling objurgations, a loud cry followed a series of screams and, as Ironfoot left his perch, closely followed by Tommy, a torrent of water drenched both of them.

They did not have to look far for the cause of the uproar. A water tanker was drawn up outside the bash and a grinning workman was playing a hose on the occupants of the neighbouring recess, where a young couple and their mongrel dog had set up house a few days previously. The young man was grappling with the wielder of the hose, the girl was screaming and the dog ran around barking while making up its mind as to who would be at the receiving end of its first bite.

Ironfoot's voice rose above the tumult. 'What the devil's going on?' he bellowed.

The second member of the two-man team, who was in charge of the operation, yelled a reply.

'Having a clean-up.'

'Turn the damn thing off,' shouted Ironfoot.

The instruction was a waste of breath. The young man continued his struggle with the man directing the hose, the girl went on screaming and the dog, now on the perimeter of the conflict, ran around in circles.

It was utter pandemonium.

Sir Godfrey Brough (pronounced Bruff) was a Very Important Personage, not least in his own eyes. He was also newsworthy. He emerged from the Royal Festival Hall surrounded by members of the press and the inevitable camera crew complete with interviewer. The group was on its way to the riverside walk where Sir Godfrey would pose for the camera against the background of the flowing Thames and deliver himself of a few well-chosen platitudes about the forthcoming visit of a famous European orchestra.

The procession was in no hurry as it wandered across the concourse towards the river bank. The VIP was naturally in the lead, beside him the interviewer. Close on their heels followed the camera operator. Strung out behind was a gaggle of reporters and photographers ready to swing into action just as soon as the moment would be ripe.

That moment was to be deferred, for the turmoil beneath the arches had now reached a point where anyone within earshot would be deaf not to have heard it. A determined Ironfoot and a tired but no less combative Tommy had joined the struggle for possession of the hose. Sir Godfrey and his retinue stopped dead in their tracks, staring in disbelief as the screaming and yelling rose to a crescendo.

Sir Godfrey, a public-spirited individual and a

staunch upholder of law and order, was outraged. He regarded this outbreak of hooliganism with disfavour and, since there did not seem to be any attempt to quell it from official sources, he decided to take it on himself to end it. He broke away from the crowd of reporters and photographers and, as fast as his short legs could carry him, sped towards the battleground. He came on the scene just as the battle for the hose had reached stalemate, neither side having gained the victory. In fact the hose had fallen to the ground where it took on a life of its own, writhing like a monstrous snake and showering everyone in the vicinity with a powerful stream of water.

Everything happened at once. Sir Godfrey and the attendant representatives of press and television came in for a fair share of the deluge, the water supply was turned off at the source, the hand-held television camera recorded the events and the photographers snapped away. Then came the crowning moment as Sir Godfrey tapped Tommy on the shoulder in an endeavour to attract his attention. A close-up showed Tommy's vengeful expression as he turned and the boom operator picked up his voice with startling clarity.

'Piss off,' he said. 'Can't you see I'm busy'

The excitement died down as the water waggon was driven away by a worried driver who felt he had attracted enough publicity. The group surrounding Sir Godfrey was uncertain as to what they should do. Was the interview to proceed? Somebody had to make the decision, but who? The young man and the girl had retreated into their bash and were engaged in sorting out their gear. Tommy and Ironfoot, similarly engaged, showed no inclination to discuss anything with anyone. It was Sir Godfrey who ended the tension. He walked up to Ironfoot, hand outstretched.

'Well, well. Who'd have thought of seeing you here. How are you, my dear fellow?'

Ironfoot turned to face his questioner. There was a smile on his face as he took the hand held out to him.

'If it isn't old Godders,' he said. 'What are you up to these days? Or shouldn't I ask?'

Sir Godfrey beamed. 'You will have your little joke, John. We all wondered what had happened to you. What's all this about?.' He waved an expressive arm which embraced the bash and its waterlogged contents.

'Quite simple,' replied Ironfoot. 'This is where I live. You must have seen it in the papers. Or do you only read the financial reports?'

'My dear chap, I had no idea. I mean - things must be pretty bad with you.'

'On the contrary. Things, as you term them, couldn't be better. This is my home and these people are my friends, and I wouldn't change anything for all the tea in China.'

'Extraordinary, quite extraordinary. I really can't believe my eyes. Honestly, John, are you trying to tell me' that you enjoy living like this?'

'Never been so happy. It's people like you I worry about. Shut away from the world in large and expensive houses, piling up possessions which you won't be able to take with you when you finally shuffle off this mortal coil, deluding yourselves that it's quite moral to amass large bank balances while millions of your fellow humans are living well below the poverty line. What was it the poet said? "You are the English. Take then the glory of a high-sounding name, for you have nothing else". Verb sap, my friend. Think well on it.'

'John, you amaze me. I don't really know what to say.'

'Then say nothing. Just think. That's what the good

Lord gave you brains for.'

Sir Godfrey, like a good cocktail, was shaken but not stirred. For a few moments he stood irresolute, then turned to the waiting group.

'Come along,' he said. 'Let's get on with the job. I haven't got all day.'

'Nor have we,' muttered one of the reporters, a remark which the VIP either did not hear or affected not to hear.

Tommy had been listening to the conversation intently. As Sir Godfrey moved away towards the river embankment the younger man turned towards Ironfoot.

'What was all that about?' he asked.

'That was Sir Godfrey Brough. We were at university together. Now he's something big in the City. Pots of money, houses all over the place, spends most of his time doing what they call good works. Man, proud of his greed, heaps up ill-gotten gains and gives to pity what he owes to justice. The immortal words of Percy Bysshe Shelley, not mine, and I agree with every word.'

'You're a funny fellow, Ironfoot. Sometimes I think you're a bit touched.'

Ironfoot laughed. 'Aren't we all, dear boy. Sane or insane, who's to be the judge. Look around you, all these miserable souls dragging out their weary lives, no hope, no dignity and no future. If that is sanity then give me lunacy any day.'

'So what's the answer?'

'The answer is where you find it. It's not for me to tell you. Think, man, think. Use your brains, sort things out for yourself, ask questions and if you come across anything worth listening to then pay attention. That is what is known as the process of learning.'

Tommy chortled. 'You're a wise old bugger, aren't you. I can't make you out. I reckon you could be living comfortably and yet you choose to hang out in a bash. What's the reason?'

'I've told you before. Freedom, that's the reason. Here I can do exactly as I please. I have no-one to tell me where I should go, how I should behave and most important of all, what I should think. And anyway, what about you? Why are you here? By choice or of necessity?'

Tommy fell silent. The only time he had unburdened himself since he left Anscombe was when he confided in the journalist, and he still felt bitter about the way he had been betrayed. Still, he thought, it was quite a different matter with old Ironfoot. He took a deep breath and plunged into his story.

'It's a sad tale, Tommy,' said Ironfoot when the story came to an end. 'You've had a very rough deal, but you're still young. The minor part of your life is behind you, the major part is yet to come. You should be concerned about what you intend to do with it.'

'What's your advice?' asked Tommy.

'I never give advice. Fools give advice and even greater fools depend on it. For what it's worth I'll give you an opinion. Listen to it and then make up your mind.'

'Alright. Go ahead. What's your opinion?'

'I haven't known you for long and most of the time you've been under the influence of alcohol. You've been too drunk to think straight, in fact you haven't bothered to think at all. If you had, you'd have realised that liquor doesn't abolish memories, it only postpones them. Before a problem can be solved it must be faced.'

'So you think I should give up the drink?'

'That's for you to decide. All I will say on the subject is that drink addles the brain and plays hell with the liver. Also it doesn't solve problems but only com-

97

pounds them.'

'Thanks for the chat,' said Tommy. 'I'm going to kip. See you later.'

He crawled into his cardboard box which had fortunately escaped the full force of the deluge and was relatively dry. Stretching out on the pile of newspapers he pulled the flask from his pocket and swallowed what remained of its contents. Rolling on to his side, he went to sleep.

Television is a remarkable medium. It brings into the living room of the viewer comments and pictures of events almost as they happen. The spot of trouble at the Bullring was deemed worthy of inclusion in the early evening news as a humorous bit in what was otherwise a rather dreary programme, for there had been little in the way of excitement on that day. The Prime Minister had hawked her usual toothy smile round a children's home, several highly-paid talking heads had done little to earn their fabulous salaries and a front bench Opposition spokesman had nattered for three minutes and said precisely nothing.

The landlord of the Anscombe Arms reached forward to turn off the set as the first picture of the disturbance at the Bullring rolled on to the screen. He saw a face that he recognised at once and heard a familiar voice telling somebody or other to piss off.

'Dora. Come here. Quick,' he yelled.

Dora Hamilton rushed into the living room, where her husband was pointing excitedly at the television set.

'Look. That's young Tommy Hutton... isn't it?'

'Good gracious! So it is. Where on earth...?'

The short sequence was over as she spoke. Josh Hamilton switched off the set.

'That was in London. Some place called the Bullring. Full of homeless people sleeping in cardboard boxes.'

'What's he doing there?'

'Ask me another. Better still, ask him.'

Dora Hamilton had never understood her husband's sense of humour.

'Don't be silly, Josh,' she said. 'How can I?'

'That's what I meant,' said the landlord of the Anscombe Arms. He hoisted himself out of the armchair.

'Now where are you off to?' enquired his spouse.

'Down to the bar. There's work to be done. I suppose you'll be going across the road?'

'What for?'

'Don't be daft. You can't wait to chew the fat with the widow Fawcett.'

Indeed, within the hour, Dora Hamilton was closeted with her friend and fellow gossip, who had also seen the news broadcast. That evening the village was alive with speculation and the conversation in the Anscombe Arms was devoted to the present state and probable future of the absent Tommy. Those who had known him intimately expressed their sorrow that he had fallen so low. Others were not so charitable. The general opinion was that Tommy had somehow brought shame upon the village.

The morning newspapers did nothing to improve the situation. Press photographers are an enterprising bunch, ever anxious to improve on their latest performances, and they had gone to town on this one. The most striking picture, a close-up of Tommy's face, lips drawn back in a snarling grimace, was accompanied by a double column news story in which Tommy's name was linked with the subject of a piece in one of the Sunday papers written by a certain Bruce Adams in which Anscombe was named as the birthplace of the man named Tommy. The inhabitants of the tiny hamlet were dismayed. Were they to expect an invasion by a horde of reporters on the hunt for a follow-up? Was the peace about to be shattered by uncaring newsmen and their intrusive cameras? They waited apprehensively for the deluge.

In the event, their fears proved groundless. The editors of the popular press did not think along the same lines as a collection of country bumpkins. The doings of Tommy Rotten, a one-day wonder, were superseded by more earth-shaking topics.

Meanwhile the man at the centre of the dirturbance, blissfully unconscious of the furore he had created, curled up on his bed of old newspapers and slept the day away.

Ann Kirby was an ordinary young woman who, like many of her contemporaries, was happy in that station of life to which fate had consigned her. She was twenty-five years of age, she had a moderately well-paid job as a computer operator in a national bank and lived alone in a small basement flat in Fulham. She had a few friends but no emotional entanglements. The two romances in her adult life had left her with a profound dislike of two men in particular and a vague distaste for men in general.

An only child, she maintained regular contact with her parents and paid a visit to Barnsley every year, but a few days in that dull northern town were usually sufficient to last her for the next twelve months and she was happy to return to the bright lights of the capital. There, in the confines of the tiny flat, surrounded by her books and her considerable collection of classical records, she spent much of her sparetime. For the rest she went out to the theatre, attended the occasional party and from time to time invited one or two of her closest friends for drinks, snacks and intelligent conversation.

On this evening in late summer she had been invited

to dinner by one of her workmates, a slightly older woman who had recently married a man some twenty years her senior. The couple had moved into a flat in Holland Park, a rambling ground floor conversion in a large Victorian house with enormous rooms and an extensive rear garden. Caroline Webster was proud of her culinary skills and had conjured up a delicious meal. George Webster, who loved wine and made no secret of the fact, kept the glasses well charged. It was a slightly tipsy trio who sipped brandy and drank coffee in the dining room with its view of the garden. A full moon hung in the sky, its light tipping the leaves of the bushes with silver and from afar came the muted murmur of traffic in Holland Park Avenue. Caroline heaved a deep, contented sigh.

'This is the life,' she said.

Her husband smiled at her affectionately. 'Glad you like it,' he replied.

Ann was not unaffected by this display of connubial bliss, nor was she surprised by a direct question from her friend.

'When are you going to get married?' said Caroline. 'You know, I can thoroughly recommend it.'

Ann pretended to consider the matter, though she knew the answer to that one and had it ready.

'I'll think of it - when Mister Right comes along. As it is, I'm quite happy with the present state of affairs.'

'Who was it said that marriage is the triumph of hope over experience?' said George.

Caroline laughed. 'Wrong, my love. He was talking about second marriages. It was that old bore Doctor Johnson. He also said marriage has many pains, but celibacy has no pleasures.'

'Wonder what he did in his spare time?' remarked George.

'Don't be coarse, darling. He was a very busy man.'

Ann looked at her watch. 'Goodness, it's almost twelve. I must be off. Don't want to miss the last train.'

Her host and hostess saw her to the door and watched her as she strode briskly down the street.

'Nice girl,' said George.

'Very,' said his spouse.

The attendant at Holland Park station was polite, sympathetic but firm.

'Sorry, miss. There's been an accident at White City. No more trains tonight.'

That was that, thought Ann Kirby as she stood outside the station. She had not legislated for a taxi ride at the end of the evening and her purse contained a mere couple of pound coins and a few coppers. There was nothing else for it but a walk to Notting Hill Gate in the hope that she could catch a late train on the District line which would at least take her as far as Earls Court. She set off up the hill at a brisk pace which unhappily was not brisk enough. She arrived at Notting Hill just in time to miss the last train on the District line.

Now it was a serious situation. She could, of course, return to the Websters and borrow the money for the cabfare home, but she decided against it. A private person herself, she was loath to intrude on the privacy of others. As she thought she walked slowly eastwards past the brightly-lighted shops and restaurants. A staggering drunk bumped into her and she felt a probing hand against her body as a gust of liquor-laden breath invaded her nostrils. Brushing the man aside, she quickened her step, striding out purposefully as though she was on her way to an important appointment for which she was already late. For one mad moment she considered hailing one of the taxis displaying a 'For Hire' light and explaining her predicament. Somehow she could not bring herself to do it.

Undecided, she stood on the edge of the pavement. The black Mercedes saloon which had trailed her from Notting Hill drew up beside her, the rear door was flung open and a man leapt out and grabbed her by the arm. Before she could cry out or put up a struggle she was hurled into the car and into the arms of a second man who gripped her tightly and covered her mouth with his hand. The attacker jumped in beside her and the car sped off along the Bayswater Road. Now there were hands everywhere, tearing at her blouse, ripping off her brassiere and fumbling beneath her skirt. A voice hissed in her ear, shut the mouth, you make noise and I cut your throat. and a brutal, thrusting finger found its mark between her legs. She stiffened in terror as a mouth closed on her right breast and sharp teeth savaged the nipple. Words ran riot through her head, no, no, this can't be happening to me, and she tried to scream as the probing finger penetrated deep into her body, but the scream was strangled at birth by the muscular hand over her mouth, then her resistance collapsed and all went black as she fainted.

The large Mercedes negotiated the one-way traffic system at Lancaster Gate and swung into Hyde Park and along the north side. The driver turned to the man sitting beside him.

'Is OK here?' he asked.

'Sure. We get her out on the grass,' came the reply.

The doors of the car opened and the four men emerged, surrounding the unconscious body of their victim. Swiftly and efficiently they transported their burden across the sandy strip and on to the greensward beneath a tree. There they clustered in lustful anticipation.

'You go first, Tony, eh?' said the driver.

The man addressed as Tony, an evil grin on his

swarthy face, unzipped his trousers to disclose a massive erection which he fondled proudly before falling to his knees between his victim's legs. At that moment Ann opened her eyes and in a vagrant shaft of moonlight caught sight of the face she would remember for the rest of her life, the narrow brow above burning dark eyes, the slobbering mouth and the massive chin and the deep scar down the cheek. As her legs were roughly thrust apart she felt the first powerful thrust. Gathering the last remnants of her physical and mental resources she took a deep breath and emitted an animal howl that tore the stillness of the night into tatters.

Tommy was taking his usual route back to the Bullring after spending the evening with his friends in Bayswater. He had not had much to drink and was consequently in a fairly sober state. He came into Hyde Park by way of the Lancaster Gate entrance and headed towards Park Lane.

Ahead of him he saw a group of figures, three men standing immobile around two others who appeared to be grappling with each other on the ground. Nothing to do with me, he thought, and altered course to steer clear of what seemed to be merely a drunken brawl. It was then he heard the scream of pure terror, a high-pitched howl which stopped him in his tracks. It could only have been made by a woman.

As Tommy would have readily admitted he was no hero, but a latent chivalrous impulse caused him to respond to the cry of a female in distress. Waving his arms and shouting furiously he burst on the group of would-be rapists in a surprise attack which caught them off guard. They scattered and the man called Tony turned his attention from attack to defence as he rolled over and struggled to his feet. In the confusion that followed Tommy ' s intrusion the one common thought in the minds of the four men was to make a getaway. They ran to their car and clambered aboard, the driver started the engine and, tyres squealing, the Mercedes sped away towards Marble Arch.

On his knees beside the woman, who was now sobbing hysterically, Tommy did his best to comfort her. ' It's alright now. It's alright. They've gone. Don't cry. It's all over. '

But it wasn't all over. In fact it was only beginning.

CHAPTER 6.

At the best of times, a police station is not what one might call a friendly place. After midnight, when darkness is the ally of the enemies of society and the thieves prowl the streets, the guardians of law and order flex their muscles in preparation for whatever the night may have in store.

Paddington Green is one of the busiest stations in the Metropolitan police area, and it was to this hive of anticriminal activity that Tommy Hutton and Ann Kirby were brought in a patrol car which had appeared on the scene of the attempted gang rape shortly after Ann's assailants had fled. The car was manned by a male constable and a policewoman, both of whom listened intently to Tommy's story. Ann, still in a state of shock, was almost incoherent as she tried to describe what had happened prior to her rescuer's intrusion. The PC decided the issue.

'Better get you two down to the station,' he said.

In the car the WPC explained the reason why they were on the scene so quickly.

'Somebody reported the disturbance. Probably a passing motorist with a carphone.' She addressed Ann directly. 'Don't worry, love. You'll be alright. Nice cup of tea and we'll get a doctor to have a look at you.'

Ann was not reassured but was in no condition to make any comment. Tommy, for his part, was content to let matters take their course. He sat silent as the car was driven rapidly down the Edgeware Road, but his brain was in a turmoil. How the hell did I manage to get mixed up in this, he thought, and for a moment regretted his hasty action. Beside him Ann shivered and folded her arms protectively across her breasts.

At the station the machinery of the law took over. Rape cases were not unusual and all in a day's work. The driver of the patrol car exchanged a few low-voiced words with the desk sergeant, Ann was whisked away by a WPC and Tommy was led to an interview room and left there with a promise that an officer would be along shortly to take a statement from him.

Even in the most efficient organisations there can occur a breakdown in communications. Detective Constable Mackie had received a brief instruction from his superior.

'Rape case, Mackie. Interview room number three. Get a statement from the fellow in there.'

John Mackie was young, alert and a dedicated thief-taker. He was not a thought reader, which explains why he entered the interview room where Tommy was seated with the fixed impression that he was about to extract a confession from an alleged rapist instead of a statement from a witness. Mackie worked on the simple principle that if Chummy had nothing to hide then Chummy had nothing to fear. It had always worked for him and he saw no reason why it should not work in the present instance.

As the DC came into the room, Tommy half-rose from his chair. Mackie looked at him with distaste, taking in his creased and wrinkled clothing, his unshaven face and the slight tremor in the hands that gripped the edge of the table in front of him. A vagrant and an alcoholic, he thought, and his first question was direct and to the point.

'Have you been drinking?'

Tommy looked at his interrogator in surprise. There was no doubting the antagonism which prompted the question.

'Just a minute,' he said. 'What's all this about?'

Mackie walked across the room and gave Tommy a violent push in the chest.

'I'll tell you what it's about, scumbag. You've been on the piss, you come across a girl and you think you'll give her one, so you attack her and get stuck in. Right? Now don't argue with me. I've come across your sort before, you little bastard.'

Tommy was terrified. He was alone in this bare room with a man who was convinced that he was dealing with a rapist and was not prepared to listen to any explanations. He panicked and made a dash for the door, a move which to Mackie was tantamount to an admission of guilt. Before Tommy was halfway to his objective, he was siezed by the shoulder and flung against the wall. As he rebounded he was met with a backhanded slap across the face. As he collapsed from the force of the blow a heavy shoe crashed into his ribs.

The proceedings were interrupted as the door opened and a man came into the room. He took in the situation at a glance.

'What the hell's going on here, Mackie?' he said.

'I was interviewing the suspect, sir. He tried to get away. I prevented him.'

Mackie's superior looked down at Tommy, who lay on his side, knees drawn up under his chin and arms protecting his head.

'This man isn't a suspect. He's a witness. You were supposed to get a statement from him, not give him a thumping.'

The DC remained silent while the other man bent over Tommy's recumbent body.

'Are you alright, sir?' he asked.

Tommy struggled into a sitting position and glared

balefully at Mackie.

'Apart from a broken jaw and a couple of busted ribs, I'm fine,' he replied.

'I'm sure it's not so bad as that. Here, let me give you a hand. By the way, I'm Detective Inspector Macandrew, and I regret this incident very much.'

'So do I,' replied Tommy. 'It's a good job you turned up.'

With Macandrew's assistance Tommy was seated once more in the chair from which he had been so roughly removed. The DI turned to Mackie.

'I'll take over now,' he said. 'Pop up to the canteen and get this gentleman a cup of tea. Don't be too long about it.'

Mackie made a hurried exit and the DI drew up a chair, seating himself directly opposite Tommy, the small table between them.

'Now, suppose you tell me what happened,' said Macandrew.

Tommy described briefly what had taken place between the DC and himself, a recital to which the other man listened without interruption, a sympathetic expression on his face.

'Would you like a doctor to take a look at you?' he asked finally.

Tommy smiled. 'It's not as serious as all that,' he said. 'I reckon I was more surprised than hurt. It was a bit of a shock - being accused of rape, I mean.'

'Yes. I can understand that. Mackie's a good officer, but he tends to hit first and ask questions afterwards. Still, so long as there's no real damage done...'

'We can leave it like that. I shan't bother to make a complaint. No use crying over spilt milk, even though it'sbetter not to spill it in the first place.'

Macandrew nodded his approval at the same time as

a knock came on the door. In answer to a call to enter, a uniformed constable appeared, carrying a tray which he deposited on the table. The two steaming mugs of tea were flanked by a bowl of sugar, and Tommy spooned a liberal helping of the sweetener into the mug that Macandrew pushed towards him. He took an exploratory sip of the hot, strong liquid.

'Well now,' said Macandrew as soon as the constable had left the room, 'shall we get on with your statement?'

In another part of the building Ann Kirby was undergoing the embarrassing process of a doctor's examination. He was an elderly man who, in the course of many years experience as a police surgeon, had dealt with innumerable cases of rape or attempted rape. He was aware that the majority of his cases involved women who were still in a state of shock and reluctant to discuss their recent terrifying ordeal. His instinct told him that the young woman who sat shivering under the blanket around her shoulders would need to be treated with considerable care. Accordingly he spoke to her in a low and comforting tone of voice.

'Now don't worry, my dear. You've nothing to be afraid of here. Just tell me what happened. Take your time.'

Ann's lower lip trembled and the tears began to flow. The doctor turned to the policewoman sitting in the corner of the room.

'Get a glass of water, please,' he said. He opened his bag, took out a small bottle from which he shook a couple of tablets into the palm of his hand and waited in silence until the policewoman returned. Proffering the tablets to Ann, he stood by while she swallowed them. Very shortly the sobs subsided.

'Feeling better now?' asked the doctor. Ann nodded and wiped her eyes with the back of her hand.

'That's fine. Now, just tell me what happened to you.'

She told her story, slowly, haltingly, beginning with the terrifying moment when she was dragged into the rear seat of the car.

'There were two men, one on either side of me. There were two men in the front. My blouse was ripped open. A hand was over my mouth and I could hardly breathe. The man on my right bit... bit my breast. Then the other man put his finger into my... into my...'

The doctor took her hand and patted it soothingly.

'I understand,' he said.

'I must have fainted,' Ann went on. 'The next thing I remember was lying on the grass. I heard somebody say "you go first, Tony", and then this man was on top of me, trying to... trying to push himself into me. I saw his face. It was ugly. He smelled of garlic...'

Revival of the memory of the most terrifying experience of her life brought back the tears and she broke into a series of heart-rending sobs as she covered her face with her hands. The doctor waited patiently until the sobbing had subsided.

'I know it's painful for you,' he said. 'Now, I must ask you this. I assure you, your answer is very important. Did he actually -er - penetrate?'

Ann pulled herself together, hands clenched in her lap. She forced herself to speak clearly.

'No... no, he didn't. There was a lot of shouting and the men ran away. Another man helped me to get up. He came here with me in the police car...'

'That's fine. Now let's have a look at your injuries.' The doctor's voice was calm and impersonal, but Ann's fears were not allayed. The prospect of her body being once more invaded by questing fingers, even though intent only on healing, was more than she could bear.

'No... no... please. I'm alright. I just want to go home.

111

I don't want to be touched. I'm alright.'

The doctor shrugged his shoulders and turned to the policewoman who had been taking notes of the conversation. In response to an enquiring look, she nodded.

'I've got all I need,' she said.

'Good. I'll leave the young lady in your hands.' He turned to Ann. 'Take things easy for the next few days,' he said. Picking up his bag he left the room.

From then on it was all routine. The policewoman assembled her notes into the form of a statement to which Ann appended her signature, she was escorted into a waiting room where she tidied herself up in readiness for the journey home, and she was in complete command of herself when a smiling constable breezed into the room.

'Ready for off now, miss,' he said.

'Just a minute,' she replied. 'What's happened to the man who came here with me?'

'Dunno, miss,' said the officer. 'Would you like me to find out?'

'If you would, please. I'd like to see him.'

'Right. Anything to oblige,' was the reply. 'Hang about. Be back in a jiffy.'

A jiffy is a very short space of time. In fact ten minutes elapsed before the constable reappeared, followed by a rather sheepish-looking Tommy. For the first time Ann took a long, hard look at her rescuer and saw a man of about her own age clad in a shabby jacket, legs encased in disreputable trousers and altogether an unsavoury sight.

'I'm sorry,' said Ann. 'I didn't thank you.'

'That's alright. Things happened a bit quickly,' was Tommy's reply.

'This officer's going to drive me home. Will you come with me?'

Tommy hesitated. He felt that he had had enough for one night and the prospect of further traumas was not one that he readily welcomed.

'Please,' said Ann. There was a note of urgency in her voice.

'Alright,' said Tommy.

'Come on,' said the constable. 'Let's get the show on the road.'

What goes through the mind of a woman who has been subject to attack and attempted rape by four men with the obvious intent of forcing her to submit to sexual intercourse with each of them in turn? As she lies on her back, legs forced apart by powerful hands while a rampant penis lunges at the vulnerable softness of her body, is she tempted to yield or does she put up a fight? The answer to these questions lies in the character of the victim.

For the greater part of her adult life Ann Kirby had cherished her independence. When she surrendered her virginity to her first lover it was a conscious decision. The subsequent relationship was conducted on her terms. They met frequently, enjoyed sex on average once a week, invariably at his flat, and it was only when he pressed her to move in with him that she ended the association. For several months she was celibate, not of necessity for she was by no means unattractive, but by choice for she had discovered that sex was not an indispensable ingredient in her life.

Her second lover was a charmer, who wooed her with flowers and cajolery but proved a miserable failure when finally she consented to spend a weekend with him in a Brighton hotel. It was a salutary experience which taught her that the best cake is not always the one with the most attractive icing. The charmer was sent packing and she reverted to her former lifestyle in

113

which sexual activity played no part. She was content with her small circle of friends and the privacy of her flat where she spent many hours alone.

This was the young woman who, within a few short hours, had suffered a shattering blow to her self-esteem. Alighting from the police car outside the entrance to her flat she seemed outwardly calm as she turned to the man who had rescued her from the clutches of her attackers.

'Will you come in?' she said. 'Please. I... I don't want to be alone.'

Tommy was undecided, which was understandable, for he was not unaffected by his recent experiences, but then he thought to himself what the hell, in for a penny in for a pound, and he got out of the car and stood alongside Ann on the pavement. The constable yelled a cheerful good-night as he drove away.

The cosy sitting room of the flat was a welcome change from the stark surroundings of the police station. Ann switched on the lights and motioned Tommy towards one of the two easy chairs stationed on either side of a low table.

'I could do with a drink,' she said. 'What about you?'

'Yes please,' said Tommy.

'Scotch or brandy?'

'Scotch'll do fine.'

'Right. Won't be a minute.'

She went out of the room and Tommy leaned back in the chair and closed his eyes. Now that the reaction had set in, he felt completely exhausted. He stretched his legs and was on the verge of falling asleep when Ann appeared carrying a tray which she set down on the table. There was an unopened bottle of whisky, two glasses and a jug of water and Ann was unscrewing the cap of the bottle as he opened his eyes. She pushed one

114

of the glasses towards him and tilted the bottle.

'Say when?'

Tommy lifted a finger as the golden liquid half-filled his glass, and she poured herself a liberal measure to which she added water. Spurning the offered water-jug, Tommy raised his glass.

'Cheers,' he said.

There was a silence as they drank, then Ann put down her glass.

'I don't even know your name,' she said.

'It's Hutton - Tommy Hutton.'

'I'm Ann Kirby. Pleased to meet you.'

She reached across the table and shook hands with her guest, and the ridiculousness of the situation hit them both at the same moment. They began to laugh and any tension that might have existed was immediately dispelled.

'I don't know how to express my feelings - about what you did, I mean,' she said.

'It wasn't much. Just a bit of shouting and waving my arms about,' replied Tommy.

'Well, it may not have been much to you. It certainly meant a lot to me. Those men. They were going to...'

'But they didn't.'

'Thanks to you.'

For a while they sat without speaking. Tommy drained his glass and set it down on the table. Ann pushed the bottle towards him.

'Help yourself,' she said.

Tommy needed no second invitation. Ann watched him as he refilled his glass, noticing the slight trembling of the hand that held the bottle and the eagerness with which he raised the brimming glass to his lips. She felt a mixture of pity and compassion and wondered how this man, obviously a drunk and a social outcast, had summoned up the courage to launch an attack on four brutal thugs without a thought for his own safety.

'Weren't you afraid?' she asked. 'Those men might have turned on you, beaten you up. Didn't you think of that?'

Tommy smiled ruefully. 'Tell you the truth, it never occurred to me. I just wanted to make a disturbance, attract attention. Anyway, they ran off.'

'Then you helped me up.' Ann blushed as she remembered that her skirt had been round her waist, exposing the lower part of her body. She hastily changed the subject.

'Do you want to ring anybody? Let them know where you are?' She indicated the telephone in the corner of the room.

'Nobody's interested in my whereabouts. I'm living rough.' There was an edge of bitterness in his voice which did not escape Ann's notice.

'Well, make yourself comfortable. I'm going to take a bath. Won't be long.'

In the bathroom she scrubbed herself vigorously then stood naked before the mirror. There were bruises on her arms and her right breast was tender and swollen, but, she said to herself, I was damned lucky. If it hadn't been for Tommy... she shuddered as her imagination ran riot. She dried herself, put on a bathrobe and returned to the sitting room.

Tommy had taken her at her word and made himself comfortable. He was curled up in the easy chair, fast asleep, one arm over his face as though to protect himself from some imagined danger. There was a look of peaceful innocence on his face and, as she stood looking at him, she felt tears come to her eyes. She spoke her thoughts aloud.

'You poor thing. You need looking after. You're a

116

mess. I'm going to make something of you if it's the last thing I do.'

She left the room and returned almost immediately with a blanket which she draped tenderly over the sleeping form. Then, turning out the light, she went to bed.

It was mid-morning when Tommy awakened from the soundest sleep he had experienced in months. Pushing the blanket which covered him to one side he swung his feet to the floor and, for a moment, wondered where he was. Somewhere close at hand there was the noise of a bubbling percolator and the fragrance of fresh-brewed coffee drifted into the room through the half-open door. Following the scent, he walked into the hall. At the same time Ann emerged from the kitchen.

'Good morning. I was just going to wake you up,' she said. 'Did you sleep well?'

Her matter-of-fact manner did much to dispel Tommy's uneasy feeling that his presence might be unwelcome in the light of day. It was, after all, one thing to be rescued from a perilous situation by a shabby down-and-out but something else entirely when that person had been invited into the home of the victim. He was at a loss for words but managed to mumble a 'good morning' in reply to Ann's greeting.

She stood to one side and gestured him into the kitchen. It was a bright and airy room with a large window and a door that led on to a small garden. Directly below the window was a table flanked by two wooden-backed chairs.

'Coffee's just ready.' said Ann. 'Sit down. I want to talk to you.'

As Tommy slid into one of the chairs, Ann placed a pair of gaily-painted mugs on the table and filled them from the percolater.

'Help yourself to milk and sugar.'

She watched him as he took his first sip of coffee, then launched into what was obviously a prepared speech.

'Look, Tommy,' she began, 'I don't want you to misunderstand me. I'd like to ask you a few questions, but if you think I'm poking my nose into your business, then say so.'

Tommy thought for a moment, then nodded.

'Fire away. I've got nothing to hide.'

'Well, first of all it's a favour. Will you stay here for a while? I... I don't want to be alone. You can have the spare room, and...'

'Hang about. I don't want any charity. I may be down but I'm not out.'

'I'm not offering you charity, Tommy. After what happened I can't bear the idea of being by myself in this flat. I promise you, there are no strings. Will you stay? Please.'

He had been married, he had fathered a child, but he was still naive when it came to women's wiles. He could see no ulterior motive in Ann's offer, nor did he look for one. Seeing the indecision in his expression, Ann pressed her point.

'I'll give you a key. You can come and go as you like. All I want is to know that you're around, that I can sleep in peace. Please... say you'll stay.'

Tommy considered the alternative, a return to the Bullring and the discomfort of his cardboard home, roaming the streets, begging for money to buy the drink which was his only solace.

'Alright, I'll stay,' he said. 'Will you promise me one thing though?'

'What's that?'

'Tell me when you're fed up with the arrangement. I

don't want to be here on sufferance.'

'Oh, yes, I promise. Come on. I'll show you your room. Then you can have a bath and make yourself comfy while I go and do a bit of shopping.'

It all seemed so simple and uncomplicated at the time, yet the arrangement was to prove to be a turning point in Tommy Hutton's life.

He was known as Wicked Campbell to the denizens of the Bullring. He was also feared. Over six feet in height and built like a prizefighter, he lorded it over his fellow dossers like a tribal chief. He carried the art of begging to the point of extortion, and there were few who had the courage to refuse his requests for 'a bit of money for a cuppa'. Not that the proceeds of his begging were wasted on anything so mundane as tea, for he had an inordinate capacity for strong lager by the pint and could easily put away twenty pints in the space of an evening. These bouts of heavy drinking were inevitably followed by incidents which involved any young female dossers who happened to catch his eye.

It was late afternoon when this brutal and insensitive monster emerged from the precincts of Bow Street Magistrates' Court. On the previous evening he had accosted a young couple in the Strand, making it plain by words and gestures that, if they failed to come up with a contribution, the consequences might be very unpleasant. The resulting scene was witnessed by a police officer who promptly arrested the offender. Wicked spent the night in the cells of Bow Street police station, was brought up before the magistrates on the following morning and was duly fined the sum of ten pounds. His worldly wealth at the time being less than one per cent of that amount, he was sent back to his cell, there to await release when the court rose at the end of the day's proceedings.

Though Campbell had been in the begging business for several months, this was his first experience of arrest and detention. From his point of view it was a gross interference with his personal liberty. He carried his deep resentment back to the Bullring where he unloaded his grievances into the receptive ears of two of his sycophants. This pair of rapscallions were a young dosser known as Pinko and his boon companion, a five foot nothing wisp of a man whom some humorist had invested with the nickname of Muscles.

Pinko, a one-time student at the London School of Economics who found the Bullring more to his taste than the lecture room, was holding forth on the attitude of the authorities.

'This is just the beginning,' he said. 'They've dragged up this Vagrancy Act. You can be nicked just for being homeless. You've now got a criminal record, Wicked. Next time you get picked up it'll be a spell in Brixton.'

'What's this Vagrancy Act,' enquired Muscles.

Pinko seized the opportunity to demonstrate his knowledge of history.

'Well, it was passed in 1824, just after the Napoleonic wars. The poor bloody soldiers had been demobbed, they had no money and no homes, so they took to the streets, sleeping rough and begging for food. Jolly old George the Fourth was on the throne. He didn't like seeing these poor sods when he looked out of the windows of the palace so bingo! the Act was passed, the ragged-arsed army was shoved into clink and that was that.'

'Things haven't changed much. They're still sweeping the shit under the carpet,' said Muscles.

Wicked was becoming bored with all the chat about history. 'Ah dinna gie a damn aboot what happened nigh on two hundred years gone. Whit the focken hell do we

120

do now?' he asked.

'Simple,' replied Pinko. 'When I was at the LSE, if we didn't like what was going on, we demonstrated against it. Occupied the premises, hung banners out of the windows, that sort of thing. The authorities soon came round to our way of thinking. We should do the same thing here, organise a march, get on the streets, let the public know what's going on.'

'So what are we waiting for?' enquired Wicked.

'Somebody to start the ball rolling,' said Pinko. 'Are you on?'

'Too bliddy right,' was Wicked's reply. 'Let's get going.'

The ill-assorted trio set out on a tour of the Bullring without further ado, making their plans as they went along. The response from the groups of dossers was immediate and very heartening. Bored with the dreary day-to-day round of sleeping, begging and drinking, the population of cardboard city was open to any proposition that would bring an element of adventure into their lives. In no time at all the bashes became hives of industry, shelter being sacrified to expediency as cardboard boxes were wrenched apart and transformed into makeshift placards covered with roughly-lettered slogans spelling out the demands of the army of the homeless.

There were a few pockets of resistance, but these were overcome by the uncompromising Wicked in typical fashion. To those who raised objections he had one reply. 'If ye're no wi' us ye're against us, an' ye ken weel whit that means.' The reputation of the giant Scotsman clinched the argument and the dissenters fell into line. When the self-appointed committee reached Ironfoot's bash, however, they ran into their first real hurdle.

'Have you made the necessary arrangements with the

police?' was Ironfoot's first question after Pinko had laid out the plans for the demonstration.

'Bugger the police,' replied Pinko. 'Before they know what's happened we'll be demonstrating outside the House of Commons.'

'I think not. You'll get no further than the end of Waterloo Bridge. The law doesn't mess about with your sort of private enterprise. They'll break up your march before it's got started.'

'We'll take a chance on that,' retorted Pinko. 'What I want to know is whether you're with us or not.'

'I'll think about it,' said the older man.

'Don't spend too much time thinking. We want action and we're going to get it. Unity is strength. Come on Wicked. You too Muscles. We've got work to do.'

Pinko was in his element. A born mischief-maker with more than a working knowledge of mob psychology, he moved about the Bullring like a Napoleon rallying his army before battle. As a consequence his tatterdemalion troops were in a state of readiness by the morning. As the clock in the tower of Big Ben boomed out ten sonorous chimes some three hundred men, women and children formed up ready to begin the march.

As the pitiful procession crossed Waterloo Bridge it was a strange and rather moving sight. Among the demonstrators was a core of men and women who had been discharged from mental hospitals into a community which neither knew nor cared about their plight. They had been coerced into joining the march and had no idea what was really happening. Shambling along, their eyes on the ground, at times leaning on each other for support, they attracted public sympathy, which was exactly what Pinko had in mind. Alongside the marchers moved small teams of young and active dossers equipped with

122

plastic buckets for the receipt of donations. There was a leavening of young mothers carrying their babies either in their arms or strapped to their backs. Make-shift placards held aloft and shouting slogans at the top of their voices the demonstrators, with Pinko, Wicked and Muscles in the lead, swung into the Strand. There they were joined by a contingent from Lincolns Inn Fields, swelling the numbers to some four hundred.

Traffic in Central London is controlled by a linked system of signal lights which react quickly to any untoward event. None the less, a collision between two vehicles in one of the busy streets of the capital can lead to a build-up of cars and other forms of transport over a wide area. The appearance of a straggling mob occu-pying one side of the Strand and moving slowly in the direction of Trafalgar Square caused chaos which spread rapidly to the surrounding thoroughfares. Near the entrance to the Savoy hotel a patrolling policeman spoke urgently into his personal radio, then moved to intercept the procession. He fell into step beside Pinko, shouting to make himself heard above the chanting of the marchers.

'You the organiser of this lot?' he yelled.

Pinko grinned and shook his head. 'Spontaneous ac-tion. We're all organisers.'

'Don't give me that. Tell 'em to stop.'

'You tell 'em,' bellowed Pinko, and promptly dived into the crowd which was already forming on the pave-ment.

The constable stood helplessly as the tide of dossers flowed on around him, then, realising that there was nothing more he could do, retired to the pavement where he once more had recourse to his personal radio. In the meantime Pinko had threaded his way through the bystanders and regained his position at the head of the demonstration.

At the point where the Strand enters Trafalgar Square a police car screeched to a halt broadside on to the approaching procession. From it sprang a uniformed inspector with a sergeant close behind him. The two men stood with arms upraised as the inspector cried 'Stop'. He might just as well have saved his breath. The procession split neatly and simply passed on either side of the obstruction as though it did not exist.

From then on it was bedlam all the way. The marchers shuffled on, exasperated motorists thumbed their horns, crowds gathered on the pavements and the chanting increased in volume. The whole of Central London was turning into one vast traffic jam as Napoleon Pinko led his ragged army into Whitehall and down towards the Cenotaph. Ironfoot Jack, who had elected to act as marshal for the infirm, the elderly and the demented, did all he could to keep his charges in order, but he was fighting a losing battle. Pressure from the rear built up as the night-time occupiers of shop doorways along the Strand tacked themselves on to the tail-end of the march.

The end came when the leaders of the demonstration were confronted by a line of police officers backed by a collection of vans and cars which effectively blocked off any further progress in the direction of the Houses of Parliament. The instructions to the police officers had been brief. Clear the streets was the command and it was carried out briskly and efficiently. In the result the march was broken up as the demonstrators fled into the side streets, falling over each other as the chanting of slogans gave way to panic-stricken screams. The mopping-up operation lasted the best part of an hour, at the end of which the area was cleared, leaving the road cluttered with discarded placards and other debris dropped by the marchers in their hasty flight to safety.

It was now time to count the cost. More than fifty of the demonstrators had been injured, the majority of them in the group under Ironfoot's care. They lay in the roadway, moaning and weeping as they nursed broken limbs and weakly attempted to stem the flow of blood from their wounds. The ambulance crews were busily attending to those who could be treated on the spot. One of them called to his mate.

'Over here, Jim. This one looks in a bad way. ' He indicated an unconscious body crumpled against the steps of the Cenotaph, blood oozing from the scalp, one leg stuck out at an impossible angle from the hip.'

Blimey. What ' s this contraption? ' said Jim, pointing to the iron hoop fixed to the boot on the injured leg.'

Never mind about that. Let 's get him on the stretcher. Looks like he's on the way out. '

CHAPTER 7.

When he accepted Ann Kirby's invitation to move in with her, Tommy Hutton's state of mind could hardly be described as reasonable. The traumas of the few hours preceding that decision had been a terrifying series of experiences which would have affected men of much greater moral fibre than a half-drunken social reject. Yet the decision had been made largely because, at the time, it was much easier to say yes rather than no.

In the unusual surroundings of the very feminine bathroom he scrubbed himself clean and donned the white bathrobe which Ann had put out for him. Returning to the sitting room he picked up the bottle of whisky and poured himself a small measure then, holding the glass in his hand, moved slowly to the wall opposite the window. It was almost entirely covered by rows of bookshelves. He ran his eye over some of the titles which ranged from hardback editions of the classics to a large and variegated collection of paperbacks, but found nothing which gave him a clue to the character of the owner, save the fact that she was a voracious reader with a catholic taste in literature.

Continuing his tour of exploration he examined the music centre and its store of tapes and discs which indicated that Ann Kirby was a lover of classical music but was not above listening to recordings of pop music by the better-known groups. There were albums of the Beatles and the Rolling Stones and a tidily arranged row of tapes of contemporary artistes, all in alphabetical order. She's certainly very methodical, thought Tommy, a place for everything and everything in its

126

place, and he contrasted this orderly and comfortable room with the bleak starkness of the Bullring where all was noise, dirt and confusion. He swallowed the rest of the whisky in his glass, poured himself another small measure and sat down in one of the two easy chairs. Leaning back he stretched out his legs and closed his eyes. In a few moments he was fast asleep, and that was how Ann found him on her return an hour or so later. She put down the bags and parcels with which she was laden and shook her guest gently by the shoulder.

'How are you feeling?' was her first question as he opened his eyes.

Tommy sat up hastily, conscious of the fact that, under the bathrobe, he was completely naked. He drew the robe tighter around him.

'Oh, I'm fine. Just having a little nap. Sorry.'

Ann smiled. 'What have you got to be sorry about,' she said. 'I told you to make yourself at home, so you do just that. Now sit up and see what I've got for you.'

She began to open the parcels, laying each object on the settee as she took off the wrappings.

'There's a jacket and trousers. I guessed the size. I got them from Marks, so I can exchange them if they're not right. Shirts, size fifteen. That OK?'

Tommy nodded. He was taken aback by the turn of events and was lost for words.

'Underwear. Socks. Couple of ties. Razor and shaving cream, toothbrush, toothpaste. That should do for the time being...'

'Hang on a minute. This lot must have cost a fortune. I can't take it,' protested Tommy.

'You can and you will. Now listen to me, Tommy. I've made up my mind. I don't know what made you into what you are, but I do know one thing. If it hadn't been for you I would have been...'

'I've told you. I didn't do anything...'

'Be quiet. Let's get things straight. I want you to stay here until you get yourself right. I'm not after your body. Do you understand?'

'Oh, I understand alright. You think you're under an obligation to me. Well, you're not...'

Ann was exasperated and she showed it.

'For Christ's sake shut up. Tommy, you're a mess. You need somebody to look after you. I've taken on the job, whether you like it or not. Now pick these things up and take them into your room and try them on. Jump to it.'

Northern determination battled with southern reticence and northern determination won the day. Without saying another word Tommy gathered up Ann's purchases and made an exit with as much dignity as he could muster. Ann gathered the discarded wrappings into a neat pile, curled up in an armchair and waited, confident in the knowledge that she had won the first battle. When Tommy re-entered the room fifteen minutes later, having shaved and dressed himself in his new garments, she stared at him in surprise. In place of the shabby wreck of the previous evening she saw a very personable young man who would not have seemed out of order in any gathering.

'Well, well,' was her first remark. 'They say clothes don't make the man, but they certainly make a difference.'

Rather self-consciously he struck what he imagined to be a male model pose, much to Ann's amusement.

'So I look alright then?'

'You look fine.'

'Everything fits. How did you manage it?'

'Easy. One of the salesmen was just about your size. He picked out the jacket and trousers. The rest was no trouble.'

This one is a very resourceful lady, thought Tommy. His experience of women was limited, for he had never been one for pursuing the female sex. Indeed, his wife had been the one and only sexual partner in his life. Now he felt unsure of himself in the presence of an obviously liberated member of the opposite sex who was making no bones about the fact that she intended to play an important part in his immediate future. Ann broke the silence.

'I fancy a cup of coffee,' she said. 'How about you? Or would you like something stronger?'

'Coffee'll do me fine. Actually I've just had some of your whisky...'

'You're welcome. Feel free to help yourself to anything you want,' said Ann quickly. 'I'll make the coffee. You make yourself comfortable.'

As she busied herself in the kitchen, switching on the coffee percolator and setting out cups and saucers on a tray, Ann thought over the events of the past twelve hours. Last night she had been a relatively care-free young woman returning to her home after a dinner party with friends. That part of her life was now over, for she knew she would never recover from the effects of the dastardly attack by the four brutal thugs who, had they been successful in carrying out their plans, would have left her a ravaged wreck on the grass of Hyde Park. She tried to imagine what her feelings would have been had she been penetrated by each one in turn, the foul breath in her face, the powerful and relentless thrusting, the spurts of semen as each one reached his climax, and oh dear God the possibility of contracting a disease.

Her mind in a turmoil, she gripped the back of a chair, holding it so tightly that the knuckles of her hand stood out white against her skin. Come on, girl, pull yourself together she murmured, and with an effort she turned to the job in hand, disconnecting the percolator and placing it on the tray, and now holding the tray steady as she passed through the kitchen door and into the sitting room.

She was quite composed as she poured coffee, though there was a slight tremor in the hand that raised the cup to her lips. Tommy sensed that she was labouring under an emotional reaction and held his peace, waiting for her to make the first move, which came after a short silence.

'I suppose you're wondering what all this is about,' she began.

'I'll be frank with you. I don't know what to think, at least not yet,' was the reply.

'I'll try to explain. I'm still confused. Everything happened so quickly. You see, I was going home. I'd been to dinner with friends, and missed the last train. Then I was pulled into this car, into the back. There were two of them. They... they did things to me. It was horrible. I think I fainted. The next thing I remember there was this man on top of me, trying to force his thing into me. Then there was a lot of shouting and the men ran off and then you were there telling me it was all over.'

Tears came to her eyes as she reached this point in her story. Tommy, certain that there was more to come in due time, remained silent.

'Then there was the police station,' she went on. 'The doctor wanted to examine me. I couldn't bear to be touched... there. I'd had enough. Do you understand?'

Tommy did not understand. Nevertheless he nodded and did his best to look sympathetic.

'I asked you to come home with me because you were the only reality in the whole business. All the rest was just a nightmare. What I remember was you, helping me up, telling me it was all over. That's the one clear picture I have in my mind. What I'm trying to say is... Oh, hell, I don't know what I'm trying to say.'

Tommy managed a weak smile. 'Then don't bother to say it. I think I know what you're getting at. Why don't you put it all out of your mind? Or try to, anyway.'

'Easier said than done. Still... let's talk about you for a change. You said you were, what was it, living rough. What's that mean?'

'Sleeping in a cardboard box underneath the arches at Waterloo Bridge, that's what. A dosser. One of the great unwashed and unwanted.'

'So how come? I mean, you're young and you look fairly healthy. What happened?'

Tommy had no intention of letting his hair down and telling the whole sad story. He had done it once. He did not like the idea of repeating that experience.

'It was a little while ago. Something I don't want to talk about. I began drinking, lost my job. I came to London, went on the booze, spent all my money and that was that. I ended up in the Bullring.'

'What was your job?'

'Draughtsman. With an engineering firm.'

'Well, you should be able to get another job easily. There's quite a demand for draughtsmen I believe.'

Tommy's answer was to stretch out his hands in front of him. In a moment they began to shake uncontrollably.

'Look at them. Can you imagine what they would be like on a drawing board? A first-class balls-up.'

'But... if you cut down on the drink? Look, let's make a bargain. Don't stop right away. Just taper off for, say, a week. Then see how you feel. What do you say?'

Tommy gave the suggestion some thought. After all,

he had nothing to lose. If things didn't turn out right he could go back to the Bullring.

'Okay. It's a deal,' he said.

In the Sheldon ward of the Westminster hospital Ironfoot Jack was recovering from the anaesthetic that had been administered when his broken and battered body was wheeled into the theatre. He did not know where he was or how he had got there. His last conscious memory was of being hemmed in by a mass of bodies and losing his footing, of falling to the ground where he was trampled by what seemed to be hundreds of booted feet and then blackness. As he slowly opened his eyes a female voice spoke from somewhere in the region of his right ear. He tried to turn his head in the direction of the voice, a manoeuvre he quickly abandoned as a stabbing pain shot through his skull.

'Just lie still,' said the voice.

He licked his lips and tried to speak, but his efforts resulted in no more than a hoarse murmur.

'Don't try to talk,' said the voice. 'Just lie still. You'll feel better very soon.'

Feel better very soon, he thought, and closed his eyes against the glare of the white-painted ceiling. He heard another voice, this time male.

'How is he, nurse?'

'Just coming round, sir.' The female voice again. It must be a hospital, wonder what's happened to me, is it serious, am I going to die, the words ran riot through his brain as he summoned up all his energies and managed to croak one word.

'Doctor,' he said.

'Ah. We're awake, eh. Now don't worry. You've had a bad accident, but you're going to be alright. Nurse will look after you. I'll come and see you later.'

There was the swish of a curtain and the sound of receding footsteps. Now agony began to invade his body and he groaned. A hand came into his line of vision and he felt a movement across his forehead as he relapsed into a semi-coma. He was aware of sounds and smells but little else. A hand was laid on his arm, he felt a slight pricking sensation and almost at once the pain receded, he had the feeling that he was floating on a soft white cloud...

He had no way of knowing how long he lay in a state midway between sleeping and waking but when he next opened his eyes it was to look into the face of the nurse who leant over him solicitously as she carefully adjusted the pillow behind his head. He opened his mouth to speak and heard his own voice as though from a great distance.

'Hello,' he said.

The nurse smiled. 'How do you feel?' she asked.

The reply came slowly, each word enunciated carefully.

'Not... so... bad. Where... am... I? What... happened?'

'You're in Westminster hospital. You've had a rather bad accident. Now don't talk too much. I'll get the doctor to see you. He'll explain everything.'

The doctor was at the bedside within a matter of minutes. He drew up a chair to a position from which his face could be seen by his patient, and spoke in a measured voice, choosing his words so that they would easily be understood.

'Now, you've been involved in a very bad accident,' he began. 'You were seriously injured. You suffered multiple fractures to both arms. Your right leg, the -er -short one, was badly damaged. Beyond repair, in fact. We had to amputate. I'm sorry.'

He paused and looked searchingly into his patient's

face as if unsure whether he should proceed or not. Evidently satisfied, he went on.

'There was some damage to the ribs, but fortunately no internal injury. You also suffered laceration to the scalp but that was superficial. No fractures.'

He paused again as his patient showed a desire to speak, moving his lips soundlessly until the words came.

'Thank... you. What... happens... now?'

'Well, we'll have to keep you here until the fractures heal. After that, you'll be transferred to Roehampton. They'll fit you up with an artificial limb. What I want you to do now is rest. If you're in pain, tell the nurse. She'll deal with it. Now try to sleep. Knit up the ravelled sleeve of care, as old Bill Shakespeare said. I'll see you later.'

The doctor departed, quite satisfied that he had put his patient's mind at rest, the nurse smoothed a pillow that did not need attention and Ironfoot Jack submerged the pain of his broken limbs in the blessed anodyne of sleep.

Pinko, Napoleon of the Bullring, had suffered a severe blow to his pride. Not only was the march on the Houses of Parliament a dismal failure, it had attracted no media attention. Added to that, his standing among his fellow residents of cardboard city had fallen to something below zero. Even his trusty lieutenants had turned against him, Wicked Campbell going to the extent of threatening to give him a thumping and Muscles indulging in a torrent of abuse for which Pinko had no answer.

The significance of the demonstration was not lost on the authorities, for the cost in terms of traffic jams and general dislocation was considerable. Under the guise of maintaining law and order on the streets the police instituted a stringent operation against the proliferation of beggars in the popular tourist spots, as a consequence of which there was a sharp reduction of disposable income amongst the unfortunate homeless. Instead of venturing on to the areas of easy pickings such as the Strand and the environs of Piccadilly, the more enterprising went further afield where the possibility of arrest was more remote. In general, however, the majority remained within the confines of the Bullring, collecting in small groups, indulging in endless argument and getting nowhere.

Given the circumstances where apathy and boredom were linked with a dearth of alcohol, incidents of violence increased. Wicked Campbell and others of his kind roamed the bashes in search of the wherewithal to slake their thirsts, and woe betide the possessor of a few cans of lager who refused to surrender them to the predators. Sporadic fighting became a nightly event and there were times when the police were forced to intervene to separate rival groups who were turning the Bullring into a battleground.

Mattie had returned to London after one of his brief and mysterious forays to another part of the country. He headed for the Bullring with the intention of looking up his old mate Ironfoot but, instead of the familiar sight of the philosopher perched on the stone parapet he was met with a very different reception. Ironfoot was conspicuous by his absence, but Wicked Campbell and the miniscule Muscles were very much in evidence, as was Lizzie, the ancient bagwoman, and it was not a scene of peace and tranquillity. The rumour around the camp was that the old crone had a hoard of cash secreted in one of her many plastic bags. Wicked had decided to test the truth of the rumour and Mattie arrived at the bash just as Campbell, holding the old crone in an iron grip, was exhorting Muscles to get on with the job of searching her belongings.

Mattie had no particular love for the foul-mouthed Lizzie, but he had no time at all for the hulking Campbell. Rushing forward, he delivered a mighty blow with his clenched fist to the top of Campbell's head and as the object of his attack released his hold on the old woman and turned to meet this new danger, Mattie launched a savage kick at Campbell's groin. It connected and the effect was instantaneous. The brutal Scot bent double, Mattie's knee crashed into his face and the fight was over. Blood streaming from his nose, Wicked crawled away on hands and knees. Muscles had already taken flight. Mattie turned to Lizzie, who crouched over her bags muttering obscene oaths as she pored over her treasures.

'You alright?' he asked.

She paid no attention to the enquiry. Mattie tried once more.

'Where's Ironfoot and Tommy?'

Lizzie looked up and uttered the one word 'Gorn.'

No joy here, thought Mattie, and was about to leave when a pale and frightened Packet came round the corner, followed by a pair of fellow dossers. All three were carrying wooden staves.

'Hello. What's up with you lot? Goin' inter battle?' enquired Mattie.

'Where've they gone?' was Packet's response.

'Campbell and the midget? I kicked their arses out of it. What was it all about?'

'They reckoned Lizzie had some dosh stashed away,' said Packet.

'They set on her. I went to get some help.'

'Very noble of yer. Well, she don't need help now.

What I want to know is what's happened to Ironfoot and Tommy.'

'Tommy disappeared a few days ago. Ironfoot's in hospital. He got hurt on the march.'

'What march?'

'Demonstration to Parliament. The law bust it up. In Whitehall. There was about fifty hurt.'

'Which hospital is he in?'

'Westminster. Sheldon ward. I went to see him, but they wouldn't let me in. Said he was in intensive care.'

'Wouldn't let you in, eh. We'll see about that. You lookin' after his duds?'

'I'm keeping an eye on them, yes.'

'Right. Carry on. If them two bastards come 'ere agin, tell 'em I'm taking a close personal interest. Got it?'

Without waiting for a reply, Mattie walked away, his long overcoat billowing around him. Westminster hospital lay on the far side of Parliament Square, a matter of a couple of miles from the Bullring. He could be there within the hour.

For the first time since he had arrived in London Tommy was relatively content. It would, however, be untrue to say that he was happy. The process of adjustment to a new way of life presented a set of problems which he was ill-fitted to solve. Though he made strenuous efforts to conquer his desire for liquor he still found it impossible to go through the day without recourse to the bottle, though he limited his intake to a few small whiskys a day.

Ann had taken a couple of days off from work but had now returned to her job. During her absence Tommy tidied up the flat and attended to the household chores, shopped for food in the local stores with money provided by Ann and in general did his best to be useful. He realised that this state of affairs could not go on indefinitely, that he would one day have to find himself a job, but for the present he shrank from the prospect of scanning the situations vacant columns in the papers or visiting the Job Centre.

He broached the subject with Ann as they sat over dinner one evening.

'You must be thinking that I ought to get off my backside and look for a job,' he began.

'Plenty of time for that,' replied Ann. 'You've had a rough passage. Wait until you're fit again. If it's money you're worrying about, forget it. You're not straining the family resources.'

'I'd like to pay my whack, just the same. I can't live off you forever.'

'Forever is a long time, Tommy. Don't be too hard on yourself. Just take it easy. Everything'll be alright.'

Alone in his room that night he forced himself to confront the situation. Did he really want to return to conformity, to be once more a member of the human race with all that such a state implied. His thoughts strayed to a recollection of some of the things Ironfoot Jack had said in the course of their discussions, statements which he had only half understood in his drunken condition at the time. He was aware that he had reached a turning-point in his life and was now in a position to rehabilitate himself. He came to a decision. No matter what it cost in terms of jangled nerves and mental torment, he would stop drinking, join the ranks of the wage-earners and become once more a respectable member of society. Let the dead past bury its dead, he said to himself, the future is the only thing that is important.

He rose early the following morning and was shaved and dressed when he sat down to breakfast. Ann commented on his appearance, asking jocularly if there was anything special on.

'Yes, there is,' said Tommy. 'I'm going job-hunting. Oh, and another thing. I'm giving up the booze. From now on it's soft drinks and mineral water.'

Ann looked at him doubtfully. 'Think you can manage it? Wouldn't it be better just to taper off, do it gradually?'

'No. I've made up my mind. It's the only way. Finish and be done with it.'

'Well, I wish you luck. I must say I admire you.'

Tommy laughed. 'Flattery will get you nowhere,' he said. 'I've got a lot to thank you for. I won't forget it.'

They left the flat together and parted company at the corner of the road, where Ann thrust a folded note into the breast pocket of his jacket. 'Just in case you need it,' she said as she mounted the bus that would take her to the City. He stood on the pavement for a few moments watching the bus as it swung into the early morning traffic of the Fulham Road.

Having had no previous experience of looking for a job, Tommy was not quite sure how he should set about it. Of one thing he was quite certain, that on no account would he go into a drawing office. Other than that he had made up his mind that he would do anything that offered a reasonable reward for a day's work. He strolled along aimlessly in the direction of the West End, pausing occasionally to peer into a shop window. A bold notice outside a restaurant caught his eye. KITCHEN HELP REQUIRED it read, and he thought why not, I'll have a go. His hope was short-lived, for the door of the restaurant was firmly locked and there was no sign of life inside.

His next stop was at a building site, where the foreman gave him a quizzical look.

'Had any experience, son?' he asked.

'Well, not a lot,' answered Tommy. 'I've - er - been working in an office. I fancy an open-air job.'

'Let's have a look at your hands,' was the next request. Tommy held out his hands, palms upward. The foreman grinned.

'No chance, son,' he said. 'You wouldn't last five minutes. I'd stick to office work if I was you.'

Strangely enough Tommy was not put out at the rejection. As he reasoned to himself he could not expect to be lucky at the first attempt. He left the site and, acting on a sudden impulse, boarded an eastward-bound bus which would take him to Piccadilly. He mounted to the upper deck from which he had a tourist-eye view of streets he had so often traversed on foot. There was the Brompton Oratory and, a little further on, the imposing frontage of Harrod's, where the doors were just opening for the commencement of business. The thought crossed his mind that there might be a job for him in the famous emporium, but a second thought banished that idea. He felt he was not yet ready to tackle the personal involvement of dealing with the public.

At the stop outside Green Park Station, opposite the Ritz hotel, he left the bus and crossed the road to the entrance to the park which was bathed in the pale sunlight of late summer. Remembering that day when he had arrived in London his thoughts turned automatically to his meeting with Mattie, the hairy vagrant who had provided his introduction to the Bullring, and he wondered vaguely where the man was now and what he was doing. Probably panhandling in the Strand or perched on the edge of a pavement somewhere pouring liquor down his throat from the large bottle which was his constant companion.

Tommy turned into the park, feeling in need of a rest.

He selected a vacant bench and sat down. There was a vague ache in his stomach, his hands trembled and his forehead was beaded with perspiration. He would have given anything in the world for a drink, but he had made himself a promise and that promise he intended to keep. Stilling his quivering hands by folding his arms and tucking his fingers under his armpits he waited for the spasm to pass. He was in agony for some ten minutes as he fought to control the revolt of a body starved of the balm of alcohol.

Finally the pain subsided to be replaced by a dull gnawing as though a devouring rat had been let loose in his belly and was nibbling at his entrails. He wiped the sweat from his forehead with the back of his hand and levered himself up from the bench. Leaving the park he began to walk along Piccadilly, forcing himself to remain upright and take slow measured steps. This is the crucial test, he thought, if I can get through this I've taken the first hurdle without falling flat on my face.

For the next couple of hours he roamed the streets and alleys around Piccadilly Circus, regarding the world around him with eyes that were no longer clouded with the effects of alcohol. He toyed with the idea of taking food at one of the numerous cafes but decided against it, not quite sure of the effect it would have on his stomach, yet he was conscious of a craving which he could not analyse. It came upon him suddenly, the memory of a film he had seen in which an alcoholic fighting the habit had resorted to tomato juice liberally laced with Worcester sauce. I'll have a stab at that, he thought, and made a beeline for the nearest pub.

The drink proved to be exactly what his tortured stomach needed and he swallowed it greedily, following it with a repeat dose. Standing at the bar he ran his eye along the line of optics, whisky, gin, brandy and the rest, and felt a quiet glow of pride that he was able to resist their allure. Now I feel fit for anything, he said to himself, and made his way out of the door and on to the street.

He had taken a few steps when he heard a voice'behind him.

'Hey, Tommy... Tommy!'

The street cleaner standing by his cart was a familiar figure with whom Tommy had been on friendly terms in the Bullring. A short fat man who had a smile for everybody, he was now waving excitedly. Tommy moved towards him.

'How are you, Mike?' he said. He pointed to the cart. 'What's all this?'

'Gone respectable, ain't I. No more Bullring, mate. Regular job, regular wages. Can't beat it.'

Tommy was highly amused. 'Makes a change I suppose. How long have you been at it?'

'About three weeks. What you doing? You look prosperous.'

'Down to my last Rolls Royce. Actually I'm looking for a job.'

'No kidding. We've got vacancies at our depot if you fancy street cleaning. Money for old rope. Shift work, six in the morning till three, three to eleven at night. Take home pay one twenty basic plus overtime...'

Tommy called a halt to the torrent of words.

'Hang on. How do I go about getting taken on?' he asked.

'Easy. Meet me here quarter to three. I'll take you to the depot, introduce you to the guv'nor. That's it. Are you on?'

'I'm on,' said Tommy. 'Meet you here. Quarter to three.'

The interview with the guv'nor was surprisingly informal. He asked a few questions, the replies to which seemed to satisfy him, and the erstwhile draughtsman became a street cleaner.

'Right. When can you start?' said the guv'nor.

'Soon as you like,' replied Tommy.

'Tomorrow morning?'

'That'll be fine, thank you.'

'You'll be with Mike here for the first couple of days. He'll show you the ropes. See you tomorrow then.'

CHAPTER 8.

To use hospital jargon the patient was 'quite comfortable', which might seem to be an unusual way to describe the condition of an elderly man with an amputated leg, broken ribs, both arms in plaster and a head swathed in bandages. Ironfoot Jack had always held to the belief that what happened to the body was of little or no importance, so long as the mind was not impaired. He now had need of all his philosophy.

His first visitor was Mattie, who had hung around the waiting area of the hospital until such time as he was allowed to enter the ward. Now he sat beside the injured man's bed and asked the inevitable first question.

'How do you feel?' he said.

For a man who had so recently been subject to major surgery Ironfoot's voice was surprisingly strong.

'My dear Mattie I am, as you can no doubt see, in a mess. They tell me that I have lost my leg, which never was a lot of use anyway. I have multiple fractures of both arms, a few busted ribs and a nasty headache. Apart from those trifling matters I am fine.'

'So how did it happen?'

'I take it you have heard about the march?'

'Packet told me. Why the 'ell did yer join it? Wasn't none of yer business.'

'No option. Some of my feeble-minded friends had been persuaded to take part. Someone had to look after them. Who else but yours truly.'

'And so...?

'It was obvious the march would be a failure. The guardians of the law saw to that. They broke up the procession in Whitehall. Everybody ran for it and unfortunately I happened to be in the way. It would seem that most of them ran over me. Hence the injuries.'

'This 'ere march. Whose idea was it?'

'That champion of lost causes Pinko. Aided and abetted by the lager-swilling Campbell.'

'Campbell, eh. Well, I've seen to 'im.'

Mattie recounted briefly the story of his altercation with the brutal Scot, at the end of which Ironfoot delivered his verdict.

'In the normal course of events I don't hold with violence,' he said. 'In this instance I would say it was justified. By the way, do you know if my belongings are safe?'

'Packet's looking after 'em. Want me to bring you anything?'

'I'm alright for the time being. Did you see anything of our mutual friend? Young Tommy I mean.'

'Ain't been seen for a few days.'

'Oh dear. I hope it's not another of his drinking sprees. The last one was almost fatal.'

At this point a nurse approached Ironfoot's bed. Mattie had by no means earned her favour when he entered the ward and she was determined to end his stay at the earliest possible moment. In her opinion, Mattie's unsavoury and anything but hygienic appearance posed a definite threat to her patients. She addressed Ironfoot directly.

'I'm afraid your visitor will have to leave now. The doctor will be here shortly.'

Mattie rose from the chair as the nurse hastily took a step backward to avoid contact.

'Sorry I can't shake hands,' said Ironfoot. 'See you soon I hope.'

'Be in tomorrer,' said Mattie. 'Take care.'

He shambled out of the ward, closely watched by a very disapproving nurse. Ironfoot gave her a quizzical look.

'Never judge by outward appearances, my dear,' he said. 'He may not be much to look at but he has a heart of gold.'

The newest recruit to the near-impossible task of keeping the streets free from litter in the City of Westminster leaned on his broom at the corner where Frith Street crosses Old Compton Street. He had spent two days in the company of his mentor, after which the cheerful Mike gave it as his considered opinion that Tommy was now sufficiently competent to be given a round of his own comprising Soho Square, Frith and Dean streets and the two sections of Old Compton Street and Shaftesbury Avenue which fell between those boundaries.

He was the type of person who took pride in doing a job to the best of his abilities. He remembered an old saying that it's better to be a good crossing sweeper than a poor Prime Minister and was amused at the aptness of the comparison. Looking at the neat pile of litter that he had gathered together with a few swift strokes of the broom and holding his shovel at the approved angle he transferred the rubbish to the interior of the nearby cart. Laying the broom and shovel neatly on the cart he took the handles and moved slowly to the next area of operation. There was time to clear another stretch of the street before he took his lunch break at noon.

The past two days had witnessed a remarkable change in Tommy's mental attitude. When, on the evening of the day on which he had been successful in getting a job he had conveyed the news to Ann, he had expected a lukewarm reception. Her reaction was one of praise that he had been so quick mixed with absolute acceptance of the lowly status of the employment.

'I think you've done wonders, Tommy,' she said. 'It's an honest job of work. No need to be ashamed of it. I'm very proud of you.'

She had greater cause for congratulation when he refused to drink wine with his dinner, for she doubted that he would be strong enough to keep his promise to give up alcohol completely. Her doubts were unfounded.

'It's great stuff, this tomato juice,' he informed her. 'Settles my stomach marvellously. Whoever invented it deserves a medal.'

The relationship between the two was now on a much more stable footing. Secure in the knowledge that her flatmate slept a matter of a few yards from her bedroom, Ann no longer feared the loneliness of the night hours. Even the unpleasant dreams had begun to fade, the scars on her mind healing with the passage of time. She did not fully understand her emotions, nor did she wish to analyse herself. She was nevertheless conscious of a growing affection for the man who had, however unwittingly, saved her from an experience that would have soured the rest of her life.

As for Tommy, he was quite happy to accept the situation. He had a job, he had hopefully defeated his alcoholism and he shared a comfortable flat on the best of terms with a young woman who, on the surface at least, was bright, pleasant and understanding. He was dimly aware of the inner tensions which Ann suffered and was sensitive to her moods, knowing by instinct when to talk and when to remain silent. Of one thing, however, he was firmly convinced. For the time being at least they had a desperate need of each other.

Platonic friendship is the gun that nobody thought

was loaded according to the cynics. However that may be, Ann and Tommy lived together in comparative harmony without the intrusion of sex. To Ann the very thought of submitting to any intimate contact nauseated her, and as for Tommy the thought never occurred to him to make advances. All his energies were directed towards conquering his addiction and doing his job. He was making satisfactory progress on both counts and looked and felt better than he had for many months. Gone was the haggard appearance and the bloodshot eyes, there was a spring in his steps and he had started to put on weight. Of even greater importance was the fact that he was slowly recovering his self-confidence.

It was at the start of his second week that he heard the news of Ironfoot Jack's accident. Memories of the Bullring had receded into a past he wished to forget, though from time to time he spared a thought for the old philosopher, wondering vaguely whether he was still in residence at the bash along with Packet and the old crone Lizzie.

His friend and mentor Mike told him the story. He himself had only heard about the incident through the grapevine on the previous day.

'There was this march, see,' said Mike. 'Old Ironfoot was roped into it. The Old Bill bust it up. Ironfoot got badly hurt.'

'Funny. There was nothing in the papers. Wonder why?'

'Well, they wouldn't print anything, would they. Can you imagine the headlines? Homeless mob marches on Parliament. Street battles at the Cenotaph. Not a good advert for the brave new Britain, eh?'

Tommy was more concerned about the condition of the old philosopher than with political discussion.

'Know where he is?' he enquired.

148

'Yeah. Westminster hospital. I was told he was pretty bad. Lost his gammy leg they said.'

'Poor old sod. I'll go down and see him tomorrow.'

'Give him my regards,' said Mike.

Though his circumstances were not particularly salubrious, the old philosopher was not at all downhearted. The plaster casts had been removed from his arms, the wounds on his scalp were healed and the only inconvenience he suffered was a desire to attend to an itch on the sole of a foot that was no longer part of his anatomy. The doctor had assured him that the condition was not unusual.

'Rather like a phantom pregnancy,' he said. 'The patient knows it isn't there. She only thinks it is.'

'If you're comparing my mental processes with those of a silly woman who thinks she's got a bun in the oven,' said Jack, with a note of scorn in his voice, 'then you're barking up the wrong tree.'

The doctor hastily assured him that no insult was intended and beat a hasty retreat. Accustomed to the servile respect of the majority of his patients, he was at a loss as to how to deal with this most unusual man who regarded the amputation of a leg as a matter of little importance and who bore what must have been considerable pain with amazing fortitude.

Feeling quite happy after his minor argument with the doctor, Jack made himself comfortable with the aid of one of the nurses and closed his eyes. In a few moments he was fast asleep. When, about an hour later, he returned to consciousness, it was to find Tommy standing by his bedside. He greeted his visitor in his usual flamboyant style.

'Well, now, look who's here. Young Tommy in person and looking fine and prosperous. I'm delighted to

149

see you. Sit down and tell me what's been happening to you.'

Tommy drew up a chair. 'Never mind about what's been happening to me,' he said. 'Look at you. How the hell did you get into this mess?'

'Let's say a minor misjudgement. It's of no importance.'

'No importance? Leave off. Well bashed up and lost a leg and you think it doesn't matter...'

'Now, Tommy, it's all over and done with, just a brief period of pain. The wounds have healed and in a few days I shall be transferred to Roehampton where they will give me a new limb which, so I'm told, will be infinitely superior to the one that I've lost. So, what's the worry?'

Tommy laughed. 'You slay me, you really do,' he said. 'From what I heard you're lucky to be alive.'

'Enough of that,' said the older man. 'Water under the bridge. What I would like to know is the reason for your remarkable transformation.'

'Simple. I got fed up with being a drunken bum, so I went on the wagon, got myself a job and a roof over my head, and that's about the size of it.'

'You make it sound very easy.'

'Wasn't all that easy. It had to be done, so I did it. No reason to pat myself on the back. Anyway, let's not talk about it. Are you alright in here? Can I do anything?'

'I'm fine. Mattie comes in most days, gives me all the news...'

'Mattie! How is the old sod?'

'Just the same. Mattie is one unchangeable factor in a constantly changing equation.'

So the chatter went on until it was time for Tommy to leave. He shook his old friend by the hand and was surprised at the firmness of the grip.

'I'll be in again soon,' said Tommy. 'Take care of yourself.'

Leaving the hospital and on his way to the bus-stop nearby, Tommy was confronted by a familiar figure. Hair waving in the slight breeze, voluminous coat flapping around the ankles, Mattie roared a greeting.

'Tommy lad. Where you been hiding. Thought you was dead.'

'I've not been hiding, you can see I'm not dead and I'm very well thank you,' replied Tommy. 'Just paid the old fellow a visit. You going in to see him?'

'That's right. Keeping an eye on 'im. On the mend 'e is. Soon be out and about.' 'Still down at the Bullring are you?'

'Off and on.'

'Packet, old Liz and the boy. They still in my old bash?'

'Yeah. No change. You look a bit rich. What yer up to?'

'Give you three guesses,' said Tommy with a grin.

'Yer got a job. Yer on the wagon. Shacked up with a bird. Right?'

'Two out of three. Well done, Mattie.'

'Yeah. I'm not just a pretty face. Listen, I gotta go in now. Let's have a meet soon, eh?'

'Right. What about tomorrow afternoon down at my old bash. About four. OK?'

'Yer on. See yer.'

With a wave of his hand Mattie turned and entered the hospital. As he crossed the road to the bus stop, Tommy wondered for a moment why he had not disclosed to his friend that he was shacked up with a bird and concluded that the question had a vulgar undertone that did not meet with his approval. Somehow he did not feel that 'shacking up' was a correct description of his relationship with Anne Kirby, nor did he agree with reference to her as a 'bird'.

The habits of a lifetime die hard. Tommy's industrial career as an engineering draughtsman had inculcated in him certain disciplines which had become part of his character. It was in his nature to make a good job of anything he tackled and he brought that commitment to the lowly but necessary work of keeping a small section of the City of Westminster clean and tidy. This brought him some small measure of appreciation from a few of the restaurateurs on his patch who showed their good-will in practical fashion. Tommy was not above accepting these perks, whether in cash or kind, and on a good day the small change in his pocket amounted to a considerable sum.

Angelo Perrotti was the proprietor of a small but select restaurant in Dean Street and one of the principal contributors to the fund for obliging street cleaners. On this particular morning he stood on the pavement before his restaurant as he supervised the unloading of a delivery of wine. The van driver and his mate showed little respect for the valuable goods they were handling, and Angelo hopped from one foot to the other as the irresponsible pair staggered between the rear doors of the van and the entrance to the restaurant. There were all the ingredients of an accident looking for a place for it to happen, and sure enough it did. The van driver tripped over the edge of the kerb, his burden crashed to the ground and the pavement was littered with broken glass as the case burst open and discharged a dozen litres of best red Tuscan into the gutter.

It was pure coincidence that Tommy was on the spot. Shovel and brush at the ready he transferred the debris to his barrow while Angelo berated the luckless perpetrator of the carnage in a mixture of imperfect English and vulgar Italian. When the tumult died and the chastened carriers resumed their work Angelo turned to Tommy, who was busily sweeping the remnants of the wine from the pavement.

'You're a good boy, Tommy,' he said as he took a handful of small change from his pocket. He selected a couple of pound coins and pressed them into Tommy's hand.

Suddenly the comparative quiet of Dean Street was shattered by a prolonged blast from a powerful horn. A large black Mercedes nudged Tommy's barrow, a furious face appeared at the driver's side window and a loud heavily accented voice left Tommy in no doubt that the barrow was not merely causing an unwelcome obstruction but also that the person in charge of the offending article was of very doubtful parentage. Not normally an aggressive person, Tommy did not take kindly to vulgar abuse.

'Alright, alright,' he yelled. 'Keep your hair on. I'll move it in a minute.'

The response was instantaneous. The door of the Mercedes flew open, the driver emerged and literally flung himself at Tommy, swinging wild punches, some of which connected. As a result Tommy found himself on his back on the pavement, staring up at a swarthy face contorted with fury, a face that bore a livid scar down one side. The attacker paused for a moment, then turned on his heel and, siezing the offending barrow by the handles, tipped it into the gutter. With a final glance at his recumbent victim he returned to the car, tucked himself behind the wheel and drove off.

Angelo Perrotti bent over Tommy and helped him to his feet.

'You alright?' he asked.

'Yeah, yeah,' replied Tommy. He was shaken but unhurt. 'What's the matter with that feller? He must be bananas.'

'That a very nasty man,' said Angelo.

'You know him?'

'Everybody in Soho know him. That's Tony Messarina. One of the Messarina brothers. Very bad news.'

'You can say that again,' said Tommy. 'Messarina, eh? Is he Italian?'

'That rubbish. Italian? These Messarinas come from Malta. Very wicked people. Clip joints and strip clubs. You keep away from them, Tommy.'

'Too bloody right I will.'

Tommy went over to his barrow and set it back on its wheels. Some of the garbage had spilled into the street, but the greater part of the load was intact. He went to work with brush and shovel, tidied up the mess and, with a farewell wave to the restaurant proprietor, went on his way.

Once the shock of the attack had worn off, Tommy was able to think about the incident calmly. Somewhere at the back of his mind was a feeling that he had seen this Messarina fellow before, and that fairly recently. Suddenly memory came back in a flood of recollection, a dark night in Hyde Park, the girl on the ground surrounded by four men, the one man who had risen from his knees, the swarthy face with the livid scar, the black Mercedes tearing off along the North carriageway, it all added up to one conclusion. This man had been the ringleader in the attempted rape of Anne Kirby. His three confederates were most likely his brothers. This is certainly a turn-up for the book, thought Tommy, and then began to wonder what he should do about it.

His morning shift ended, Tommy returned to the

depot. His friend Mike was reporting for duty on the afternoon shift, and Tommy related to him the story of the incident outside Perrotti's restaurant.

'Bloody hell,' said his friend at the end of the recital.

'You've run foul of a right lot there. These Messarinas are poison. Four of 'em, real wicked bastards. They're the guvnors in Soho. Poncing, running whores, protection rackets, you name it, they're in it. My advice to you, Tommy lad, is keep well away from them. You was lucky to get away so easy. You might have got a knife in your ribs.'

'Do you reckon they might have another pop at me?'

'Shouldn't think so. It was Tony who gave you a thumping, you said. He's probably forgotten all about it. Lay low, say nothing and keep out of his way, that's my advice.'

'Thanks, Mike,' said Tommy. 'See you later, eh?'

Arriving at the Bullring to keep his date with Mattie, Tommy was welcomed by the man himself backed by Packet and the boy. Lizzie was in her usual corner, muttering to herself and searching through a collection of carrier bags for whatever she thought she had lost. Tommy's first enquiry was about Ironfoot Jack's condition.

'Comfortable,' reported Mattie. 'Goes to Roehampton termorrer. Giving 'im a new leg. Quite excited 'e is.'

'I'll bet,' said Tommy. Mattie reached for the litre bottle which was conveniently to hand.

'No good offering you one,' he said.

'No thanks,' replied Tommy. 'I told you. I'm on the wagon.'

'Well, 'ere's to crime,' said Mattie. Removing the cork, he applied the neck of the bottle to his mouth and took a monstrous swig. Wiping his whiskers with the back of his hand, he emitted a resounding belch.

'That's better,' he said. 'Now then, Tommy. How goes it with you?'

'Mustn't grumble. Got a nice little job and a room in a friend's flat. No complaints really.'

The conversation was interrupted by the old bagwoman, who had been listening intently to what Tommy had to say.

'Got a job, 'ave yer?' she said. 'Gone up in the world. Too good for the likes of us.'

'Shut up, Lizzie,' said Mattie. The old crone, lips working over toothless gums, did not take kindly to Mattie's rebuke.

'Won't bloody shut up. Speak me mind, I do,' she retorted. 'You clear off, Tommy Rotten. Go back to yer posh mates.'

'Come on, Tommy. Let's go for a stroll,' said Mattie.

'Can't talk in front of 'er. Silly old cow.'

The two men walked away from the bash towards the walkway beside the Thames. Leaning their elbows on the parapet they stood in silence for a few moments. Out on the water a tug towed a string of barges up-river, moving slowly against the ebbing tide.

Tommy broke the silence. 'You know Soho pretty well, Mattie?'

'Should do. Spent enough time there. What's on yer mind?'

'The name Messarina mean anything to you?'

'Not 'alf. Four brothers. Real bastards. Own most of the manor. Maltese ponces, knife merchants. Slit yer throat soon as look at yer. Not mixed up with 'em are yer?'

'In a way, yes,' replied Tommy. He described briefly the incident of the morning, and Mattie nodded wisely.

'That's Tony Messarina all over,' he said. 'Vicious sod. You was lucky. Might 'ave got knifed.'

'What, in broad daylight? Come off it.'

'They've done worse than that. Carved a feller up once. Right in Shaftesbury Avenue. Middle of the day.'

'Didn't they get nicked?'

'No chance. Old Bill knew who done it. No witnesses. No nicking.'

Tommy fell silent as he looked across the river to the leafy beauty of the Embankment Gardens and the stately rear view of the Savoy hotel. There was one question on his mind. Should he take Mattie into his confidence, tell him the whole story and ask his advice or should he sweep the sorry mess under the carpet and forget about it. He decided to take the plunge.

'Remember the other day? You asked me if I was shacked up with a bird,' he began. 'Well, I'm not really, not the way you think. I'm living in this young woman's flat, but there's nothing between us. It was like this.'

Tommy went on to recount the story of how he had come to the rescue of Anne Kirby on that unforgetttable night in Hyde Park, how she had taken him into her home, supported him as he searched for a job and helped him to go on the wagon.

'That's the position, Mattie,' he said. 'Now comes the crunch. This Tony Messarina. I thought I'd seen him before somewhere. Then it came to me. He was one of the four who attacked Anne. It all adds up. I reckon the other three were his brothers. What should I do about it? Should I tell Anne? Or would it be best to forget all about it and go on as if nothing had happened?'

Mattie seemed in no hurry to reply and Tommy waited patiently until his friend chose to speak. Finally Mattie came out with his opinion.

'Got to tell 'er, Tommy. She's a right to know. What

'appens after? Up to 'er. She wants to 'ave a go at 'em, so be it. Need any 'elp, let me know.'

'Thanks, Mattie. You're a pal. Where do I find you if I want to get in touch?'

'Be around 'ere. Staying in London. Keeping an eye on the old feller.'

'Give him my regards when you see him.'

'Will do. Yer off now?'

'Yes. See you soon, eh?'

'Good luck,' said Mattie, and on that note the two men parted.

Tommy was in no hurry to return to the flat. He felt he needed some time to himself to go over in his mind the events of the day, to digest the information he had gleaned from his colleague Mike and to consider Mattie's advice. He walked slowly over Waterloo Bridge and turned into the Strand where he paused to buy an evening paper. Then, acting on impulse, he crossed the road and, for the first time in several weeks, went into a public house.

The bar was large and sparsely populated, the bartender a slovenly character who slouched over to attend to the needs of his latest customer. He did little to conceal his contempt when Tommy ordered a tomato juice.

'Just a tomato juice?' said the ornament to the licensed trade.

'With Worcester sauce,' replied Tommy.

The business at the counter concluded, Tommy carried his drink to a small table near the door. He sat down, unfolded his newspaper and idly perused the headlines. Finding nothing of interest, he put down the paper, took a sip of his drink and gave himself up to his thoughts.

His first and most immediate problem was the way in

which he would break the news of his discovery to Anne. How would she take it, he wondered, this re-opening of wounds which had scarcely healed. Would she want to go all out for revenge, or decide to let the matter drop, and if she opted for revenge, what were the implications. With only a hazy idea of police procedure, he nevertheless was aware that he and Anne would become involved as witnesses, possibly be called upon to identify her assailants and in general be subject to much inconvenience for a considerable length of time. It was not a pleasant prospect. There was also another factor to be considered. The Messarinas were definitely not the kind of people to overlook interference with their activities, and it was a safe bet that they were surrounded by thugs who were well-paid to protect their employers' interests.

The pub was now beginning to fill up with home-going workers taking a few drinks before facing the long and uncomfortable journey to the bosom of their wives and families. I've exhausted the possibilities of this situation, thought Tommy. He swallowed the remainder of his tomato juice and walked out into the Strand.

Anne Kirby realised that the flat was empty as soon as she closed the front door behind her. She had grown so accustomed to being welcomed by Tommy when he was on early shift that his absence caused her some concern. Ever present in her mind was the fear that one day Tommy would fall victim to the habit that had led to his downfall, would take that one drink which, in any reformed alcoholic, would be the first step on the road back to dependency. She wandered aimlessly round the flat, went into the kitchen and made herself a cup of instant coffee which she took into the sitting room, then sat gazing into space, telling herself over and over again that she was being stupid, that very shortly she would hear the sound of a key turning in the lock of the front door and Tommy would be home.

As she sat and waited she tried to analyse her feelings about this man who had become part of the fabric of her life. Up to now she had taken him for granted, her only emotion being concern for his well-being, but she had come to appreciate his kindness and his gentle ways, to understand the fierce fight he had waged against his addiction. She remembered how she had vowed to make something of the disreputable wreck whom she had taken under her wing in a quixotic move that belied her natural commonsense, and told herself that she did not for one moment regret her decision. Now, sitting alone with only her thoughts for company, she faced the fact that the loss of Tommy's companionship would be a blow from which she would not easily recover.

She looked at the clock on the mantelpiece. Half past seven, she said to herself and as tears began to moisten her eyes she murmured under her breath, for God's sake, Tommy, come home, please come home. As if in answer to her prayer there came the sound of footsteps from outside, the door of the flat was opened and a voice called 'Hello. Anybody at home?'

Anne leapt to her feet and rushed into the hallway as Tommy closed the door behind him. As he turned towards her she burst into tears, standing there a piteous figure, arms down by her sides. He stared at her in consternation, not knowing what had brought on this strange behaviour, so out of character with her normal down-to-earth manner.

'Hey, come on, what's the matter?' he asked.

'I was just... worried. I thought something had happened to you. You were so late...

160

Not quite sure how to deal with this situation, Tommy took her hand and led her into the sitting room.

'Now you just sit down. I'll make us a cup of tea and then you can tell me all about it.'

He disappeared into the kitchen as Anne sank into a chair. By the time Tommy came in with teapot and cups on a tray she had recovered her composure.

'You could have telephoned,' she said. 'It's not like you to be late. I was very worried. You might have had an accident...'

Tommy was genuinely contrite. 'I didn't think,' he said. 'Look, something happened today. I had to find out a few things before I told you about it. Sort of make some enquiries.'

Anne sipped her tea, realising that she had given way to panic over something that was entirely the product of her imagination.

'I'm alright now, Tommy,' she said. 'I was a bit silly. I've got to be honest with you. I thought you might have gone back on the booze.'

'No chance. I've finished with that lark. I'll tell you what it's all about and then we can decide what to do.'

'I'm all ears,' said Anne.

'Well, it was like this. I had a bit of bother this morning. In Dean Street. My barrow was in the way of some bloke's car. I was about to shift it when this feller jumped out of the car and set about me. Took me by surprise. Laid me flat on my back.'

'Just like that?'

'Right. Just like that. But that's not the whole story. You remember those characters who attacked you?'

'That night in the park? That's something I'll never forget.'

'Well, this fellow was one of them. I'd have recognised him anywhere. Nasty-looking piece of work with

161

a scar down his cheek. Anyway, I went to see one of my old mates at the Bullring after I finished work. He knows a lot about Soho. He told me that this chap was one of the Messarina brothers. They're gangsters, run strip clubs, prostitution, extortion rackets - you name it, they're in it. Four of them, come from Malta.'

Anne listened to the recital with growing feelings of unease. Ever since her ordeal she had tried to put the experience out of her mind and had succeeded to some extent. Now the memory was back in all its horror. Her voice trembled as she asked the question.

'Oh, Tommy, what shall we do?'

CHAPTER 9.

Crime is a twenty four hour a day business. Those who commit crimes take no account of hours. They are on duty night and day looking for opportunities, spying out the land, laying plans and making preparations for doing the business. They take no account of hours nor do they log overtime; they stay with the job until the operation is completed, when they decamp with their considerable rewards or get nicked as the case may be.

The picture is the same on the other side of the fence, where the guardians of the law strive to tip the balance of the scales of justice in their favour. They also labour night and day in the constant war against lawlessness. Also, because the process of the law demands it, they keep strict records so that "anything which is said may be written down and given in evidence".

Detective Inspector Ian Macandrew was a good policeman in that he believed in the principles of law and order and in the administration of justice in a fair and equal fashion. On his manor of Paddington he was known as "straight" to both criminals and colleagues. His memory was prodigious, his paperwork impeccable and, having reached the rank of Detective Inspector by the age of forty-five, he was in line for promotion before retirement.

When the call from Tommy Hutton came through, it was at the end of a tiring day during which he had had to cope with several arrests and the consequent flood of paperwork. That he was tired was understandable, but there was no evidence of fatigue in his voice as he requested the switchboard to put the caller on the line.

'Mister Macandrew?' said the voice. 'My name's

Hutton, Tommy Hutton. I don't know if you remember me...'

'Yes, Mister Hutton, I remember you. What can I do for you?'

'That rape business. In Hyde Park. A young woman called Anne Kirby.'

'Yes. You were a witness. You had a slight - er - disagreement with one of my colleagues.'

'That's right. Well, I've found out who the four blokes were who did it.'

Macandrew pulled his notebook towards him and picked up a pen.

'Right,' he said. 'Who are they and how did you find out about them?'

Tommy briefly recounted the circumstances in which he had recognised Tony Messarina. Macandrew listened intently, occasionally making a note on his pad. When Tommy ended his little speech, Macandrew gave his verdict.

'You say you can positively identify this Tony Messarina. What about the other three?'

'Anne could identify them. She remembers their faces.'

'Yes. Of course. She would,' said Macandrew. He took a quick look at his list of engagements for the morrow.

'I think it would be best if you and the young lady came in to see me,' he continued.

There was an exchange of whispers at the other end of the line, then Tommy spoke. Whenever you like.'

'Excellent. Would tomorrow morning suit you? Say eleven o'clock?'

'We'll be there,' said Tommy.

Macandrew replaced the receiver and sat back in his chair. This is going to be a nasty one, he thought. The

Messarinas were not the ordinary run of mindless thugs. They were, as he well knew, cunning and resourceful. Moreover they were sufficiently wealthy to afford the very best in the way of defence counsel should they be brought before a court. In the meantime it wouldn't be a bad idea to get the latest on the Messarinas. He picked up the telephone, and the switchboard answered almost immediately.

'Get me Inspector Davis at West End Central,' he said.

The call from Davis came through within a matter of minutes.

'How are you mate?' said Davis cheerily. 'What's going on in your neck of the woods?'

Macandrew laughed. Davis' cockney accent always amused him, as did his jokey manner. The two men had often worked together and enjoyed a rapport that made their joint efforts agreeable.

'I need a bit of help,' said Macandrew.

'You've come to the right place. Just pour out your heart to uncle Colin. Difficult problems we solve right away. The impossible ones take a little longer. Fire away.'

'The brothers Messarina. What's the latest on them?'

'No change. They're still a pain in the arse. I've been trying to feel their collars since forever, but they're too fly. What's your interest?'

'They might be in the frame for rape. Got any recent mug shots?'

'Sure. A whole gallery of them.'

'Can you get them over to me first thing in the morning?'

'No sweat. They'll be on your desk when you get in.'

'Thanks, Colin.'

'Let me know how you get on, eh?'

'I'll do that little thing,' said Macandrew, and rang off.

For a while he sat deep in thought. This wasn't going to be an easy one, but there was a way out. He could interview Hutton and Kirby, hear what they had to say, put them off from taking any further action and sweep the lot under the carpet. In the meantime he had had enough for the day. He marshalled the clutter of papers on his desk into a tidy pile and left the office.

Tommy put down the phone after his conversation with Macandrew.

'Well, that's that. I hope we're doing the right thing,' he said.

Ann, sitting upright on the settee, rubbed her hands together, a nervous movement which was an outward indication of inner turmoil. She was re-living that dreadful night, could feel once more the hands that invaded her body, the culmination of events which found her on her back, legs forced apart, dreading the violation which was about to take place. She had a vivid mental picture of the dark, evil face, the prominent scar down the cheek, in her nostrils was the smell of garlic-laden breath. She began to shiver and Tommy looked at her in some alarm. She had always presented herself as a calm and dependable character, very sure and deliberate when she was called upon to make decisions in her day-to-day life. Now she was another person, a frightened little girl facing unknown dangers. Tommy sat by her side and took her hand.

'Look, Ann , I'm sorry. I didn't think it would upset you so much,' he said. 'Tell you what, let's call it off. I'll ring Macandrew, tell him I made a mistake. What do you say?'

Ann took a deep breath and squeezed Tommy's hand

tightly. After a while the shivering stopped as she brought her emotions under control.

'No, Tommy,' she said, her voice low and determined. 'I want to go through with it. Animals like that, they should be put away. I'll be alright. Its just that...'

'I know. It won't be pleasant for you. Don't worry. I'll back you up every inch of the way.'

Anne managed a weak smile and relaxed her grip on Tommy's hand. Now that the die had been cast she was prepared to set the wheels of the law in motion and do all she could to make sure that her attackers would be brought to justice. She had little knowledge of police procedure, but she had great faith in the power of the authorities who administered justice, for she had never had reason to doubt that, in the end, right would triumph over wrong. It was a philosophy of which she would have great need in the days ahead.

Tommy's voice broke in on her reverie. 'I've got an idea,' he said. 'Why don't we eat out tonight? Don't know about you, but I could murder a curry. Alright?'

Anne's reply was almost immediate. She rose to her feet and went towards her room.

'I'll just get my coat,' she said.

The Indian restaurant was a few minutes walk from the flat. It was typical of the many ethnic eating places which had sprung up in the neighbourhood, flock-papered walls, clean white tablecloths, shining glasses and solid cutlery. There were few diners and Tommy and Anne were able to choose a corner table where they could talk without being overheard. A cheerful waiter with a Peter Sellers accent took their order and they settled down to talk.

'Good idea, this,' said Anne. 'Better than mooning around in the flat thinking all sorts of things about tomorrow.'

'Couldn't agree with you more,' replied Tommy. 'Does take your mind off problems. Being among people stuffing their faces, well, it's sort of ordinary, isn't it? Look at that chap over there. You'd think there was nothing wrong in his little world.'

Anne followed her companion's gaze to the opposite side of the restaurant where a solitary diner presided over a table which appeared to support samples of every dish on the menu. He was a very large man with an appetite to match, or so it would seem by the way he shovelled enormous spoonfuls of food into his mouth. Anne watched in fascination, then giggled.

'What's so funny?' said Tommy. 'I was just thinking of a rather rude joke about fat men.'

'Well, let's hear it.'

'Oh, no, I couldn't. Perhaps I'll tell you later.'

She was saved further embarrassment by the arrival of the waiter who rapidly covered the table with a multitude of dishes, finishing off the performance with a flourish as he polished a brace of warm plates and set them before his customers.

'Golly, that smells good. I feel like a little girl at a party,' said Anne.

'That's what you are,' said Tommy.

Conversation ceased as they loaded their plates from the numerous fragrant dishes set before them. Spicy meat curry was added to perfectly cooked patna rice and topped by a savoury concoction made from the humble lentil and known as dahl. There were crispy poppadums, something called Bombay Duck which may have originated in Bombay but which bore no resemblance whatever to a feathered fowl and many other and equally delectable additions such as lime and mango pickles. As they ate, Anne cast surreptitious glances at the man sitting beside her, and contrasted him with the pitiful

168

wreck that he had been only a few short weeks ago. Never in her wildest dreams did she imagine that he would not only conquer his alcoholism but that he would hold down the menial job he had taken on. She felt a quiet pride in the knowledge that she had been in some part responsible for a seeming miracle.

As the meal progressed, unpleasant memories faded. They both drank mineral water, which surprisingly had much the same effect as sparkling champagne in uplifting their spirits.

The meal at an end, Tommy insisted on paying the bill.

'My treat,' he said. 'You've done enough for me. It's time I started doing something for you.'

They walked back to the flat, still in high spirits. Anne took Tommy's arm, making a physical contact with him for the first time since she had taken him into her home. She did not regard the action as strange or untoward, but she was aware that there was now a new aspect to the relationship, that on the following morning they would embark on a joint venture when they kept the appointment with Macandrew.

Tommy, for his part, was only slightly surprised by what he took to be merely a friendly gesture. Over the weeks he had spent as her guest there had grown up an easy brother and sister attachment, each respecting the other's privacy. He knew that Anne had suffered an enormous shock, that it would be some time before she recovered from the mental and physical damage that was the aftermath of the brutal assault upon her. She had more than once told him that his presence in her home was a great comfort to her, that she felt safe knowing, to use her own phrase, that 'there was a man about the house'. Tommy had jokingly said, on one occasion, that he could not see himself in the role of a knight in shining armour. Her only reply was a withering look indicating her displeasure at his self-denigration. He took the hint and also took great care not to repeat the offence.

Back at the flat they said their goodnights before retiring to their respective beds. Neither of them referred to their appointment with the Detective Inspector on the following morning. It was as if they had tacitly agreed not to spoil the memory of a delightful evening.

Inspector Maeandrew looked at his watch and noted that the time was quarter to eleven. Spread out on the desk before him were a number of photographs which he began to examine with great care. They were excellent prints and they all had one thing in common. They all featured one or other of the Messarina brothers, sometimes individually, at other times as members of a group which included some of their associates, criminal and otherwise. As he studied the prints he was filled with a sense of revulsion, knowing that all these dark-faced and evil creatures had committed crimes without number and had gone unpunished. He could put a name to all four of the brothers. There was Antonio, the eldest, easily identifiable by reason of the massive scar on his cheek, then came Alberto of the round, chubby face and bulging stomach. The younger end was represented by Mario and Gino, born within a year of each other and sufficiently alike to be mistaken for twins.

Macandrew , then a Detective Sergeant, had served a stint at West End Central at a time when the Messarina brothers were serving their apprenticeship to crime. Their Maltese father was already well-established as a pimp who controlled the activities of some twenty Soho whores. The toll he exacted from them had made him a wealthy man and an important figure in the Soho hierarchy of villains. When he died the mantle of his wealth, power and prestige fell upon the shoulders of his sons, who carried on the family tradition, luring young girls into prostitution by the use of terror and violence while at the same time building up a small army of thugs who carried out the brothers' orders to the letter.

The money rolled in and was put into use in the rapidly growing empire of vice and corruption. Properties were bought and turned into strip clubs and centres for the distribution of pornographic literature. The prostitutes were housed in rooms above these premises which made it easier for the thugs who collected the bounty to keep tabs on their charges. By the time the elder brother had reached the age of thirty the Messarinas were the acknowledged rulers of Soho. None dared to question their authority, their victims suffered in silence and the police were impotent, for witnesses to their crimes were few in number and too terrified to open their mouths.

Placing the photographs in a neat pile on his desk, Macandrew went over in his mind the pros and cons. He now was in a position to mount an official attack on the notorious brothers but certain conditions must be met. First; there should be evidence that a crime had been committed and then the perpetrators should be identified beyond a shadow of doubt. Given that the victim was able to make a positive identification supported by other evidence, charges could be brought subject to the approval of the Director of Public Prosecutions. Much depended on the strength of the evidence and the character and courage of the witnesses. Well, said Macandrew to himself, let's listen to what Anne Kirby and Tommy Hutton have to say and go on from there.

His visitors were ushered into the Inspector's office on the dot of eleven o'clock. He rose to welcome them, hand outstretched, a smile on his face.

'Pleased you could come along,' he said. 'Sit down and make yourselves comfortable.'

As he took his seat behind the desk he found it hard to conceal his amazement at the change in the man whom he had last seen a drink-sodden derelict with shaking hands and dulled eyes. Whoever had been responsible for this had done a good job, he thought, then turned his attention to the files before him. Finally he looked up and began to speak quietly but forcefully.

'Now, Tommy, you say you've identified one of the men who attacked Anne,' he began. He used the Christian names deliberately as a way of putting the two at ease.

Tommy nodded in confirmation. 'That's right,' he said.

'Tell me about it.'

Tommy described the incident outside the restaurant in Dean Street in detail.

'I see. And you're quite sure? No doubt in your mind at all?'

'Absolutely sure. I got a good look at him. He was coming towards me.'

'What about the other three?'

'They scattered. I didn't get a sight of their faces.'

Macandrew picked up the pile of photographs and turned his attention to Anne.

'Now then, Anne,' he said. 'I'd like you to look at these photographs and see if you recognise any of the faces on them. Take your time. No hurry.'

Anne moved her chair closer to the desk. Her hands trembled slightly as she turned over the prints one by one then, going back over them once more, she selected four and passed them to Macandrew.

'They're all on there,' she said. 'All four of them.'

Tears welled in her eyes and she groped in her handbag for a tissue. Macandrew waited patiently for the weeping to subside. Anne pulled herself together.

'I'm sorry,' she murmured. 'It's... it's...'

Macandrew was all sympathy as he rose from his chair, moved round the desk and, standing behind Anne, laid the four prints in front of her.

'I know this is an ordeal for you,' he said, 'but I'd like you to identify each of the men separately. Do you feel up to it?'

As Anne nodded there was a knock on the office door. In answer to Macandrew's call, the door opened and a woman PC entered carrying a tray which she set down on a corner of the desk.

'Ah, a nice cup of tea. Let's take a little break, shall we,' said Macandrew.

They drank the strong brew in silence, after which the Inspector returned to his task, standing slightly to one side of Anne as she pointed to the faces which were inscribed indelibly on her memory.

'This is the one who dragged me into the car,' she said, pointing with a forefinger. 'That's the one who was sitting in the back seat, the one that... that... bit...'

Macandrew placed a soothing hand on her shoulder.

'Alright, that's enough for the moment,' he said. 'No... no. Let me go on. That one was sitting beside the driver. He was watching. Licking his lips. He was... horrible. That was when I fainted.'

Macandrew urged her on. 'And then?'

'When I came to I was lying on my back. The one who had been driving was on top of me, trying to... I remember one of them said "you go first, Tony".'

'Can you point him out?'

Anne pointed to the grinning face with the prominent scar on the cheek.

'That's him,' she said. 'I'll never forget that face as long as I live.'

Macandrew was satisfied. Anne had correctly identified the four Messarina brothers to his satisfaction. Nevertheless he was intent on extracting every piece of information possible from someone who he was sure would prove an excellent witness.

'Can you remember anything about the car?'

'It was very roomy in the back. It was black. There was a sort of star on the front. I saw it through the windscreen.'

'Anything else?'

'It smelled very new. Real leather.'

Macandrew filed the information in his mind. A black Mercedes saloon, fairly new. He turned to Tommy.

'The man who assaulted you in Dean Street. What car was he driving?'

'A black Mercedes saloon. I'm pretty sure it was the one I saw in the park.'

Macandrew gathered the photographs together. He resumed his seat, quite happy with the result of the first step in his enquiries. Yet, as he well knew, it was only the first step. There was still a long way to go.

'Fine, you've both done very well,' he said. 'However, this is only the beginning. Identification from photographs is good enough for me, but that doesn't mean that it's good enough for the courts. Before a prosecution can go forward there will have to be an identity parade.' He gave Anne a searching look. 'Do you feel up to it? Confronting these men, I mean?'

Anne needed one word to reply. 'Yes,' she said.

'That's all, then. Thank you for coming in. I'll be in touch.'

As the door closed behind the departing couple Macandrew picked up the phone.

174

'Get me Inspector Davis, West End Central,' he said.

In an alleyway branching off Wardour Street in the heart of the West End can be found the Club Cucaracha, owned by Tony Messarina and patronised by the night people, a peculiar mix of villains, stars of stage, screen and television, monied idlers and tired businessmen squiring their buxom doxies. It was a recent acquisition by the elder Messarina who had for some time been searching for a suitable centre of operations to provide cover for his illegal activities.

The retiring proprietor, after a brief and uncomfortable interview with Tony and his brothers, had handed over his highly profitable enterprise in return for an undisclosed consideration. Those in the know swore that no money changed hands, nor was any explanation forthcoming from the late owner of the club. After transferring control he had disappeared, no one knew where, though there was some conjecture that he had become part of the concrete piling supporting a high-rise office block in the City. There was, however, no evidence to prove this theory and speculation died a natural death behind a wall of silence.

Entrance to the club was by means of a discreet door sandwiched between an Italian restaurant and a betting shop, both part of the Messarina empire. Membership cards were closely scrutinised by two characters whose dinner jackets were under constant strain from their considerable muscular development. Their battle-scarred faces bore welcoming smiles only for genuine members in good standing. As for the rest, they stood as good a chance of entering as a camel passing through the eye of a needle.

The Club Cucaracha was a high-class joint and Tony Messarina saw to it that the standards were maintained.

The premises were spacious, the lighting low key, the food and wine excellent, the service impeccable. A well-paid and very professional trio of piano, bass and drums provided a musical background for the gyrations of the punters who shuffled round the dance floor, and there was a long bar on a raised section for the convenience of those members who preferred to survey the scene rather than be part of it.

The administrative offices were situated at the rear of the premises. They consisted of a series of small rooms in which the day-to-day business was transacted and a larger room which was the preserve of the brothers and to which entry was permitted only to a favoured few. Here, in surroundings of extreme luxury, the brothers foregathered to count and share out their ill-gotten gains, to exchange information and to lay plans for the further extension of their operations.

It was shortly after one o'clock on a Sunday morning, and the brothers were about to call it a day. They had been in close conference for a couple of hours during which time they had mapped out a rough programme for the coming week. The proceedings had been informal, as they always were, with the elder brother Antonio lolling in a comfortable armchair as he pondered on the contributions made by his younger brothers. Like a general in command of a military expedition he listened carefully, came to a conclusion and issued his orders, certain in the knowledge that they would be carried out to the letter.

The raid came with startling suddenness. One moment all was quiet and peaceful in the back room, then the door was flung open and what appeared to be a small army burst in. In fact, the army consisted of five men, three in the uniform of the Metropolitan police and two in plain clothes. The brothers were out of their chairs in an instant.

'What-a bloody hell is this' roared Tony. 'Get outa here. Is a private club.'

'And this,' said Inspector Colin Davis, 'is a police raid.' He turned to one of the uniformed men behind him.

'Right, sergeant. Get on with it.'

The sergeant stepped forward. 'Alright, you lot. Up against the wall.'

The brothers displayed some reluctance to move, but hastened their steps as the three uniformed officers closed in on them. They stood in sullen silence as they were searched thoroughly. Meanwhile the Inspector and his colleague were busy examining papers on the low table which occupied the centre of the room. Deciding there was nothing to warrant further inspection, Davis turned his attention to the four brothers. His first remark was addressed to Tony.

'I'd like to see what's in that safe,' he said. 'Hand over the key.'

Tony began to bluster. 'You got no right...'

Davis cut him short. 'Don't talk to me about rights. You want to do this the hard way, that's fine by me.'

Tony produced a bunch of keys from his pocket. Separating one from the rest, he unhooked it from the key-ring and handed it to the sergeant who passed it in turn to Davis.

The safe was large, old fashioned and dominated the corner of the room. Davis operated the key and swung the door wide open to reveal a remarkable sight, neat stacks of Treasury notes almost filling the upper shelves, the lower part a jumble of files and account books.

'Well, now, what have we here,' said the Inspector. 'I thought there was a recession.' Slowly and deliberately he proceeded to remove the stacks of notes and pile them on the adjacent table. This action proved too much for Tony, who let out a strident scream and launched himself towards Davis. His progress was brought to an abrupt halt by the sergeant who seized him by the shoulder, swung him round and delivered a devastating punch to the midriff. Doubled up and in agony, Tony collapsed on the carpet while Davis smiled approvingly. He motioned to his plain-clothes assistant.

'Give me a hand with it,' he said. 'Count it and make out a receipt.'

Still gasping for breath Tony hauled himself from the floor. The sergeant laid a restraining hand on his shoulder.

'What you do with my money?' he yelled.

'Proceeds of crime I shouldn't wonder,' replied Davis cheerfully. 'Prove rightful ownership and you'll get it all back.'

As the sergeant roughly shoved him back into line with his brothers, Davis picked up the telephone and dialled a number. When the connection was made he spoke briefly.

'The Maltese falcons are caged,' he said. 'It's over to you now.'

At the other end of the line Ian Macandrew uttered a few words of thanks and hung up.

CHAPTER 10

There comes a point in every man's life when he sits back and takes a long, hard look at himself and asks himself a number of questions. Chief among them concern three fundamental issues. What have I done with my life thus far, where do I stand at present and how do I see the future? Tommy reached that important juncture on the Sunday morning following the interview with Macandrew, when he and Anne Kirby had committed themselves to bearing witness against the Messarinas.

Tommy was alone in the flat, Anne having gone to visit a friend in hospital. She had said that she would be back in the late afternoon and Tommy had time on his hands. For a while he pottered about the flat then, around midday, decided to take a stroll. He had no real purpose in mind as he closed the door of the flat behind him; he was only conscious of a desire to be out and about, to see what was going on in the world, to be part of the human experiment that was taking place around him.

He wandered aimlessly through a series of back streets where the usual Sunday activities were in full swing. Some of the owners of the many cars parked at the roadside were busy with bucket and sponge, giving their vehicles the weekly spruce-up. The residents of the bed-sitters emerged from their lonely rooms, some on the way to the local pub, others doing a spot of shopping for items forgotten on the previous day. There was an autumnal nip in the air and Tommy quickened his pace as he came into the bustling area of Earl's

Court where the usual crowd of idlers were gathered at the entrance to the underground station.

For a while he toyed with the idea of patronising one of the many small cafes in the vicinity but decided against it. Instead he went on his way up the Earl's Court Road towards Kensington High Street and the gates of Holland Park. There, he thought, he would sit on one of the benches and, surrounded by green grass and trees reminiscent of the countryside, do a little thinking.

Holland Park is probably the most pleasant of the many small green oases which dot the capital. Even in the height of summer it is never unduly crowded. On this autumn Sunday the numerous benches were largely unoccupied and Tommy chose a spot where he could sit quietly without fear of interruption. There he gave himself up to his thoughts.

He remembered vividly that other park into which he had staggered when first he came to London, and contrasted the drunken wreck he had been with the man he was today. What he had done, of course, was to run away from a crisis instead of facing up to it, to seek an answer to his problems in drink. Remembering the tone of the article in the Pictorial, he had to admit that there was an element of truth in the description of him as a snivelling object who deserved neither pity nor sympathy. Now that was all changed. He had conquered his addiction to alcohol, he was doing a job of work and he had the support and encouragement of the woman who had done so much to help him regain his self-respect.

Thinking about Anne, he tried to analyse the relationship between them. Living in the same flat, seeing each other every day and retiring to their respective rooms at night had paved the way to an easy interdependence which placed no great strain on either of them. Neverthertheless, they were both going through a stage of recovery from traumatic experiences which would only be healed by the passage of time. He had a feeling that his future was somehow linked with Anne's but what that future had in store he could only guess.

There was, however, one matter which he intended to see to without delay. He held out his hands in front of him, spreading the fingers wide. Not a tremor, they were as steady as rocks. So to hell with cleaning the streets, he would go back to the job he knew, a job which had brought him great satisfaction in the past. Back to the drawing board he murmured to himself, and flexed his fingers in anticipation as he pictured the blank sheet of paper before him, the orderly arrangement of T-square and set square, the pencil sharpened to a fine point and the first clear line setting the datum for the third-angle projection.

He had no idea how long he had been sitting on the park bench. A glance at his watch told him that the time was one o'clock and a slight rumble in his stomach said it was time to eat. He rejected the idea of returning to the flat for a lonely snack, electing instead to eat at a fast-food emporium in the High Street. With a couple of hamburgers and a large coffee inside him and feeling at peace with the world, he hopped on to a Fulham-bound bus.

When Detective Inspector Colin Davis had planned the raid on the Club Cucaracha for the early hours of Sunday morning he had done so advisedly. He was well aware that the elder Messarina would lose no time in assembling his legal battalions, but he equally well knew that the weekend was not a favourable time for rapid communication. With the brothers safely locked up in the cells at West End Central under the pretext of helping the police with their enquiries, Dixon would have time and to spare to arrange an identity parade, to formulae charges and generally attend to what had to be done in order to bring his prisoners before a magistrate. He was under no illusions about the future course of events. Tony Messarina had already made the permitted telephone call and it would be only a matter of time before his solicitor would turn up claiming the right to see his client. The rest would be a battle of wits which Davis was convinced he would win.

He had already spoken to Macandrew and been assured that his witnesses would be available to attend in order to go through the process of identifying the brothers. Now all he had to do was wait until Macandrew returned his call confirming that he had made the necessary arrangements. So far so good, thought Davis, and he leaned back in his chair. Patience was part of the stock-in-trade of a good policeman.

Tommy was waiting in the flat when Anne returned from the hospital.

'How was the patient?' he enquired as she flung her coat and handbag on the settee.

'Oh, she's fine. Should be out in a couple of days.'

'I'll put the kettle on. Bet you could do with a cup of tea.'

'Love one. They offered me a cup at the hospital. It wasn't fit to drink.'

'I know. I've had some. Hang about. Won't be a jiffey.'

As he got up to go to the kitchen the telephone rang. Anne picked up the receiver.

'Hello. Who is it?' she said. She listened for a few moments then put her hand over the mouthpiece and turned to Tommy.

'It's mister Macandrew. Says that the Messarina brothers have been arrested. He wants us to identify them.'

'When?'

Anne removed her hand from the mouthpiece.

'When would you like us to come along?' she asked.

The voice at the other end of the line spoke at some length. Anne nodded her head from time to time then turned to Tommy again.

'They're being held at West End Central. Could we be there in an hour. He'll send a car for us.'

'That's fine by me. How about you?'

'I'm OK.' She spoke into the telephone. 'That'll be alright, mister Macandrew. We'll be waiting.'

As she replaced the receiver Tommy looked at her with some concern. Her colour had faded and her hands were trembling.

'I'll get that cup of tea. You sit down,' he said. He went into the kitchen and returned shortly carrying the two cups which he set down on the table. They drank in silence, which was finally broken by Tommy.

'It's going to be a bit of an ordeal for you, isn't it?'

Anne put on a brave face, but she was feeling anything but brave at the thought of coming face to face with the four beasts who had so cruelly mistreated her. However she had made her decision and was determined to abide by it.

'I'll be alright, Tommy,' she said. 'Don't worry about me.'

He was reassured to some extent as the colour came back to her face and her hand no longer shook as she lifted the cup to her lips.

'I am worried about you,' he said, and there was a note in his voice which she had not heard before, a tender and caring note which somehow made her feel good.

'Tommy... please. I've got to go through with it,' she said. 'No more arguments...'

'That's OK. I'm right with you. All the way,' replied Tommy hastily. 'I owe you a lot.'

Anne forced a smile. All through her life she had been independent, determined to pursue her chosen path to wherever it might lead, confident in her ability to cope with any problems she might encounter. Now she was in need of support.

'Correction,' she said. 'We owe each other a lot. I'm not sure what would have happened to me if you hadn't been around after...'

'That's all in the past. Let's get this thing over with and then we can think about the future. Tell you what, Anne. I'm going to get a proper job. Get back into my trade. Back to the drawing board.' He held out his hands. 'Look there. Not a tremor. What do you think of that, eh?'

'Tommy, it's wonderful. I'm so happy for you.'

'You and me both. Come on, then. Get yourself ready. That car should be here any minute now.'

Anne drained her cup, rose to her feet and gave a mock salute before disappearing in the direction of her room.

They were collected by a police car driven by a uniformed constable. Beside him sat the WPC who had been present on the night of the attack in Hyde Park, and it was obvious that she had been well briefed by Macandrew.

'Now don't you worry, love,' she said as the car sped through the light Sunday evening traffic. 'The Inspector'll be at West End Central. He'll look after you.'

'What are they like, these identity parades asked

Anne.

'Piece of cake, love,' said the WPC cheerily. 'All over in a few minutes. You just go down the line, touch chummy on the shoulder...'

'Chummy? Who's that'' queried Anne.

The WPC laughed. 'Sorry, dear. that's what we call the villains. Sort of general nickname. Anyway, tney'll tell you what to do.'

At the station everything possible was done to put Anne and Tommy at ease. They were ushered into an office where they were greeted by Macandrew and introduced to Inspector Davis.

'I'll just put you in the picture,' Davis began. 'Now downstairs we've got a dozen fellows who all look pretty much the same. In among them are the four Messarinas. All you have to do is go down the line. If you recognise any of the faces, just touch them on the shoulder. You've nothing to be afraid of. There'll be a uniformed officer right beside you. It's just a matter of routine. Any questions?'

'No,' said Anne. Tommy shook his head.

'Right, then,' said Davis briskly. 'Let's get it over then, eh?'

The twelve men were indeed very similar in appearance. The dark Mediterranean faces were impassive, they stood silently as Anne passed down the line. At the end she paused and retraced her steps. She had no difficulty in remembering the faces of her assailants, and there was no hesitation as she touched each of the Messarina brothers on their respective shoulders. The last one to be identified was the elder, the man she had heard addressed as Tony. He showed no emotion as she came to him, but there was a tension in the air as Anne shrank from the contact. The look of hatred on the scarred face was in itself evidence of recognition and of guilt.

Anne's escort hustled her away, supporting her by the arm as her legs started to give way. Now it was Tommy's turn. He walked down the line, identified Tony Messarina at once and unhesitatingly, showing no interest in the rest of the line-up. He joined Anne, Macandrew and Davis in the latter's office.

'Now that was just fine,' said Davis. 'You did very well.'

'What happens now?' asked Tommy. Anne was too shaken to take any part in the conversation.

Macandrew provided the information. 'The four of them will be charged. Various offences, including attempted rape. They'll be kept in the cells overnight and brought up before the magistrate at Bow Street in the morning.'

'Do we have to be there?' was Tommy's next question.

'Not necessarily. The Messarinas will be represented. Their solicitor will ask for an adjournment, which will be granted. Then he'll make an application for bail for his clients. We'll oppose it, naturally, but the magistrate may grant bail, we can only guess. It would help me if you were available on the telephone tomorrow morning.'

Tommy glanced at Anne, who gave a nod.

'That's OK. We'll be at the flat,' said Tommy.

'Thanks. Now I think you've had enough for one day. There'll be a car to take you home, and I'll ring you in the morning.'

As the door closed behind the departing couple, Davis turned to his colleague.

'Think they'll be alright?' he asked.

Macandrew pursed his lips.

'The young woman looked a bit shaky. Don't know

how she'll perform in the witness box, but we'll have to see. Hutton seems to be well in control. Make a good witness I think.'

'He only identified Tony Messarina.'

'True enough. Still, guilt by association, eh? Not the first time it's been put forward.'

'So all we have to do now is wait for Bertie the shyster. What's the betting he'll be here within the hour?'

Macandrew grinned.

'No takers,' he said. 'It's a stone cold racing certainty.'

Known throughout the criminal world as Bertie the shyster, his name was Bertram Harvey, his occupation solicitor and Commissioner for Oaths. His clientele was drawn from the top echelons of Britain's most notorious villains, his considerable fortune deriving from the contributions they made to his exchequer. The leader of a gang of robbers, having separated a few million pounds of specie from its rightful owners, was not averse to spending a large percentage of the loot on legal advice and, in the event that he was brought before the courts, the sort of defence that only Bertram Harvey could supply. Bertie the shyster possessed a criminal mind. He was also himself a criminal. The accounts he rendered for his services, subject to the scrutiny of the Taxing Master, were modest. His actual fees were enormous, paid in cash and hidden away in bank accounts as far afield as the Bahamas, the United States of America and the safe havens of Switzerland and Lichbenstein.

Bertie received the news that the Messarina brothers had been arrested as he dallied with an obliging nymphette in the bedroom of a suite in a Brighton hotel. He had many secrets from his wife, the pursuit and ravishing of youthful flesh being one of them. As he rose from the bed and hurried into his clothes he looked at the gold Rolex decorating his left wrist. If he put his foot down he could be in London by nine o'clock. With a last regretful glance at the shapely figure of his latest conquest and a promise to her that he would be in touch, he left the suite and the hotel and climbed into the Jaguar parked a few yards from the entrance.

As he pointed the nose of the powerful car towards the road to London he speculated on the circumstances that could have led to the arrest of a bunch of gangsters who were, in his opinion, untouchable. He had advised them over the years, as he had advised their father before them, and had taken the handsome retainer with a clear conscience. It was largely due to his influence that the brothers had avoided trouble over the many years that they had operated their nefarious enterprises.

He was prepared for anything when he entered Inspector Davis' office at West End Central. He greeted the two officers with a polite 'good evening'. Macandrew and Davis sat in stony silence.

'I believe you have four of my clients in custody,' he began.

'That's right,' replied Davis.

'Habeas corpus?' said Harvey.

It was question and statement rolled into one.

'Afraid you're a bit late, old chap,' said Davis. 'Your clients have been charged. They'll be kept in custody until tomorrow morning. They'll be brought up before the magistrate at Bow Street.'

They've worked a real flanker on me this time, thought Harvey. Aloud he said

'Quick work Inspector. What are the charges?'

'Your clients will tell you. I take it you'll wish to see

them,' said Davis.

'Certainly. Now, what about police bail?' replied Harvey.

Davis' reply was courteous but firm. There was a twinkle in his eye.

'You should know better, mister Harvey. Habeas corpus. Works both ways, doesn't it. I'll get an officer to take you down to the cells.'

There was no more to be said and Harvey retired from the field. As he was shepherded from the office by a uniformed constable Davis winked at his colleague.

'Round one to us I think, Ian,' he said.

Macandrew's reply was cautious. 'There are still a few rounds to go. Bertie's a cunning bastard. He'll try every trick in the book. We'll have to be on our toes to win this one.'

In the car that took Anne and Tommy back to the flat she sat huddled in the corner of the rear seat. During the journey she did not utter a word, nor did she thank the officer who had driven them home. In the sitting room she sank into a chair without bothering to remove her coat and, hands folded in her lap, stared blankly at the wallpaper.

While not fully understanding the cause Tommy could sense her distress and maintained a sympathetic silence. His experience of the workings of the female mind was limited and he had no idea what to do about Anne's unusual behaviour. One thing he did know, however, was that she had screwed herself up to identifying her attackers and was now suffering the reaction. He tried to put himself into her place. How would he feel, he said to himself, if he had been savagely attacked and then, some time later, been called upon to face and then identify the brutes who had assaulted him. The speculation brought no satisfactory answer. The truth of the matter was that he could not cope with the situation. He went into the kitchen and made a pot of tea.

She was still sitting in the same position when he came back into the sitting room. She displayed no interest in the cup of tea he placed before her, but her eyes were filled with tears which ran unheeded down her face, streaking her cheeks with ribbons of mascara. She made no sound, there were no sobs, no signs of hysteria, there were only the tears still streaming from brimming eyes as evidence of a deep distress. What the hell do I do now, thought Tommy. Should I go to her, put my arm round her shoulders, say comforting words, risk her recoiling from my touch...

The question was decided for him as Anne suddenly leapt to her feet and rushed from the room. He listened intently. She had gone into the bathroom and, from the faint sounds he heard, he judged that she was brushing her teeth. Then came the slam as she closed the door of her bedroom and after that there was silence. Tommy leaned back on the settee and closed his eyes. He too was not unaffected by the events of the evening. Recalling the mad expression on Tony Messarina's face his imagination ran riot as he pictured Anne repeating the process of identification four times, looking into the eyes of each of the four brutes, conquering her repugnance as she put out her hand to touch them. What were the memories invading her mind and assaulting her senses; and if this was her reaction to this preliminary contact, what would happen when she faced them in a courtroom. He had no doubts about his own performance, for he had made up his mind that whatever he could do to bring about the downfall of the villainous quartet would be done without thought of the consequences and regardless of the risk.

He must have fallen asleep, for the next thing he remembered was opening his eyes as a noise disturbed him. All the lights in the room were switched on and Anne was standing before him in her nightdress holding out her hand. Words poured from her mouth, come to bed, Tommy, with me, I can't sleep alone, I want you to hold me, please, Tommy, please...

Still half-asleep Tommy allowed himself to be led into her bedroom. Anne was whispering to him urgently. '

Take your clothes off. Come to bed. Hold me.'

As if in a dream he did as he was told. A trembling Anne took him in her arms.

'Hold me tight, Tommy. Just hold me.' She murmured over and over again. After a while her trembling ceased and she breathed deeply and easily as she relaxed. Tommy remained motionless, holding her close to him, feeling her warm body against his own. She fell asleep.

Later in the night she reached for him, fondling him, her warm hands exciting him, her lips nuzzling his face. They came together tenderly and it was wonderful, the most natural thing in the world as they pleasured each other to that final ecstatic thrust as they climaxed together.

'Don't go away. Stay there. Inside me.'

Linked together they stroked and kissed and finally slept. Later, as drawn broke, they came into each other's arms once more, Anne murmuring endearments as they made gentle love.

It was ten o'clock in the morning when they surfaced to face a new and momentous day. Dressing gowns over their night clothes they breakfasted in the kitchen. In contrast to her sullen silence of the previous evening,

Anne was bright and cheerful. In a matter-of-fact voice she referred to the events of the night.

'Well, we've taken the plunge now, Tommy. How do you feel about it?'

'Very happy. Top of the world, in fact.'

'No regrets?'

Tommy paused and selected his words carefully before making a reply.

'I think it was fated that it would have to happen. We were both in need of something and that something came about last night. We're on the same plane. I can't really find the words. I just know we understand each other far better than we ever have done.'

Anne knew intuitively of the inner thoughts that Tommy wanted to express. She was quite clear in her mind about the reasons that impelled her to invite him to her bed. It was neither love nor passion. In her forthright Yorkshire way she had come to a decision about resolving what she saw as an anomaly, a man and a woman living in close proximity without indulging in sexual activity. It was in the car on the way home from West End Central that she made the decision to 'put things to rights'. She did not regret her action and was joyful that everything had turned out so well, that she and her new lover were compatible physically as well as mentally. She did not look too far into the future. She was quite happy in the present.

'We should be hearing from Macandrew soon,' she said.

'That's right,' Tommy replied. 'I reckon the proceedings will be over by noon. He'll probably ring from the court.'

'What do you want to do this afternoon?'

'Let's wait until we hear from Macandrew and then decide. That alright with you?'

'Fine. I'll just get on with a bit of tidying. The flat's in a mess.'

Tommy jumped to his feet. 'Good idea,' he said. 'I'll give you a hand.'

The call from Macandrew came through shortly after midday. He spoke to Tommy at some length. The information was to the effect that the Messarina brothers had been brought up before the magistrate, their legal representative had asked for an adjournment for a week which had been duly granted, there had been a successful application for bail despite police objection and Tommy and Anne would be required to attend at Bow Street magistrate's court on the following Monday.

'So that's that,' said Anne. She did not appear to be unduly disturbed. 'I'll take a week's leave from the office. What about you?'

'I'm chucking my job in. Tomorrow morning I'm out hunting for a job in a drawing office. There's plenty about.'

'There's also a recession.'

'Doesn't bother me. A good draughtsman can always get a living. As long as there's an engineering industry there'll be a call for good men in the drawing office. That's where it all begins.'

'So what about this afternoon?'

'There's an old fellow in a hospital in Roehampton who'd be glad of a visit. Feel like playing the Lady Bountiful?'

'Yes. Let's spread a little happiness. We shouldn't keep it all to ourselves.'

Queen Mary's Hospital at Roehampton is famous all over the world. Equally famous is the adjoining factory where, in co-operation with the hospital's orthopaedic surgeons, a team of dedicated engineers provide artifi-

193

cial limbs for those who have been deprived of the originals. It was there that the air ace, Douglas Bader, was fitted with the manufactured legs that enabled him to fly again to his greater glory and the considerable discomfiture of the Luftwaffe in World War Two.

The newest patient at Queen Mary's was a favourite with nurses, doctors and the technicians charged with the task of providing him with a working substitute for a lost leg. He endured pain with fortitude, behaved towards staff and fellow patients with unfailing politeness and brought to the business of conquering his disability a remarkable enthusiasm and a willingness to learn which earned him approval from all sides. Ironfoot Jack, known to all and sundry as Professor, was in his element.

He was aware that he had a long and painful course of treatment before he would be at ease with his new appendage. Although the stump had healed the scar tissue was still tender and he could only wear the harness which was part of the artificial limb for a short time each day. However, the wheelchair which stood beside his bed gave him a degree of mobility and he took full advantage of this. The hospital was a whole new world whose inhabitants were not the sort of people one would meet every day. They were a never-ending source of study for the alert and enquiring mind. Ironfoot and his wheelchair were to be seen careering through the wards and along the corridors-at all hours as he did his rounds as diligently and regularly as the doctors.

His daily tours were not without motive. When he had abandoned his cushioned life as an academic to live amongst the most deprived members of society he had been animated by a desire to explore the human condition. Now his horizons expanded as he talked with men and women condemned to face a future where they would be classified as disabled. He had always held the view that bodily afflictions could be overcome by strength of mind, a philosophy he preached at every opportunity. Though his ideas met with a mixed reception his enthusiasm was undiminished.

He was sitting in his wheelchair, the artificial leg on the bed beside him, when Tommy and Anne came into the ward. He greeted Tommy with evident delight.

'Well now, young Tommy,' he said. 'It's a pleasure to see you. And the lady...'

'Anne Kirby. A friend of mine.'

The old philosopher took Anne's hand and pressed it warmly.

'Forgive me if I don't get up. As you can see I'm in a temporary condition of instability, on the hop so to speak. However, I shall soon be on equal terms with the rest of humanity with the help of this contraption.'

He gestured toward the artificial limb.

'But I'm forgetting my manners. Draw up a couple of chairs and sit yourselves down. I'm in the mood for a good old chat.'

The old man's good humour was infectious and Tommy and Anne entered into the spirit of things.

'Tommy's told me so much about you,' said Anne. 'I've been looking forward to meeting you. I'm sorry about your...'

'A mere peccadillo. I've still got one good leg and a pair of excellent arms. Anyway, that's enough about me. How are you getting along, young Tommy? Still keeping Westminster tidy?'

'Not for long. I've decided to jack it in. Going back to my old trade.'

'That's the stuff, my boy. I wish you all the luck in the world.' He turned his attention to Anne. 'I've a feeling that you had a hand in this, if you'll forgive the impertinence.'

'Not really,' Anne replied. 'It's all Tommy's idea, but I must say I agree with him. He's wasting his time sweeping the streets.'

'Perhaps you're right, my dear. Still, time is never wasted as long as lessons are learned.'

Tommy's attention had strayed to the contrivance lying on the bed. He reached over, picked it up and inspected it with interest. He spent some time examining the section of the leg which controlled the ankle movement.

'Nice bit of work,' he said. 'Tried it out yet, Ironfoot?'

'Indeed I have. Two sessions a day for the past week. Just beginning to get the hang of it.'

Tommy waggled the ankle joint, testing the spring reaction against the palm of his hand, an operation which he repeated several times.

'Had any trouble with this part?'

'Well, now you mention it, yes. If I had a toe I'd have stubbed it frequently. Why do you ask?'

'Just curiosity. I'd like to meet the bloke who designed this...'

'The bloke who designed it is standing right behind you.'

Tommy turned his head. The remark had come from a tall, grey-haired man in a white coat who had approached the group silently on rubber-soled shoes. Ironfoot greeted him in his usual effusive manner.

'My dear John. What a pleasure. Meet my friends. Anne, Tommy, this is mister Cartwright from the factory next door. He's responsible for making these goodies.'

Tommy and Anne acknowledged the introduction,

shaking the hand that was held out to them. Cartwright smiled pleasantly as he addressed Tommy.

'So what would you like to say to me?'

Tommy laid the artificial leg on the bed and rose to his feet. He pointed to the spot on the leg where a spring connected two parts of the assembly.

'Just a small thing. That spring. I don't trust springs. Too much trouble with varying tensions. Looks to me as though gravity would do the job better. Now if there was a weight, free moving, activating the foot movement...'

Cartwright had listened as Tommy spoke. Now he broke in.

'Very smart of you to spot that. Matter of fact it's been on my mind, something of a problem. I take it you're an engineer, mister...'

'Hutton. I'm a design draughtsman. Look, I don't mean to tell you how to do your job.'

'I'm sure you don't, but I'm always willing to listen to somebody who knows what he's talking about. Who are you with?'

'Nobody at the moment. I was with Anderson's of Crawley for eight years.'

'Ah, yes. I know of them. Very good people. Why did you leave them?'

Tommy hesitated before answering the question. He was sure that there was some ulterior motive in Cartwright's mind but for the life of him he couldn't determine what it was. His questioner resolved the doubt.

'Forgive me for being so - er - nosey. The fact of the matter is that we're very short-handed in our drawing office. How would you like using your talents in a very worth-while job?'

'I reckon I'd like it very much, but...'

'But me no buts. Could you come in and see me at the factory, say one day this week? Give me a ring.'

Cartwright produced a card from his pocket and scribbled on it, then handed it to Tommy.

'This is the direct line to my office. Now I won't take up any more of your time. I'll look forward to seeing you.'

With a wave of his hand he turned and walked away. The silence which followed was broken by Ironfoot.

'Made quite an impression there, young Tommy,' he said.

'Looks like it,' said Tommy.

'You'll give him a ring?'

'Oh, sure. Something might come of it. Anyway, we'll see. Wouldn't mind having a bash at the artificial limb lark. Bit of a challenge, isn't it?'

The conversation was interrupted by the appearance of a stout and cheerful Jamaican lady. She piloted a tea trolley to the foot of the bed.

'Afternoon, Professor,' she said, a broad smile almost splitting her face in two. 'You an' yo' friends like a nice cuppa?'

Ironfoot beamed. 'We'd like nothing better, my dear Prudence. Pour away.'

When the tea had been poured and delivered and the tealady had taken her departure, Tommy looked at Ironfoot enquiringly.

'What's all this professor business?'

'Red tape, dear boy, red tape. When you enter these establishments they want to know all about you. If you don't tell them, they soon find out. My shady past in the city of dreaming spires has come to light, a fact of which I am suitably ashamed.'

'Don't see what you have to be ashamed of. I think I'll call you Professor from now on. The title suits you.'

198

Ironfoot's face wrinkled in a rueful grin.

'Ah, well, such is academic fame. Now how about some gossip. What are you and this delightful young lady up to?'

'Remember telling me one day that life is for living. Me and Anne are doing just that.'

For the rest of the time to the end of visiting hours the three indulged in cheerful and inconsequential chatter. On the steps of the hospital building Anne, having said their goodbyes to the old philosopher, laid her hand affectionately on her companion's arm.

'You know, Tommy,' she said. 'I think this is your lucky day.'

'Looks like it, doesn't it,' replied Tommy.

CHAPTER 11

Relations between men and women are not easy to define. The happily married couple may present a picture of connubial bliss to the outside world yet behind the curtains of the matrimonial home there are strange and complex forces at work. It was a cynical sage who remarked that one could search the world in vain to find two people more unsuited to be joined in holy matrimony than a man and a woman.

Anne Kirby was an intelligent young woman, but her experience of men and their ways was limited to a couple of liasons conducted on her own terms. They were short-lived, ended abruptly and taught her little. When she invited a disreputable alcoholic wreck to share her home she was in a state of confusion where emotion triumphed over logic and fear conquered prudence. Her behaviour was irrational but was understandable. She did not want to be alone.

Her decision to take a hand in the rehabilitation of a homeless, drink-sodden outcast from society was dictated by a sense of obligation. Tommy Hutton, albeit unwittingly, had nevertheless come to her rescue when she had abandoned all hope and she owed him a debt that she was determined to discharge; and when Tommy announced that he was going on the wagon she was delighted. It gave her even greater pleasure when he went to work as a humble street cleaner.

It came as a shock when Tommy revealed to her that he had identified one of the men who had taken part in that terrifying incident in the park. What impressed her above all else was his obvious concern about whether he should inform her of his discovery, knowing that it would re-open old wounds. His support for her stand in deciding to go to the police and the way he stood by her during the ordeal of the identification parade drew her closer to him. She was not sure whether she loved him, was in love with him or just cared deeply for him. She invited him into her bed because she wanted him.

They had returned from the visit to Roehampton in high spirits. Anne was captivated by the gentle courtesy of the old man and wanted to know all about him.

'Tell you the truth I can't make him out,' said Tommy in reply to her questioning. 'All I know is he was a professor at Oxford. Threw it all up to go and live with the homeless under Waterloo Bridge. He talked a lot about freedom but I couldn't make head nor tail of his arguments.' There was a twinkle in his eye as he went on, 'anyway they were way above the head of a street sweeper.'

'You can cut that out,' replied Anne. 'You're not a street sweeper any longer. I bet that chap Cartwright offers you a job when you go and see him. You are going to give him a ring, aren't you?'

'Oh, sure. First thing in the morning. I dunno, though. I don't know anything about artificial limbs.'

'You spotted something about the professor's leg, didn't you? It seemed to impress Cartwright.'

'Oh, that was just commonsense. A design weakness. Sooner or later somebody would have seen it.'

'But that's the point. It was you and not somebody else. I could see that Cartwright was impressed. I think today was your lucky day.'

'Maybe. Let's see what happens, eh?'

'I know what's going to happen. Mark my words. Cartwright wouldn't have asked you to ring him if he hadn't been interested. I think he's already made up his mind.'

'Proper little know-all aren't you,' was Tommy's laughing retort. He could not deny that he was touched by Anne's display of confidence and, looking back over the period of their association, he recalled the unstinted support she had given him as he fought to overcome his addiction. Impulsively he took her hand.

'You're a good person, Anne. I'll do my best to make you proud of me,' he said.

In the back room of the Club Cucaracha a different kind of conversation was taking place. The Messarina brothers had not taken kindly to their arrest and temporary incarceration. It had come as an unwelcome shock to them, for they had thought they were untouchable. That anyone should have the temerity to bear witness against them was a pill that they found hard to swallow.

Tony was speaking. His face was dark with fury and his eyes glittered with hatred as he addressed his brothers.

'We gotta do something a bit quick,' he began. 'That bloody cow, she put the finger on us. We gotta shut her big mouth.'

Alberto, as usual the lazy and easy-going member of the quartet, attempted to pour oil on the troubled waters.

'What you worried about, Tony?' he asked. 'One silly bitch and one know-nothing cunt, what they can do? Nothing. Bertie wipe the floor with them in court. We walk away from it. After, we teach the idiots a lesson, give them some aggravation.'

The elder Messarina turned on his brother, his face distorted, the livid scar on his cheek taking on a life of its own as he ground his teeth.

'Don't you talk like a prick, Alberto. These two

pieces of shit, they make monkeys out of us. Everybody laugh, look at the Messarinas, ha-ha-ha, you think I take that from them. Madonna mia, I piss all over them. So, Alberto, you shut the mouth, you hear. No more mess about, no more take a chance. We fix the bitch first, then the feller. Understand?'

The three brothers exchanged glances. As long as they could remember, Tony had been the boss and they had always obeyed him without question. He had passed sentence of death on the woman who had dared to go against him, to bear witness in a court of law that he, Antonio Messarina, had committed a crime. So the woman was as good as dead. It only remained to be determined how, where and in what manner her life would be ended. The planning could safely be left in Tony's hands. There had been occasions in the past when it had been found necessary to ensure that certain persons disappeared without trace. Tony had planned the operations, his younger brothers had joined him in executing the plans and everything had gone like clockwork. There was no reason to suppose that this latest venture would be anything but successful.

'Now, listen to me,' said Antonio Messarina, and his brothers hung on his every word. 'This is what we do...'

Tommy approached the interview with Cartwright in an optimistic mood. He had telephoned that morning and, after a brief conversation, had arranged to present himself at the factory at three o'clock in the afternoon. Wearing a recently-purchased dark blue suit he left the flat with Anne's good wishes ringing in his ears. Arriving at his destination, he was conducted at once to Cartwright's office, a spacious room at the front of the building where the principal furnishings seemed to consist almost entirely of bits and pieces of artificial limbs. A functional drawing board occupied a prominent position in a good light from one of the two large windows, a desk piled with drawings stood in a corner and three chairs were ranged against the wall adjacent to the door.

Cartwright's greeting was warm and friendly. He shook Tommy's hand and motioned him to one of the chairs, then perched himself on a corner of the desk.

'Glad you could come along,' he began. 'I was very interested in the remarks you made about your friend the professor's new leg. You seemed to think the design could do with some improvement.'

'Well, yes,' replied Tommy. 'It was only a little thing. You see, the old man said that he was having trouble with the foot. Kept stubbing his toe. What I mean is stubbing where his toe would have been if he had one.'

Cartwright laughed. 'I see what you mean. Go on.'

'I noticed there was a spring that controlled the movement of the foot. I thought that maybe if there was a counterweight instead of the spring...'

'Just a moment,' said Cartwright. He hoisted himself from the desk and went over to where several artificial legs lay in a heap on the floor. Selecting one of them, he picked it up and returned to his perch, laying the leg across his knees.

'This is a similar limb to the one we've provided for your friend,' he said. 'Would you like to show me how you think it could be improved?'

Tommy got up from the chair and took the leg from its position on Cartwright's knee. Laying it on the desk he actuated the foot by pressing the palm of his hand against what would have been the toe end of the foot. Cartwright slipped from his seat and stood beside Tommy in order to have a clear view.

'I don't want you to think I'm trying to tell you your job,' said Tommy. 'It's just that I don't like coil springs. You never know where you are with them. The performance is variable, you see. Now if you used the force of gravity in place of the spring you'd have a constant force, one that doesn't change.'

'So?'

'I'd take out the spring and substitute a calculated counterweight. Free moving. Just heavy enough to counterbalance the weight of the foot section. Now, when the bloke who's wearing the leg swings the stump forward the toe comes up. Then when he puts his weight on the the heel here the toe automatically goes into its normal position. See what I mean?'

Cartwright rubbed his chin thoughtfully. 'I've got to hand it to you, young man. I've been in this business over twenty years and solved a lot of problems. You come along and find a solution to something that's been bothering me for some considerable time. What's more, you find it in five minutes. Remarkable.'

Tommy embarrassed by this fulsome praise from a man so much his senior, felt awkward.

'It's nothing really,' he said.

'I had a lot to do with small mechanical movements in my last job. Just a habit, letting gravity do the work I mean. You know, like the weights and pendulum on a grandfather clock.'

'I take your point. The principle is there. What matters is how one adapts it. That's where engineering intelligence comes in. There's a lot of difference between a grandfather clock and an artificial limb.'

'They can both mark time,' said Tommy, and Cartwright laughed with him at the juvenile joke.

'You said you were with Anderson's of Crawley for eight years,' said Cartwright.

'That's right. Went there straight from school, into the drawing office. They were very good to me, gave me time off to take the City and Guilds exams.'

'Could I ask you why you left them?'

Tommy debated with himself for a moment. Should he tell this sympathetic man about the tragedy he had suffered, how his wife and child had been killed, the whole sad story? On the spur of the moment he decided against it.

'There were... personal reasons. Nothing to do with the job. I was very happy, getting along well, but something happened. It was a very personal thing, just me, nobody else involved...'

'I understand. Let's leave it at that. Now I'll tell you why I asked you to come along and see me. I'm always on the lookout for suitable people for my design team. It's quite a demanding job, every day a fresh problem, but what we are doing here is important and worthwhile. How would you feel about joining us?'

'Well, it's a new line for me. I don't know anything about artificial limbs...'

'But you do know something about engineering design, I'm convinced of that. I have a feeling that you'd fit in very well. Look, I'll tell you what I have in mind. I'll give you a start at fifteen thousand a year. Give it a month to see how you like it. What do you say?'

'Yes, mister Cartwright... and thanks...'

'Never mind the mister. The name's John. We don't stand on ceremony. It's Tommy, isn't it? Now come along and I'll introduce you to your colleagues. Won't take long. There's only five of them.'

He climbed to the top deck of the bus that would take him from Roehampton to Fulham and made his way to a seat at the front. Sitting there, high above the streets through which the huge vehicle ploughed its way, he pondered on the events of the past few days. No doubt about it, he thought, it was a lucky chance which had led him to visit old Ironfoot and again it was sheer chance that his visit had coincided with Cartwright's presence on the ward. He wondered whether there was some significance in these coincidences. Was he now reaping some reward for his successful struggle against alcoholism? Was there somewhere a benevolent Fate planning a new life for him? A quotation came to his mind, there is a divinity that shapes our ends, rough-hew them as we may.

From the moment that he entered the drawing office to be introduced to John Cartwright's staff he felt at home. There was something about the calm atmosphere prevailing there that took him back to those care-free days at Anderson's. His fingers were itching to pin paper on drawing board, to handle the tools of his trade, to turn rough sketches into finished work with clear and precise lettering of sizes and tolerances. He looked forward to the following day when he would treat himself to the finest set of drawing instruments money could buy.

He alighted from the bus at Fulham Broadway. It was only a short walk to the flat and he covered it in double-quick time. He was almost running as he came to the last few yards. Anne, who was watching an early evening programme on television, rose to her feet and switched off the set when she heard the sound of his key in the lock of the front door. She went to meet him as he literally bounced into the sitting room.

'How did it go?' was her first question.

Tommy, slightly out of breath, hesitated before replying, but she knew by the look on his face that it was good news.

'It was great. Fabulous. Cartwright offered me a job on his team. Fifteen thousand a year. What about that?'

His enthusiasm was infectious. Anne embraced him and laid her cheek against his. He held her close as she murmured in his ear.

'Oh, Tommy, I'm so glad for you. You deserve it. This is only the beginning. Just wait and see.'

They broke away from each other. Anne, ever the practical one, took his hand and led him to the settee.

'Now sit down and tell me all about it,' she said.

Tommy needed no urging.

'That Cartwright's a great bloke,' he began. 'Made me feel at home right away. We had a good old chat. He took me into the drawing office. Introduced me to the team, five of them, first names all round. A real matey atmosphere. I'm going to enjoy working there.'

'So, when do you start?'

'Next week. Cartwright's going to give me a ring. There's one or two arrangements he has to make, like getting in a board for me and so on.'

'Fifteen thousand a year, that's three hundred a week...'

'Less tax,' interrupted Tommy.

'Even so, that's not bad.'

'No, not bad at all. Guess what I'm going to do tomorrow morning?'

'You tell me.'

'I'm going out to get the finest set of drawing tools that money can buy, that's what.'

The Ford Escort van parked across the street from Anne Kirby's flat had been there since early morning. It was not a very conspicuous vehicle. The casual passer-by would have taken it for the transport of a self-employed decorator, it had that sort of look. The two

208

dark-skinned young men sitting side by side could have been discussing what to do about the dry rot in the wainscoating. The fact that their eyes never left the entrance of the basement flat opposite was neither here nor there.

Mario and Gino had received precise instructions from their elder brother. They were to keep watch on the flat and, when they were certain that the woman was alone, they were to get into the premises and snatch her. They were then to put her in the van and drive to the warehouse near Blackfriars Bridge, from where they would telephone to confirm that the their task had been successful. After that, Tony would take over.

It was a little after nine o'clock when Tommy made his appearance. As he walked briskly down the street two pairs of eyes watched his progress until he disappeared from sight round the corner. Gino, in the passenger seat, looked at his brother.

'We go now?' he said.

Mario started the engine and, after a glance in the wing mirror, swung the van across the street and drew to a halt in a vacant space outside the flat. As Mario descended the few steps that led from the pavement to the front door, Gino opened the rear doors of the van and lugged a rolled carpet from the interior. Flinging it over his shoulder, he followed his brother, who already had his finger on the bell-push.

In the kitchen Anne, slippered and with a dressing gown over her nightdress, was about to wash up the breakfast dishes. When the bell pealed she wondered for a moment who would be calling at this hour in the morning, decided that it was probably the postman and, passing down the short passage from the kitchen, slipped the catch on the Yale lock. Mario, in the lead, kicked the door wide open and burst in, closely followed by Gino.

As Anne opened her mouth to scream a hand was roughly clapped over her face, she was pinned against the wall and a voice hissed in her ear, you make noise I cut your focken throat.

Anne was terrified, yet an instinct told her to keep command of her senses. In that instant when she came face to face with Mario she knew with an awful certainty that she was helpless and alone. This time there was nobody to come to her rescue, and the powerful arms that held her precluded any attempt to fight back. She closed her eyes and pretended to faint as Mario dragged her into the sitting room and kept them closed when Gino forced a gag into her mouth. Limp and unresisting she did not struggle as her hands were tied behind her back and her ankles lashed together. Her captors worked swiftly and in silence, and her world went dark as they wrapped her in the carpet that had so recently decorated Gino's shoulder. She felt herself being lifted and carried for a short distance, then roughly thrown down on a hard surface. She heard the slamming of doors, the sound of a car engine bursting into life and was conscious of motion as the vehicle accelerated through the gears.

She was in acute discomfort, the dryness in her mouth accentuated by the gag, the bindings around wrists and ankles beginning to bite into the naked flesh. She forced herself to control the trembling in her limbs as her mind tried to grapple with the situation in which she found herself. The questions beat in her brain. What were the Messarinas up to? Did they intend to keep her from testifying against them? If so, how would they do it? Keep her imprisoned? They couldn't do that forever.

On one matter she was quite clear in her mind. Whatever was to come she intended to face it clearly and logically, to weigh up the pros and cons and pit her wits and intelligence against the animal cunning of her captors. Having arrived at this conclusion she concentrated all her mental and physical resources on fighting against the pain in her arms and legs. It was not easy. So far as she could determine she was in a confined space, probably the back of a small van, being rolled from one side to the other as the vehicle negotiated corners. There was no way she could control her movements. She gritted her teeth, consoling herself with the thought that there must be an end to her plight. She prayed that it would come soon.

It was not long before her prayer was answered. Her mobile prison came to a halt, there was the sound of doors opening and closing and once more she was lifted and carried over a short distance before being dumped unceremoniously on a soft surface. Faintly through the folds of the carpet came the murmur of voices, then busy hands unrolled the covering and she was able to take stock of her surroundings as the gag was removed from her mouth and her legs and arms released from their bindings.

She was lying on her back on a mattress in the corner of what was obviously a large warehouse. Crates and boxes were stacked indiscriminately on the cement floor, and high overhead a single electric bulb shed a dim light on the scene. She turned her head towards her captors who stood side by side, broad grins on their faces. She now knew with dreadful certainty that she was in serious trouble, perhaps in danger of her life and her heart sank. Summoning up all her courage she licked her lips and spoke in a hoarse whisper.

'What the hell are you playing at?' she said.

The brothers exchanged glances and burst into laughter. It was Mario who answered her question.

'You make trouble for us, lady,' he said. 'Now we

teach you a little lesson, you don't mess with the Messarinas no more. You understand?'

She swung her legs over the edge of the mattress and made an attempt to rise, but her legs refused to support her and she ended up in a sitting position. She pulled her nightdress down over her knees and wrapped her arms across her breasts.

'You'd better let me go,' she said. 'I'm under police protection.'

Mario turned to his brother and mockingly repeated her words, which led to another outburst of laughter. When the merriment had subsided Mario spoke once more.

'We don't give monkey's fuck for police. Now you shut the mouth, right? No more talk. We wait for Tony to come.'

Huddled on the edge of the mattress, head bowed and still in a state of shock, she told herself over and over again, keep calm, don't give up, where there's life there's hope. That she could expect no mercy from her captors was certain, but what did they intend to do with her? She shuddered as her mind went back to that night in the park, the hands that invaded her body, the terrifying moment when her legs were forced apart, the panic-stricken scream wrenched from her throat as she struggled vainly against the weight of the body pinning her to the ground...

She forced herself to think logically. She was utterly alone, there was no gallant knight to rush to her rescue, no Tommy emerging from the gloom shouting and waving his arms to distract the attention of her attackers...

She had to make up her mind. She was not equipped to fight so she had to submit. She had read somewhere that a prostitute in the way of business could minister to upwards of twenty men in a single night.

She made the decision. She would do whatever was required of her, divorce her mind from what was happening to her body, make a pretence of enjoying the proceedings which would not last for ever, could not indeed be carried further than the gratification of lust. Whatever indignities she would be made to suffer, and she was sure there would be many, she was determined to survive.

From a distance came the sound of a door opening and closing. Hurried footsteps rang out on the concret floor. She raised her head as Tony Messarina and his brother Alberto came into view from behind a pile of packing cases and joined their younger brothers. There was a murmur of conversation, then Tony approached her, a broad smile on his face.

'Good morning, lady,' he said with mock politeness. 'You not so cocky now, no? No nice policeman to hold your hand. What you got to say?'

She tried one last despairing desperate shot, though she had little hope that it would be successful.

'Look, let me go. I promise I won't go to court. I'll tell the police I made a mistake...'

'You bloody right you make a mistake. You make plenty trouble for us, but we nice people. Forgive and forget, eh? So you give us nice friendly fuck, we take you home, you forget all about us. What you say?'

Her reply was simple and immediate. She rose to her feet, shrugged off her dressing gown and nightdress and stood naked before her captors.

'Come on, then. Who's going to be first?' she said.

Tony licked his lips, then slowly and deliberately loosened his belt and let his trousers fall around his ankles. His erect penis sprang into view and he fondled it proudly.

'You like, lady?' he said. 'Lovely prick, eh? Now I screw the arse off you. Lie down and open your legs.'

She did as she was told. Over and over the words hammered through her brain, there's nothing to be afraid of, it's just a fuck, nothing new, you've done it before. As the panting Tony lowered himself on to her she closed her eyes.

Then came the first powerful thrust followed by a frenzied lunging to which she began to respond as she became aroused. The tempo quickened and suddenly it was all over as, with an animal howl, Tony came to a climax, his hands grasping her buttocks as his semen spurted into her. The watchers licked their lips in anticipation as their elder brother slowly withdrew and rose to his feet. He was breathing hard, thin lines of spittle forming at the corners of his mouth as he gestured to Alberto.

'Now you go,' he gasped.

Alberto moved forward and sat on the edge of the mattress. Very deliberately he unzipped his trousers, took out his penis and grabbed a handful of his victim's hair. Not for him the expenditure of energy in playing the beast with two backs. He had long ago discovered the delights of fellatio. Drawing Anne's head between his legs he caressed her lips with the tip of his penis, then it was inside her mouth and he was chanting 'suck it, suck it, suck it' and she obeyed, the odour of stale urine in her nostrils, gagging as the thing in her mouth grew larger, then the hand tightened on her hair and she almost choked as he ejaculated. She rolled away as the hand relaxed its grip, coughing and spitting to rid herself of the slimy mess from her throat.

There was to be no respite. No sooner had Alberto released his grip than Mario leapt on her, thrusting a hand between her legs and poking his fingers simultane-

214

ously into her anus and vagina. She wondered vaguely what he intended to do, but the busy fingers worked away until she drew a shuddering breath and came to orgasm.

This was the moment Mario had been waiting for. Heaving her body over so that she lay face downwards he hissed in her ear, now I fuck you up the arse, and proceeded to bugger her.

It was a new experience for her and, though at first it was slightly painful, she was relieved that she was no longer obliged to respond to Mario's rapid penetration. Furthermore it was not long-lasting. Already excited after having watched his brothers perform, Mario quickly reached his climax. When he withdrew she lay quietly face down, head resting on her arms. She heard voices raised in argument as young Gino protested that he had no wish to play his part in the orgy. Good, she thought, that's one less to cope with.

Now Mario was standing over her and she turned her head to meet his gaze. There was a wolfish grin on his face and his tone of voice was soft and ingratiating.

'One more time with Tony,' he was saying. 'One more time then we let you go.'

She turned on her back. All she wanted to do was to get the whole thing over, to leave this depressing place behind, close her mind to all that had happened and take up her life from the point when she had been abducted. Now Tony was on her once more, thrusting away, hands caressing her breasts, squeezing the nipples, then straying to her neck, thumbs pressed against her throat blocking off her breathing, he was going to kill her. Panic took over. She grasped at his wrists but there was no strength in her fingers. Her final paroxysms coincided with his last purposeful thrust. She died as his semen flooded into her.

Tony Messarina stood by the body of his victim.
'She won't talk to nobody no more.' he snarled.

CHAPTER 12

Tommy had spent a pleasant couple of hours touring the Euston Road, browsing in the many shops specialising in the provision of drawing office equipment. He knew exactly what he wanted and in the end he found it, a superb set of drawing instruments in a velvet-lined leather case at a price which made a considerable hole in his savings. To him it was not merely a commercial transaction, a simple exchange of money for goods; it was a symbol, a beginning of a new life when he would put behind him all the traumas of the past.

He made his way back to Fulham as quickly as the bus could carry him and burst into the flat with a cheery 'Hello. Anybody at home?' There was no reply. With a feeling of foreboding he made a rapid tour of the rooms. There was an eerie emptiness about the place and his fears grew as he made a more thorough inspection. The bed had not been made and there was no sign of Anne's nightdress and dressing gown. A quick search of the wardrobe showed that all her street clothes were still in place. In the kitchen the electric kettle was cold to the touch and the dishes of the previous night remained unwashed. In the sitting room, half-concealed by an armchair, lay a solitary slipper.

He put two and two together and came up with the simple answer. Anne had been abducted. But who had done it - and why? There was only one explanation. The Messarina brothers, determined to prevent Anne from testifying against them, were making sure that the main witness for the prosecution would not take the stand. The dreadful realisation dawned on him that she was in the power of ruthless men who would not stop short of murder to protect their skins. He felt a bitter regret that he had ever embarked on this perilous journey of revenge. Another thought occurred to him. Surely the police would have realised the dangerous predicament their informants had placed themselves in, and was it not up to the authorities to give them some protection.

He stood irresolute in the centre of the sitting room. There was need for action, but what was the first step to be taken? The question answered itself. Macandrew should be informed that his principal witness had disappeared, that all the signs indicated that she had been kidnapped. He went over to the telephone, lifted the receiver and dialled the number that would put him in immediate touch with the Inspector's office.

Macandrew answered on the third ring and Tommy poured out his information in a rapid flow of words to which the Inspector listened for a while without making any attempt to interrupt. When finally the flow dried up, Macandrew spoke.

'Right, Tommy. I've got the picture. I'd like you to get over here right away. I'll send a car for you.'

Tommy's reply was short and positive.

'Don't bother. I'll get a taxi.'

He put down the receiver and stood by the telephone for a full minute during which time his thoughts ran riot. A fury was steadily building up in him, rage against the brothers who had invaded his peace and security, anger that the police, who should have taken steps to ensure that their witnesses enjoyed protection, had failed in their duty and above all a deep resentment that Anne should have been taken from him and must be in grave danger. He was now quite certain that she was in the hands of the Messarinas and he shuddered to think what she might be suffering. The thought that he might never see her again spurred him into action. Rushing from the flat, he emerged into the street and ran as fast as his legs would carry him towards the main road.

Inspector Ian Macandrew was a worried man. The news that Anne Kirby had vanished, presumably the victim of an abduction, brought home to him the fact that he had been very careless in not ensuring that his witnesses were properly protected. There was no doubt in his mind that the Messarina brothers were responsible and he was equally certain that Anne Kirby was no longer in the land of the living. He picked up the telephone and asked to be connected with his colleague at West End Central.

Colin Davis received the news in shocked silence. He was not slow to realise the implications in this turn of events.

'We've dropped a right clanger here, Mac,' he said.

'You're telling me,' replied Macandrew. 'We'll have to get a move on with this one. Look, Hutton's on his way to me now. Should be here any time. I'll get what I can from him and then bring him over to you. In the meantime you'd better start the hunt for the Kirby woman. Don't think there's much hope, but we'll have to go through the motions.'

'She'll be a goner by now I reckon. Those bastards don't mess about,' said Davis. 'Still, I'll start the wheels rolling. There's an outside chance she may still be alive.'

'Right, go ahead. I'll be over within the hour.'

Macandrew put down the receiver and leaned back in his chair. He was not relishing the prospect of the coming interview with Tommy Hutton. The man would be bitter and angry and in no mood to accept reassurances and sympathy. He would have to be handled with kid gloves and, though Macandrew was sure he could cope with the situation, he nevertheless felt some uncertainty about the outcome.

His worst expectations were realised when Tommy was ushered into his office. Ignoring the outstretched hand and the conventional greeting of the Inspector, Tommy burst into a furious tirade against the Metropolitan Police in general and Inspectors Macandrew and Davis in particular.

'You knew what these people are capable of,' he said. 'You should have given us some protection. God knows what has happened to Anne. She might be dead by now. You should have known those bastards would stop at nothing...'

His voice broke and he was on the verge of tears as he visualised Anne as a corpse floating in the river or lying by the roadside somewhere in the country. As if reading his thoughts, Macandrew spoke in a low and gentle voice.

'Now we don't know for certain what's happened to her. There may be an explanation. If so, we'll find it. The search has started already, there are men out on the streets looking for her. Look, Tommy, pull yourself together, sit down and tell me exactly what you found when you got home.'

Tommy's fury began to evaporate and he sank into the nearest chair. Macandrew's gentle voice and calm manner went some way to allaying his fears. After all, he said to himself, we're on the same side, there's no point in ranting and raving, the milk has been spilt and we've got to find a way to unspill it. He took a deep breath and launched into a description of the events of the morning.

'I went out about nine o'clock,' he began. 'I told

Anne I'd be back around noon, and she said she'd be waiting. I went up to Euston...'

'What for?'

'Oh, I've got a new job. Drawing office. Had to get a set of instruments.'

'I see. Go on.'

'Well, I got back to the flat about twelve. I thought there was something wrong as soon as I opened the door. I called out but there was no reply. I did a quick scout round but the place was empty. The bed wasn't made, the dishes weren't washed. It wasn't like Anne to leave things in a mess. Then I checked on her wardrobe. All her street clothes were there, but there was no sign of her nightdress and dressing gown. There was one slipper on the floor of the sitting room.'

'Any signs of a struggle?'

'No. Furniture all in place, nothing disturbed.'

'So what did you do then?'

'Got on the phone to you.'

'Did you notice anything suspicious when you left the flat in the morning? Anybody hanging about, anything like that?'

'No. There was nothing unusual.'

Macandrew, who had been standing during the course of the conversation, returned to his chair behind the desk.

'Well, it looks as though your friend has been abducted,' he said. 'I'm very sorry, but make no mistake, we'll turn London inside out to find her. Now what I'd like you to do is to come with me to West End Central and have a chat with Inspector Davis. Is that alright with you?'

'Sure.'

'Right then. Let's be off.'

In the car that took them to the West End Tommy sat

in the rear seat, silent and alone with only his thoughts for company. In the passenger seat beside the driver Macandrew made no attempts at conversation save for a few remarks to the man at the wheel. Arriving at their destination, with Macandrew leading the way, they passed through the maze of corridors that finally brought them to the office of Inspector Colin Davis.

No time was wasted on preliminaries as Macandrew opened the proceedings.

'From what Tommy here tells me, there's no doubt that Anne Kirby has been abducted. Time, after nine and before midday. No signs of a struggle in the flat. Street clothes all in place, nightdress, dressing gown and one slipper missing. That's about it from my end.'

Davis nodded and shot a sharp glance at Tommy.

'Anything else you can tell me?' he asked.

Tommy shook his head, an action which did not seem to satisfy Davis, who continued his questioning.

'Everything alright with you and the young lady? No disagreements between you?'

'Hang about. What are you getting at? You don't think that I...'

'In a case like this everybody's a suspect, boyo.'

In the circumstances it was a particularly insensitive remark and Tommy reacted to it immediately.

'What the bloody hell are you talking about?' His voice rose to a shout. 'You know as well as I do that the Messarinas have got her. You should be getting up off your arse and looking for her instead of asking me bloody stupid questions.'

Judging by the expression on his face, the outburst did not please Davis, and even Macandrew arched his brows in surprise. As for Tommy, all his frustrations and anger accumulated since Anne Kirby went missing came out in a torrent of words.

222

'You two have landed me and Anne right in the shit. We didn't know what we were up against. You should have told us, given us some protection. You're coppers for Chrissake, you know the score, you know what these bastards are capable of. Look, I want nothing more to do with you. I wish to God I'd never come to you in the first place. None of this would have happened. Sod both of you. I'm off.' With that he jumped up and was out of the door in a flash.

Davis rose from his chair as though to follow but stopped when Macandrew raised an admonitory finger.

'Let him go, Colin,' he said. 'He'll be back.'

But Tommy, standing on the pavement outside the police station, had no intention of returning. From now on, he said to himself, I'll do things my way, and the first thing I'm going to do is get hold of Mattie. He hailed a passing cab and told the driver to take him to the Festival Hall.

Cardboard City was in a turmoil. The residents of the Bullring had been given summary notice to quit in order that the damage done to the supports of Waterloo Bridge could be repaired. Under the watchful eyes of uniformed police they wandered aimlessly around the site, gathering together their meagre possessions and preparing for a mass evacuation. Some of the well-established inhabitants raised feeble objections but to no avail.

Tommy arrived at the place he had once called home as the evacuation was getting under way. Lizzie, the ancient baglady, sat forlornly among her collection of parcels, mumbling under her breath as she checked and re-checked their contents. Nearby the massive figure of Mattie bent over the pile of books and papers which belonged to the absent Ironfoot. He looked up from his task as Tommy approached and his whiskers parted in a

223

smile of welcome.

'Now then, Tommy lad,' he said. 'Got 'ere just in time. Give me a hand, eh?'

'What's going on?' asked Tommy.

'Order of the boot. Sodding bridge falling down. C'mon. Let's get out of 'ere.'

'Where to?'

'Got a squat. Long Acre. Three of us. Good mates. Ironfoot's gear'll be safe there.'

Mattie bent once more to his task and Tommy joined in. The job was soon completed and two tidy piles, tied with odd pieces of string, lay ready for transportation.

'Hang about. I'll get a cab,' said Tommy.

'Cab? Leave off. We'll walk. Only a cock-stride,' was the reply as Mattie hoisted the heavier pack on to his shoulder and strode off. Carrying the lighter load, Tommy followed.

The squat in Long Acre was a commodious basement under an empty office block which Mattie and his mates had converted into a semblance of home. Three mattresses were ranged against one wall, there were scraps of carpet on the concrete floor and a paraffin stove in the centre of the room spread a gentle warmth in its immediate area. A couple of dilapidated easy chairs completed the furnishings.

Mattie deposited his load and sank into one of the chairs, motioning Tommy towards the other. When they were both seated Mattie produced the litre bottle from the depths of his capacious overcoat, took a gigantic swig of the contents and held out the bottle invitingly in Tommy's direction. Tommy shook his head.

'I've given it up. Gone on the wagon,' he said.

'All the more for me,' replied Mattie, and took another huge gulp from the bottle before returning it to its home. He wiped his whiskered mouth with the back of his hand.

'Right then,' he said. 'So what's doing? How yer getting on?'

Tommy needed no further invitation. He poured out his story in detail, ending with a description of the scene in Davis' office. Mattie, who had listened in silence and without interruption, shook his head sadly.

'Big mistake, Tommy. Never trust rozzers. All bastards. Wot yer wanna do about it?' he said.

Tommy answered through clenched teeth.

'I want to get that bastard Tony Messarina. He's killed Anne. I know it.'

He paused for a moment and then went on.

'No, I don't want him killed. I want him smashed to pieces. I want him to suffer for the rest of his miserable life. I want you to help me.'

'Don't want much do yer, son. Gang boss. Army o' minders. No chance, no chance at all...'

'There's got to be a chance,' interrupted Tommy. 'He's got to be on his tod sometimes. I'll cripple him if it's the last thing I do. If you won't help me I'll go it alone. So what is it? Yes or no?'

What could be seen of Mattie's forehead wrinkled in thought. He was not averse to violence, regarding it as the best and quickest way of settling a disagreement. He came to a decision. 'Alright, Tommy. We're mates, ain't we? I'm with yer. Let's get on with it.'

In the back room of La Cucaracha Tony Messarina sat behind his desk. It was close on midnight and he was alone. It had been a good day as was evidenced by the neat stacks of banknotes before him, all ready for transfer to the safe. This was a task he enjoyed, picking up the bundles of notes and depositing them with loving care beside their neighbours on the crowded shelves.

He had cause to feel pleased with himself. That morning Bertie the shyster had telephoned him with the news that the police had withdrawn the case against himself and his brothers. The principal witness against them had disappeared and had not been traced. So far so good. When the heat has died down, he said to himself, we'll attend to the boyfriend, teach him a lesson he would never forget.

He was still relishing the prospect of inflicting grievous bodily harm on the lunatic who had dared to set himself up against the Messarinas when the telephone rang. He picked up the receiver and, before he had time to acknowledge the call, a hoarse voice was shouting in his ear.

'We got trouble, boss,' said the voice. 'Down the stripper in Dean Street. Better get down here sharpish...'

There was a sound of raised voices in the background and the line went dead. Tony slowly replaced the receiver. He was not unduly perturbed. In his line of business trouble was never far away, but he had no doubts about his ability to handle any situation. First making sure that the safe was securely locked, he reached for his overcoat.

Mattie stepped out of the phonebox and joined the waiting Tommy.

'Right. It's on,' he said. 'Now listen. Messarina will be leaving the club any minute now. He'll come out the back door. If anybody's with him we don't do nothing. If he's on his tod we do the business. Got it?'

'Right,' said Tommy, and tightened his grip on the heavy hammer in his gloved hand. Mattie was similarly armed. The two men slipped round the corner and took up their positions at the end of the alley which ran along the rear of the club. In the dim light from an adjacent street lamp they watched as Tony Messarina emerged from the rear door of La cucaracha. He turned to operate the locks , heard the sound of hurried footsteps and half-turned as two shapes loomed up in the semidarkness, then his world turned black as Mattie"s hammer made contact with his head. He went down like a log.

The ensuing seconds were packed with action. Mattie turned the unconscious body face upward and he and Tommy went to work with their hammers, working in unison to a pre-arranged plan. First the ankles were shattered, then the shins as the hammers rose and fell. Kneecaps were reduced to a splintered mess, ribs were stove in and the elbow joints on both arms smashed to a bloody pulp.

'That's enough,' gasped Mattie. 'Let's scarper.'

Tommy looked up at his friend, face contorted and eyes blazing.

'One for the road,' he said, and rained a series of blows on the gangster's groin then followed Mattie's lead in tossing his hammer on the ground.

News of the attack on Tony Messarina spread through Soho like wildfire. Among the criminal fraternity of the area the gang boss had been thought to be untouchable, though he had many enemies who rejoiced in his down-fall.

Inspector Colin Davis was among the first to hear of the incident, and he lost no time in visiting the hospital to which Messarina had been taken. He received the news that the victim of the attack was in intensive care and, as the first step in his enquiries, interviewed the doctor in charge of the case.

'The injuries are very serious,' said the medico. 'I suppose you know that two hammers were used?'

'I do. They were found on the ground beside the body of the victim. What's the extent of the injuries?'

'Well, both legs are shattered below the knees. Both patellas smashed, pelvis broken, several ribs with some lung penetration. Both elbow joints. There's a deep fracture of the skull...'

'Do you reckon he'll survive?'

'It's a toss-up. If he does live he'll be a vegetable. So far as we can determine there's severe brain damage. He's in a coma at present.'

'So he can't be questioned?'

'Afraid not.'

'I see. Well, thanks a lot, doctor. You'll let me know if there's any change in his condition?'

'Most certainly, Inspector.'

Davis returned to his office from where he immediately telephoned his opposite number at Paddington.

'Heard about Messarina, Ian?' he said.

'I have indeed,' replied his colleague. 'I'm coming round to see you right away. Alright?'

'Sure.'

Davis put down the receiver. So far as he was concerned the case was already closed and would show on the record as just another unsolved gangland attack. He had no illusions about the perpetrator. That young fellow Hutton had certainly taken the law into his own hands. Rough justice, he thought, but justice all the same.

Following the successful foray into Messina territory, Tommy took Mattie's advice and holed up in the Long Acre squat.

'There'll be people looking for you,' Mattie had said. 'Don't know what the brothers will do. Wait and see. Keep yer head down.'

'What about the police?' asked Tommy. 'What do you think they'll do?'

'Bugger all. Good riddance to bad rubbish. All in favour. Villains kill each other, saves police time an' public money. Make yerself comfortable. I'll get some grub in. See yer.'

Left to himself, Tommy had time to think. His original fury had abated to some extent, though he did not regret the violent attack on the elder Messarina. On the contrary, he was aware of a change in himself, a feeling of power that was a direct result of his triumph over the evil creature who had brought sorrow into his life. Strangely enough, he had no fear of the consequences of his action, for he had proved to himself that he could be capable of violence if the need arose. He knew that he owed a lot to Mattie, whose assistance had been invaluable, but he also knew that he had played his part and inflicted his share of the damage.

He spent two days in almost solitary confinement. Mattie flitted in and out of the squat bringing provisions and bits of information and the other two squatters were conspicuous by their absence, having no doubt been advised by Mattie to keep out of the way for the time being. On the morning of the third day Mattie brought the glad tidings,

'In the clear, Tommy boy. The Messarinas 'ave fucked off. Back to Malta. Tony's finished.'

'Finished?'

'Still in hospital. Brain damaged. Won't never walk or talk again so I've heard.'

'Best news I've had for a long time. Hope he lives for ever. What about the police?'

'Told yer. Don't give a monkey's. No enquiries or anything.'

Tommy fell silent and his friend watched him with

some concern. Ever since the attack on Messarina Mattie had wondered what effect the incident would have on a man who was not by nature offensive or given to violence and was very surprised at Tommy's calm reaction to the news about the gang leader. He was certain of one thing, however, that young Tommy Hutton had undergone a radical change and was no longer the quiet and unassuming fellow he had known in Cardboard City. It's a queer world, he thought as he abandoned further speculation. He lugged the litre bottle from its home and drank deeply. It was one answer to many questions.

Tommy broke the silence.

'Wonder how old Ironfoot's getting on,' he said.

'Funny. Wondering the same meself. Orter yo and see 'im.'

'That's an idea. Why don't we go now? I could do with a breath of fresh air.'

Mattie heaved his huge body from the chair.

'You're on,' he said. 'Let's go.'

The old philosopher was in his element. A problem presented was a problem to be solved, and he had revelled in conquering the new method in walking forced upon him by what he referred to as "my tin leg". The progress he made had surprised his teachers, who regarded him as their favourite pupil and gave him every encouragement of which they were capable. As a result the patient progressed by what might be called leaps and bounds.

When Tommy and Mattie entered the ward, Ironfoot demonstrated his walking skills by meeting them halfway. The two men stared in surprise at this display of agility and, the greetings over, settled down round their friend's tidy bed.

'It's a miracle,' said Tommy. 'Nobody would believe

that you've got an artificial leg.'

'I would,' said Ironfoot and joined in the laughter that followed the remark. 'It's no miracle, Tommy,' he went on, 'just a matter of application and the triumph of mind over matter. Now, what have you two been up to. Tell me all the news.'

In a few staccato sentences Mattie related the recent happenings in Cardboard City.

'Don't worry about your gear,' he said. 'I've got it safe.'

'Dear me,' said the old man. 'It looks as though I shall have to find a new home when I leave this place.'

'Got a squat. You're welcome,' said Mattie.

Tommy broke into the conversation.

'It's a bloody shame. What's going to happen to the poor sods who've been turfed out? Where the hell will they go?'

'They'll find somewhere,' said Mattie.

There was an uncomfortable silence, ended by the old philosopher.

'I've had a lot of time for thinking while I've been here,' he said. 'I've come to the conclusion that I've been a very selfish man. I've pursued my own way of life without regard to what has been happening to my fellow men, particularly those unforunates without homes and without hope. Now that I have a new leg I think it's time for a new life. Now here's what I've been thinking.'

'Go on,' said Tommy. 'I get your drift.'

'Well now, let's suppose that some charitable persons got together, acquired some sort of large building, fitted it out with simple beds and washing and cooking facilities and provided shelter for as many homeless people as possible. How does that sound to you?'

'Crazy,' said Mattie.

'Cost a bomb,' said Tommy.

'The cost is immaterial. I am not without means as you both must have suspected. Would you be willing to help me to set this scheme up?'

'Won't be easy,' said Tommy. 'What do you think, Mattie?'

'You want to do it. I'm with yer,' was the reply.

'Right. Professor, we're on. When do we start?

'Actions speak louder than words. You can start right away.'

Reaching into the locker adjacent to his bed-the old man fumbled for a moment then, with cheque book and pen in hand, turned to Tommy.

'I'm going to give you a cheque for twenty thousand pounds. Pay it into your bank. As soon as it's cleared you can start operations. I'll be leaving the hospital in a couple of days. I'll join you then. Satisfactory?'

'Very. We won't waste any more time. See you,' said Tommy.

'Oh, by the way, give John Cartwright a message. Tell him I shan't be going to work for him. I've found a better job.'

Within a few days Operation Help the Homeless was in full swing. Tommy had wasted no time in a search for suitable premises and had signed a six month lease on a massive warehouse on the south bank of the Thames near Blackfriars Bridge. The estate agent was glad to get it off his hands, asking few questions when Tommy offered the full rent in advance and happily handing over the keys.

Now Tommy and Mattie stood side by side at one end of the building surveying the capacious interior. The concrete floor was littered with debris and there was dust and dirt everywhere.

'Have to get the place cleaned up before we can make a start,' said Tommy.

Mattie was sanguine.

'No sweat. Get some mates down here. Day's work, that's all.'

'Right, get going,' Tommy replied. 'I'll get the electric and gas and water turned on. See you later.'

By the following day a transformation had been brought about. Mattie's mates included an electrician, a carpenter and a plumber, men who were glad to exercise the skills which society had rejected. Under Tommy's supervision they set about laying pipes and cables, installing panel heaters and the rest of the paraphernalia which would turn the cold warehouse into a warm and comfortable haven for its future occupants.

The work was well advanced when the old philosopher turned up out of the blue. Wearing a sober business suit under an expensive overcoat and carrying an elegant walking-stick, he was the epitome of the successful City gent. He was greeted happily by Tommy and Mattie who, truth to tell, were becoming worried about funds. Their fears were laid to rest.

'Not to worry, dear boys,' said their benefactor. 'I shall be seeing some of my wealthy acquaintances over the next few days. They will be only too pleased to ease their consciences by contributing to a worthy cause. Just get on with the work and leave the finances to me.'

He was as good as his word, returning from his forays daily with a briefcase stuffed with cash and cheques. Freed from financial strictures, Mattie went on a spending spree. A plethora of beds, blankets, kitchen equipment and trestle tables poured like a tide into the warehouse. In keeping with his position as chief buyer to the project, Mattie had effected a change in his appearance. His whiskers shaved off, hair neatly trimmed and his bulk crammed into a suit which fitted where it touched. When he first appeared in his new guise, he was only identified by his voice.

Christmas was approaching and the gang of workers pulled out all the stops. By mid-December only the finishing touches remained. When finally the warehouse was ready to open its doors to the homeless, who were already queuing outside, Tommy, Mattie and the Professor made a last tour of inspection. Assured that everything was in order, Tommy gathered the workers around him for a briefing.

'We have accommodation for two hundred people. Any in excess of that number will have to be turned away. Sorry about it, but that's the way it is. If there's any trouble I want it settled quickly and quietly. There's enough of you to make sure that violence is unnecessary. Understood?'

There was a chorus of agreement, and Tommy looked at his watch.

'Right. Open the doors in half an hour's time.'

He turned to Mattie and the Professor.

'Come on, let's get down to the far end. We can keep an eye on things from there.'

As the minutes ticked away Tommy was conscious of a great sense of achievement. The Professor, for his part, had his doubts.

'You know, we're only scratching the surface of a huge social problem,' he said.

'All right,' replied Tommy. 'But at least we're doing something. Just wait and see. This is only the beginning.'

BORN ROTTEN.

JOE CANNON.

This bizarre novel is a powerful, gripping and exciting story which tells of the bruitality and violence of London's underworld as it is today.

Joey Bello, the anti-hero described by the title, takes the reader into the criminal haunts of London's Soho, the subculture of Notting Hill where racial tensions fuel sporadic outbreaks of violence, the eerie night-life of the West End, and the strange other world of the expatriate villian basking in the Spanish sun.

As the Bello saga unfolds, the reader is transported into the battle-ground of international crime, where billions of pounds, dollars and other currencies swell the pockets of traffickers in drugs and vice, where conspiracy, extortion corruption and murder are commonplace. Here the Mafia, a criminal octupus, spreads its tentacles worldwide.

BORN ROTTEN throws a searchlight on international crime and in doing so opens up a new era in crime fiction.

Paperback price £4.50 net U.K.

YELLOW BRICK PUBLISHERS. 2, Lonsdale Road, Queens Park. London . NW6 6RD.

ENGLAND'S TOUGHEST VILLAIN

JOE CANNON

Gripping, exciting, and often horrifying, this is the story of Joey Bello, an ex-criminal, who wages his own personal war against corruption in the highest places: the untouchable echolons of our own police force and especially the Mafia.

Joey Bello fights on his terms. He meets violence with violence, bruitality with bruitality.

ENGLAND'S TOUGHEST VILLAIN opens a window into the sub-culture of the underworld, introducing the reader to a side of life which he would ordinarily and otherwise not see: a world of theives jargon and evil deeds, where danger lurks in dark corners and where the threat of death is ever-present: a world in which a sawn-off shotgun is no respecter of persons: where a .45 automatic is a great leveller.

Paperback price £4.50 net U.K.

YELLOW BRICK PUBLISHERS. 2, Lonsdale Road, Queens Park, London. NW6 6RD.

JUDGE ME NOT

JOE CANNON.

In this book, the final volume of the trilogy following
BORN ROTTEN and ENGLAND'S TOUGHEST VIL-
LAIN, the saga of Joey Bello continues.
Here the author draws on his considerable knowledge of
sophisticated crime to give a picture of computer frauds
carried out by Bello and his confederates. While not
being a guide to the essential elements of this type of
crime, the fiction presented here has a basis in fact, as
any computer hacker will know.
A chapter of the book is devoted to a fictionalised
account of the probable circumstances surrounding the
murder on the Costa del Sol of Great Train Robber
Charlie Wilson. Amid a welter of speculation, the author's informed opinion is as good as any and better
than most. He opens a window on criminal activity
which has hitherto been securely locked and bolted.

Paperback price £4.50 net U.K.

YELLOW BRICK PUBLISHERS. 2, Lonsdale Road,
Queens Park, London. NW6 6RD.

AUTOBIOGRAPHY

GANGSTER'S LADY

ELLEN CANNON.

The story of ELLEN CANNON'S life tells what it's like being a member of one of Notting Dale's largest families and because of the family tie, the support from the Mafia.

This book is packed with incidents. As her man rose through the ranks of villainy and became a major gangland figure, she was introduced into the society of London's top Jollies of the Underworld. She learned to play the game of the Gangster's Lady in strict accordance with the rules.

Whatever knowledge she had of the secrets of Gangland she kept it to herself-

Now for the first time she's telling all-

She pulls no punches and gives a documented account of the violent life with her husband.

She is a remarkable lady.

Paperback price £4.95 net U.K.

YELLOW BRICK PUBLISHERS. 2, Lonsdale Road, Queens Park, London. NW6 6RD.

COUNTERFEIT MAN

PHILIP GRANT

Why is handsome Hugo Lansing, top U.N. official so alarmed when he discovers that Elizabeth Tasker, his secretary and lover, has flown from New York to Frankfurt, close to his birthplace on the Rhine? What could she have discovered? Why are the Security Services interested? Does it concern the origins of the Lansing family?

Lockhart, ex-Interpol and Scotland Yard, is sent to find out what she knows and is soon enmeshed in deadly intrigue among the monuments and castles atop the Rhine.

The trail leads to the British Museum, an English Stately Home and back to Germany where Lockhart fights for his life with a pathological killer before the awesome secret of Hugo Lansing is revealed.

Paperback price £4.50 net U.K.

YELLOW BRICK PUBLISHERS 2, Lonsdale Road, Queens Park, London. NW6 6RD.